Praise for

THE EMERGENT

"*The Emergent* is a tale of blood, loss, family, and departures that orbits a continent, its casualties and its letdowns. It is a story for those of us who will never be sure if we only imagined that hand at the shoreline reaching for us."

—SALAR ABDOH
Author of *Out of Mesopotamia*

"A woman's bold reckoning with memory, and pursuit of all its drifting pieces. *The Emergent* is just that—an aching recognition of how family narratives persist, holding us in their loving embrace, or imprisonment."

—MARC PALMIERI
Author of *She Danced With Lightning*

"*The Emergent* is a haunting first-person narrative about young Kat's shattered family and their complex histories. The title of this sensitive, evocative novel says it all: life is about our emergent selves and the stories we tell and hear along the way."

—SUSAN SHILLINGLAW
Author of *A Journey into Steinbeck's California*

"Holmberg has created a compelling and thoughtful novel that is a beautifully crafted and complex narrative. *The Emergent* causes one to wonder if they will be bystanders in life, or if they'll jump in—allowing the mysterious mosaic of life to create something fascinating."

—EMILY KEEFER
Author of *The Stars on Vita Felice Court*

"*The Emergent* is not to be rushed through, if you can help it. Each paragraph is lovingly crafted, and I deeply enjoyed Kat's Holden Caulfield-like alienation. As I read, I began wondering how real any of our ideas about our personal histories are."

—TIM GERSTMAR
Author *of The Gunfighters*

"For a novel that moves so swiftly from one American coast to the other, and back again, interestingly it is the obscure neighborhoods of San José that inform the soul of Holmberg's polyphony of a novel, *The Emergent*. As a Californian, I love this book. I love it because it's the California I know but almost never read about. In this way, I see it on the bookshelf between Helena María Viramontes' little masterpiece *Under the Feet of Jesus* and Leonard Gardner's beautiful *Fat City*. It's that good."

—GEORGE MCCORMICK
Author of *Inland Empire*

The Emergent

by Nick Holmberg

ISBN 978-1-64663-619-8

Published by

◪ köehlerbooks™

3705 Shore Drive
Virginia Beach, VA 23455
800–435–4811
www.koehlerbooks.com

THE EMERGENT

Thanks for reading!

NICK HOLMBERG

— Nick

VIRGINIA BEACH
CAPE CHARLES

Dedicated to those still searching for their voice.

All things that move and breathe with toil and sound
Are born and die; revolve, subside, and swell.
—Percy Bysshe Shelley, "Mont Blanc"

*L*ook at the headless chickens and fingerless hands, vines and a screaming child, dark glasses and grease and sweat—theft. Vinyl-recorded symphonies and the roar of buses and trucks do not stifle these things. The world and the music entwine themselves deeply.

This is a birth or some fleeting pleasure.

Wake. Run.

Tell this to anyone.

No one notices. No one listens.

Burrow in tunnels under towers.

An old man looks at the darkness, a young man reads a book, a young woman rubs her bruised thighs. An old woman looks at her passport and pulls her luggage closer.

And the tunnels become oceans. The oceans are people, and the people are obscured.

This is a birth and some abject horror.

Wake. Swim. Feel the salt sting scrapes and cuts and burns.

Tell this to anyone.

Notice. Listen.

1.

THE REASSURING WHISPERS STOPPED. And I went searching for them. I wandered the streets and avenues for a week and stayed on the subway at night. Back and forth, over and over, between the Bronx and Brooklyn or Queens and the Bronx or northern Manhattan and South Ferry. I found the whispers, but they weren't calm anymore. So that's why I got off the train here in Marble Hill.

Okay, fine, Lilly. I needed a job and a place to stay, so I answered your ad.

I don't know why I'm here in New York. The last thing I remember clearly is that my friend Alma disappeared. After that, it's been like walking through a dream. Or a dream within a dream.

It was about six weeks ago. Tramping through downtown San José, rubbing newspaper ink off my fingers, listening to a new CD on my battered Discman, I tried to think about anything that could settle my nervous stomach: Had Richard Jewell really planted the bombs at the Olympics a few weeks ago? Would Fiona Apple's "Sleep to Dream" make sense if I kept listening to it? Had the downtown scenery of my childhood always changed so dramatically from west to east? On one side of the San José State campus, new and old business towers stood beside giant cranes. The campus itself was a confused mass—the angular library looked like a hospital, a vine-covered lecture hall impersonated a church, brick-arched faculty offices resembled classrooms, a white stucco classroom building seemed like a Spanish mission, and redbrick dorms loomed like prison cell blocks. On the other side of campus, old Victorians clashed with Craftsmans and square apartment complexes—all in various states of disrepair.

I waited at an intersection as detoured evening rush-hour traffic bottlenecked along the road. I felt my stubbly scalp; even after four months, I wasn't used to it. I took off my earphones. Over the grinding gears and idling engines, a long guitar solo danced from the little white house across the street where I'd lived until April. The odor of charcoal and lighter fluid mingled with the traffic vapors.

Alma sat on the front steps. Her navy-blue tank top, loose blue jeans, and black Doc Martens made her white skin glow. Shoulder-length platinum hair caught the light of the midsummer afternoon sun. She was talking with a young woman in a pale sundress. After I crossed the street, a dirty-blond hellion careened on her trike through some well-worn tracks on the corner of the lawn of Alma's rented house. Her dress flapping, the little girl belted a wicked laugh and tore off down the sidewalk.

"Ella!" the woman yelled. She bolted after the little girl, stopping for a second to shrug a "sorry." I waved and smiled. The woman turned and ran off to catch Ella.

"That Ella's mom?" I asked Alma.

"Adopted, but yeah," Alma said, her black eyes following the pursuit. "Name's Coral. Nice lady. She's moving soon to be with her sick grandfather."

"New hair?" I asked. I kissed her on the cheek, smelling sandalwood and cigarettes.

She said, "Yeah. Cut it out of boredom. Besides, my natural shade was dirty looking. Thought I'd brighten things up a bit."

"It worked," I said as I sat next to her. "What are you doing out here?"

"Place is crawling with people. And Loskie." Her face twisted. She lit a cigarette. "Has he always treated me like this?"

I opened my mouth, took a quick breath, pressed my lips together.

Alma continued: "I must have gone five or six times to the corner store for him today—beer, wine, wine opener, ice, garlic. Fifteen minutes ago he demanded another bottle of Jack. I've been sitting out here ever since." She paused. "Enough of my drama. Where have you been all summer? Why didn't you drive here?"

"In this traffic? I wouldn't have driven even if I still had the car."

She gasped. "You sold the '66? What the hell?"

"Yeah . . . I just couldn't afford it anymore." I took a drag off Alma's cigarette.

"Hey, cool hair. It highlights your ears." She turned to watch the traffic. "So, where'd you go?"

I gave back the cigarette and watched a beat-up Datsun pickup lurch and stall in traffic. "Traveled up and down the coast, spent time in San Francisco. I wanted to go to New York City, but it'd be too tough to find a job."

Alma scratched her shoulders until dry skin flaked. "Do you really hate yourself that much to want to live in the filth of all those people?"

"You've never been to New York."

"Neither have you. And I don't know why you'd want to. I can hardly stand San José. I was thinking of escaping this city, escaping the people. Instead, I got busted."

"Jesus, Alma," I groaned. "Again?"

She hung her head, bangs covering her face. "Month and a half ago."

A man's voice rose above the music: "Yaaaa, you're damn right!"

Alma sighed. "I had two shots and a beer. It's not like I was drunk."

"They're never gonna let you drive again."

Alma stared at the brick steps. "I just got out of jail. Ten days. That's why Loskie's throwing this party. But I gotta say, spending one night in the drunk tank should have counted for four days in jail. The women in the tank were dirty and mean from their oncoming hangovers."

Again, the man's voice pierced the music: "Haaaaa! Yer goddamn right!"

I rolled my eyes. "Well, should we go in?"

"I guess." Alma stubbed her cigarette on the step. "They're all his friends, though. Nobody really knows me."

Around the corner came Coral, carrying the trike and a screaming Ella. Coral threw the trike on the lawn. Struggling up the steps to the house next door, Coral shrugged again and smiled at us. Alma and I laughed. Ella bit Coral's shoulder, and Coral yelped. They disappeared into the house.

I followed Alma and her sandalwood-cigarette scent. In the living room, we made our way around three huddled folding chairs and a makeshift coffee table—a plank laid across two empty blue milk crates. Atop a small TV-VCR combo, a stern-looking couple glared at us from the cover of an empty VHS box, a fighter jet streaking under their faces. Music and yelling from the backyard echoed off the hardwood floors. Holes ravaged the doors to the hallway and into the kitchen.

"Walls are bare," I said. Only scuffed smudges—some of boot soles, most of handprints—decorated the white walls.

"Yeah," Alma said, scratching below her collarbone. "My sketches came down when you left. But I won't let Loskie put his stuff up. Airplanes would cover the walls. He really wanted to fly."

"Jesus. Can you imagine him at Top Gun? 'That's right, Ice . . . Man. I *am* dangerous.'"

"How many times did we watch that damn movie?"

We laughed. Walking into the kitchen, we were surrounded, invaded by the noise from outside. Barbecue smoke rolled through the open door in slow, regular waves. The music stopped, and the yelling outside wound down to a murmur. I bumped the kitchen table and knocked over an empty beer can as I opened a window to clear the room of smoke. Alma popped the tops off a couple of Keystones. We sat at the table, swigging from the silver aluminum.

"So, where exactly did you go this summer?" Alma asked, red marks appearing near her collarbone where she'd just scratched.

"Did some traveling before I sold my car."

The woman I'd met in the spring rose from a nearby corner of my mind and loomed. A silence persisted, and the smoke continued to flow into the kitchen. I looked toward the door. Then I found Alma's big dark eyes.

I smiled and said, "Sorry about that."

"About what?" She rubbed the raised red scratches on her chest.

"I was just spacing out for a second." I chuckled. Then I lied: "I . . . I went up to Oregon and down to LA."

"Rare!" a man yelled, moving near the back door. "The only way to have it. Sear it superhot, trap those good flavors."

A distant voice responded.

Alma scrambled toward the stove, snatching up her copy of *Metro* magazine and tossing it on the dirty cold burners. She stared down at the cover photo; the voice from outside kept mumbling. I stared at Alma, but her blond bob guarded her. She crossed her arms and started scratching her shoulders again.

"Yeah," the man squawked, "I got two types, and I won't cook 'em any other way. What? This is my house. You don't like the way I cook, don't eat. Hell. More for me. What?"

The distant voice murmured another question. Alma leafed through the weekly, turned it over and started again, pretending to read about restaurants and upcoming downtown shows. I opened my mouth but didn't say anything.

"Like I said," the man shouted. "There are two types of meat at my parties: blue and red."

The man stumbled over the threshold and spilled meat juice and Jack Daniel's on the light-blue linoleum. His drab brown hair matted with sweat, he stood barefoot in jeans and a barbecue-stained Hawaiian shirt. Light-blue eyes stared at me. After a brief pause, Loskie said, "Speaking of rare, holy shit." He smiled crookedly. "Where the hell've you been?"

"Away."

Loskie set down a platter of steak with a foil tent perched on top. Red and purple saturated the large cutting board. Congealed fat and blood ran onto the off-white Formica. Then he lurched toward me. I started toward the door, but he wrapped his arms around me from behind, cold whiskey splashing my arm. He rested his head on mine.

"Well," Loskie said, "we missed you."

I stood still in the damp, boozy embrace. He let go and I wiped the liquor off my arm. Alma stared at the magazine, her shoulders looking as if they would bleed soon. Loskie gulped a long drink and eyed his knife rack.

"Goddammit!" he exploded.

Alma jumped, and I retreated. He stomped around, opening and slamming every drawer in the kitchen.

"What's the matter, honey?" Alma whispered, now rubbing the raised red streaks on her shoulders.

"I told you," he said, pulling out a chef's knife from a narrow drawer. "Put the goddamned knives back where they belong or they'll get dull. You're such a . . ." He took a deep breath and faced Alma, then staggered toward her and took her in his arms. He said, "I yuv you," and kissed her with a loud smack. Alma gazed up at him, smiling weakly as she stroked his cheek. I sat again, keeping an eye on the knife in Loskie's hand.

After taking another swallow from his cup, Loskie paced the kitchen, running the long blade of the knife across a sharpening steel with surprising speed and precision. Then he stopped and glared at me. "Where've you been?"

Wincing as he continued to rasp the steel together, I said nothing. The smoke had become even thicker in the room.

"What?" he said. "Can't talk? Won't talk, more like. Always did think you were better than everyone else." He started hacking into the rare meat. Steaming red juice flowed over the side of the cutting board. He shook his head. "Whatever." Then he turned to Alma. "Why's it that you still hang out with her?" He turned back to me. "Why's it you never say anything?" Loskie repeated louder, "Why's it you never say anything?"

I gulped my beer, the can echoing metallic and empty when I placed it on the table. "I don't need this." I stood up.

"Wait. Don't go." Alma rushed to my side. "I have to talk to you." Her arm around mine, she guided me toward the back door. Under her breath, she said, "Don't mind this bastard."

"What'd ya say?" Loskie said, and stopped cutting.

We skirted by him. He did a full turn, long fork in one hand, chef's knife in the other.

"Nothing," Alma said. "C'mon, Kat."

"That's what I thought," Loskie said. As we walked out to the backyard, Loskie shouted, "Hey! I'm almost outta Jack. Where's my bottle?"

Alma didn't answer.

Three guys stood just outside, guarding the door and a keg of Tied House beer. Each wore black shades, dark blue jeans, and a perfectly ironed, navy, short-sleeved button-up and had neck tattoos that seemed faded against their brown skin. Their cologne filled my nose as we squeezed past. More eyes stared at us from the yard. All kinds. But all belonging to people like Loskie: townies from the bar where he hung out. And groups of men—some fat, some muscular, all of them tattooed—milled around the large yard of dirt and dead crabgrass; I even recognized a few of the men from the bar, but not enough to talk to them. Most were armed with red plastic cups and cigarettes and uniformed in greasy white T-shirts with mechanic's coveralls; some had unbuttoned their coveralls and folded them down to the waist. A dark mestizo man, somewhat older than the others, stared at us. Taking off his bright-orange shirt, he revealed a broad chest entirely tattooed with an ancient map. He lit a cigarette and lay down on a weight bench and lifted the barbell. Three small white women with various bright hair colors and facial piercings sneered from the picnic table where they sat.

Alma and I kicked up dust from the dead grass as we sidestepped through the chattering and laughing mass of flesh. The music started again. We sat next to each other in broken plaid lawn chairs in a corner opposite the scoffing women. A hint of twilight crept into the yard. Through the tall chain-link fence I saw plastic slides, jungle gyms, tricycles, bikes, and the green grass in other people's yards grabbing up the remaining sunlight. From behind a tree next door popped the hellion Ella. Clothed in nothing but floral-print underpants and a coat of dirt from face to feet, she smiled and waved frantically. We waved back, and just as quickly as she had appeared, she disappeared screaming into the house.

"That kid remind you of anyone?" Alma said.

I glanced at her knowingly. Then I said, "So, two DUIs, huh?"

"Yeah. Two times. They'll never let me drive again. Those classes you drove me to—remember? after my first DUI?—those should have been punishment enough. Can you believe I'm on probation just for having a few drinks?"

I ignored her last question. "I'd rather die than sit in jail thinking about what I've done."

"Don't be so dramatic. I wouldn't rather be dead," Alma responded. "But I agree with you. It was torture sitting in the cell for ten days, regretting, playing over and over again my brief lapse in judgment."

I frowned. "A 'brief lapse'? What a copout. That's like saying the weather is the cause of being happy, melancholy, introverted, or homicidal."

Alma shifted her weight. "But don't you think there are things beyond our control that affect our decisions and moods? Our environment has a greater effect on our actions than you're admitting, Kat. Think about it: if I wake up from a wonderful dream and say to myself it's going to be a great day, that doesn't make it a reality, because if I walk out the door and the rain drenches me, I sure as hell am going to be in a bad mood."

"Read the newspaper and bring a fuckin' umbrella." I smiled. "We have to know how we'll react in situations: either control an impulse or avoid the situation altogether."

Alma shifted her weight again. "What are we supposed to do? Live in a box? Develop a religious impulse control? It seems unrealistic not to consider the desperate situations that drive people to kill, or steal, or beat the crap out of someone. Or drive drunk."

The crowd shuffled across the dead grass toward the meat that Loskie set out.

After a few minutes, I asked, "Why're you still living with him?"

"I don't know. The cheap rent?"

I frowned at her.

"Okay," she said as she glanced at me, digging her fingers into her palm. "I know you're thinking I'm full of crap right about now."

"Yep."

"Well, I'm scared. That's why I asked you here. I don't think I can do this on my own. I feel totally trapped. I know I should've gotten the hell out of here a long time ago—right around the time you moved out, actually. But it really hit me when I was in jail last week. I thought about the night I got busted again. I was out with Loskie, down at the bar. He was playing pool, and I started talking to this woman, Marylou—cute, done-up makeup, fresh tattoos, jet-black hair—and we started talking about traveling. And she'd been all over the place. She'd hiked the rain forests of Costa Rica and the deserts of the Australian Outback; she'd rafted down the Colorado and the Amazon; she'd even stayed with families in the Italian and Irish countrysides. I wondered how she did it, how she got by and fed herself. I mean, she'd grown up her whole life in San Francisco—Pacific Heights—but when she turned eighteen, she took off. Almost no money and only a few sets of clothes packed in her little backpack. She said she just figured she could rely on the kindness of strangers."

Alma paused, glanced at me, and continued.

"So anyway, I told Marylou she was full of it. She said I'd be surprised at how willing people are to help a wanderer. She said, 'Experience is valuable currency,' that people wanted to live through her by hearing about the places she'd been."

Alma stopped and looked at me. I wondered why.

She went on. "So it all started to sound possible to me. I was completely caught up in her story. I told her I needed to get out of San José. Then Loskie stepped between me and Marylou and said, 'What the hell?' and grabbed my arm and pulled me outside. The next thing I knew, he was squeezing my arm and yelling at me, telling me that I loved him and I couldn't leave him, not after all that we've been through. A bouncer separated us, but not before I called Loskie a bastard and backhanded him. Next thing I knew I was in the car and getting pulled over by the cops. I'd run a stoplight."

"Damn," I whispered. "What the hell are you still doing here?"

"I told you I'm scared. What am I going to do? Sleep in the park? Before I got sentenced—and while I was in jail—I thought I'd run into Marylou again and ask if I could tag along with her. She'd talked about taking a train to Crater Lake and camping."

I looked at her out of the corner of my eye.

"I know, I know," she said. "I mean, a woman like that staying in a place like this for that long? For someone like me?"

"You could have stayed with me."

Alma shook her head. "You don't know how many times I picked up the phone. But then I'd remember how I let Loskie come between me and you."

I was stunned that she felt like that. I'd known her my whole life. And I'd done far worse things. Like . . . well, I'll just leave it at that for now.

Alma continued: "The day after, Loskie bailed me out and said he was sorry. But when I got convicted a month later, I went to county lockup and had a lot of time to think. I thought about how I've been . . ." She stopped talking and swallowed hard. Her eyes glistened as she looked at me. Then: "And I thought a lot about you. I figured you had the car and you really don't like your job." She paused again, faced forward. "I guess I thought I'd just throw some of my stuff in your car and we'd go somewhere. But you got rid of the '66."

Ella appeared again beyond the chain-link fence, wearing nothing but a smile. But her mischievous grin left her face. She shrieked and ran away, her little white butt offset by a thick layer of dirt on her face, chest, and legs.

I laughed and looked at Alma. She was gazing at me, black eyes glimmering. She mouthed, "Help me."

"What the hell's goin' on here? You two really are dyking out, aren't you?" Loskie stood before us, smiling. "Just kidding. Hey, Kat. Saw-ry you had tuh see that in the kitchen. Really. I don' like it when we get like that." He kissed Alma loudly on the cheek, sloshing a little whiskey on her arm.

I stayed quiet.

He swayed, tumbler of whiskey in one hand, platter of parcooked flesh in the other. He stared at me with one eye shut. Then he slurred, "So, quiet girl. How d'you like yer meat? Red 'r blue?"

"I'm a vegetarian." I stared through the chain-link fence as if Ella would appear for comic relief.

"Since when?" Alma asked.

I scowled at Loskie.

"Well, there's lotsa salad an' corn."

I glanced at Loskie and then away, saying, "Not really that hungry."

Loskie breathed through his mouth and stared at me with his one open eye. Finally, he said, "Why're you even here then?"

My stomach gurgled. Then I looked right into Loskie's eye.

Before I could speak, Alma said, "To see me."

Loskie swayed a bit; his face contorted. Then he turned, spilling meat juice on the dead grass, grumbling.

Alma fumbled with the pack of cigarettes. She plucked two and gave one to me. Her hands trembled as she lit them. Loskie sat with the three small women at the picnic table across the yard. He had his hand over one eye, scowling in our direction. I stared right back at that drunk bastard. The three women all walked away. Alone, he glowered at us, blinking his one eye.

I didn't look away from him. "What is his problem?" I asked.

Alma dug at her shoulders again and whispered, "Who cares?"

I followed Alma toward the back door through the thinning crowd.

Loskie cried, "Hey! Where the hell's my Jack?"

The door rattled when Alma pushed it shut. In the bedroom, Alma slid the bolt into place and stood by the door. The streetlamp lit the room.

"I am so sick of this," Alma sniffled. "All I've wanted to do since you got here is . . . all day . . . every day. But everything I think, everything I say, everything I do is . . . is . . ."

I took Alma in my arms, and she began to weep. Racket outside; more people had arrived to the party. The music and voices outside echoed throughout the house. I held Alma in the yellow light, smelling cigarettes, body odor, and the fading scent of sandalwood. I led her over to the bed and we lay down. I ran my fingers over the raised lines on her shoulder. Then I stroked her cheek and her ear. Alma quieted. The din of music and chatter outside filtered in.

I asked, "You awake? You okay?"

"Yeah. Just thinking about what to do."

"And?"

Alma sighed. "I don't know. I want to go back to Santa Cruz for school, but I don't think I can get my grant money anymore. I've been thinking about the traveling you did this summer, but you sold your car. So I don't know what the hell I'm gonna do. I could go anywhere. Anywhere but here. Maybe north on Highway 1 until I find a place where I feel safe, wherever that might be."

I said, "Why don't you just leave right now?"

Alma sat up on the edge of the bed and lit two more cigarettes. I joined her when she handed one to me. She said, "Will you go with me?"

Suddenly the music outside stopped. Loskie shouted, asking people why they were leaving.

I said, "All roads lead to . . . I just don't know if I can do it."

Alma put out her cigarette. We sat on the bed in the shadows cast by the streetlamp through the blinds.

Finally, I said, "But I want to know that you're okay. So I don't know how that's going to work."

A thump rattled somewhere in the house.

Alma touched my cheek. Then she took my hands in her own. "Katherine," she said, "let's get out of here right now."

"Where to?"

"I don't know. Let's just leave now. I've already thrown some stuff in my backpack. We could take the bus to the coast and go camp on the beach; or we could go up to the city."

The streetlamp outside flickered. Alma's eyes were wide. Something rattled in the front of the house.

"What're you saying?" I asked.

"I'm saying we should get the hell outta here. Together. I don't really want to go to San Francisco—to me it's just another dirty city—but there's a school up there that I could transfer to. And you could find a better job. We can stay there until I finish school and then get out of there, go see the world. In the meantime, we'd be safe . . . in the Castro . . ."

A question tinged her voice as she trailed off. She let go of my hands. We sat in silence for a moment.

Then I said, "I lied earlier. I didn't go to Oregon or LA. In April, I met a woman, Thalia, and spent a lot of time in the Castro with her. And I really didn't like it very much. The people there think people like me are cowards, indecisive at best."

A siren wailed in the distance, came closer, then receded. Someone coughed in the living room. Alma started to scrape the underside of her forearm.

I took her hands and squeezed them. "Alma. I've known you my whole life. I love you . . ." Finishing the sentence with "like a sister" sounded stupid—cheap even—so I stopped.

"I'm confused."

"It's like this: I left Thalia because to her, all roads led to San Francisco, to the Castro, to all that it's supposed to represent. When I started going there with Thalia, it was the first time I'd ever really felt like part of something. But pretty quickly I felt trapped in an either/or world. Thalia was no better. She thought she could convert me from being bi, like it's some sort of religious choice. She wanted me to be staunchly militant just like her. So we spent more time in the city being activists than we did being two people who liked each other."

As I told Alma these things, I thought I knew what I was talking about and that I had to push Alma away in order to push her toward something real. But now I'm not sure I did the right thing.

Alma replied, "I don't really understand. Isn't this the very thing that we should stand up for?"

"It is, but I can't. I'm done with that scene."

"Okay, fine. We don't have to go to the city. I just want to get out of here. With you."

"I can't."

Alma breathed unevenly. Then she said, "You remember how we used to go to that beach with Mom? I never understood why you didn't go in the water with us. Even now, just sitting here, I can feel the water, the mist, the cold gray sky. A hundred yards out, the waves swelled past me and crashed toward you. I want you to be beyond the breakers with me, with me in the act of physical, spiritual strength. Sure, with its bad eyesight, a shark might come take a bite out of your ribs or legs, mistaking you for food. And what about the cold, right? You might cramp up so you wouldn't be able to swim ashore, dying a horrible, salty death."

"Are you trying to persuade me?" I asked, chuckling.

"I'm just trying to say that these unknowns can be handled in two ways. You can stay on the beach and watch, imagining what might—but probably won't—happen. Or you can offer up your mere physical existence for the chance to be a part of something bigger than yourself."

"What was the last class you took? Religion?"

"It doesn't matter. What I'm saying is if we were together, we would be less afraid of sharks and drowning, of assholes like Loskie."

I didn't say anything. Alma suddenly seemed like a different person, and I couldn't—can't—figure how she'd gained all that insight. I've read a hell of a lot more than her. But I've never read any philosophy like that.

Somewhere in the house came a sound like a body being dragged across the floor.

"Alma!" Loskie screamed. "Where are you, goddammit! Where the hell are you?"

Alma rushed to the window, opened it, and pushed out the screen.

"C'mon," Alma whispered. "Get out the window."

The door handle jiggled and Loskie shouted, "Open up! I know you're in there licking that bitch's box." He banged on the door.

"Get out," Alma repeated.

I climbed down. When I turned around, Alma was closing the window.

"What about you?" I said, almost choking on my words. "C'mon."

"No. I'll be okay." Her black eyes flashed. "I'll call you later."

The banging on the door continued. And the window closed.

I turned and ran home.

How could I do that to her?

The next morning, around ten o'clock, I woke up wondering what the hell I had done. And I've been asking myself that question for weeks now. I called her, but she didn't answer.

How could I have left her there with that maniac pounding on the door? And I let her stay to be devoured or drown. I called again. No answer.

Why didn't I call the cops? Had I helped kill her? All this swirled in my head throughout the day as I wandered the apartment, going to the door about a hundred times to go looking for her. But I waited.

That night, I called again. Loskie answered, "Alma?" I hung up. For the rest of the weekend, I forced myself to stay in. I smoked cigarettes, telling myself that I had to be around if Alma came by. I called a few more times on Sunday.

Finally, long before I had to be at work that Monday, I decided to go by Alma's house. Maybe she was angry at me for abandoning her; after all, she had not come by my place. I had to make her understand that I hadn't left her, that I just wanted for her to get herself out of the situation. I had to make sure she was okay. I walked across the campus and somehow smelled fall in the distance.

As I crossed the street, I saw a barefoot, shirtless Loskie sprawled on top of the front steps. His unbuttoned pants exposed dark pubic hair. An empty bottle of Jack lay on its side near his head. I realized his car was gone. Had Alma stolen his car? I stepped over his heaving frame and searched the house until I was sure that Alma—or her lifeless body—was not there.

Again standing over Loskie's body, I noticed a taxi. The young mother, Coral, was leaving her upstairs apartment with two large suitcases. Somehow she managed to wheel them both to the taxi with her sleeping hellion, Ella, on her shoulder. Coral spotted me.

"Where'd Alma go? I saw her leave earlier."

I shook my head.

She shrugged and, with a weary arm, waved and got into the taxi. I never got a chance to ask when Alma had left and how.

I know you're still wondering why I came to New York, but I can assure you that it wasn't to find Alma. She would never come here.

I just don't know how to talk about why I'm here, especially with someone like you. I mean, you own your home, you're a nurse, and you run a community clinic. I've never known anyone like you. What could you possibly want from someone like me?

Not long after Alma disappeared, so did I.

The sun rose above the clouds, a growing slash of orange in the east, faint blue layers pursuing black, the purple line between darkness and light creeping westward behind me.

A brilliant yellow blinded me. Then I navigated a sea of Tuesday commuters to downtown Manhattan, Liberty and Greenwich Streets. I was alone on top of the South Tower and facing north. Red, blue, orange, yellow, green, brown subway lines glowed beneath the surface, running up and down and in and out of the island. And a troupe of millions of street performers failed eternally on the grid of streets below, singeing their hair while breathing fire, dropping juggling balls and each other, trying to impress people who carried cameras and their old people and young people and pocket-change pity.

Out of all of those performers emerged a woman, an acrobatic contortionist, completing perfect flips and somersaults and twists. She contributed to the ever-flailing performers, who then stumbled and pivoted and gawked at all the buildings and bridges, knowing nothing of their history. From that tower, I tracked each of the performers and lost them one by one at the manmade banks of the East River, the harbor, the Hudson. Or they wandered up the widening island only to become concealed by a muggy haze of skyscraper tributes to man's majesty, tributes to getting lost, to loss itself. I was urged to go down there. To be a performer. Or the woman. Or the haze obscuring the concrete.

I saw these things.

I still see them from time to time.

I am telling the truth. It wasn't until a few days later that I found myself leaning over my sketchbook, hiding my ever-narrow eyes behind my black bangs, thinking about how much I liked my funky hair but also wondering why I cut my hair in a way that shows off my big, ugly ears when I push my bangs behind them. I came to the conclusion that people were stupid for taking pride in things they have no control over, like nice, normal-sized ears. At least you know for certain where a hairstyle comes from.

Water from a nearby fountain sprayed my sketchpad. Pencil lines blurred, paper warped. I became aware that I was sitting in the grass and of the people around me talking business or travel or politics or crosswords or how to take the subway to the Empire State Building. Training the hair out of my face, I suddenly felt exposed and had to get out of Bryant Park; I needed a place to stay. I frowned at my smudged drawings; as I got ready to go, I was considering throwing out the whole sketchbook. Then I noticed a tall brown-eyed man with sun-darkened brown skin standing next to me.

"What're you drawing?" he asked with a slight Southern twang.

"What?" It was the first time anyone had talked to me in days.

"Your drawing. I'm intrigued. What is it?"

"Anyone can see I'm no good, so I'm calling your bullshit."

"Well, you're onto me," he said, and laughed. "Name's Pablo. Friends call me Berlin." He extended his hand and I shook it.

"Berlin?"

"Most of my friends are military. We go by last names. You know, like athletes?"

"Not really. I don't really like sports. You're military? You don't look it." He was bald with long, dark sideburns that sprouted exactly even with the tops of his ears and gradually grew thinner until they came to fine points just under his cheekbones.

He smiled. "I got out in '92. Now I spend my time sculpting this look." He framed his face with his hands, puckered his lips, and widened his eyes.

I laughed. "You're a little nuts."

"Maybe. There's lots of chemicals in Iraq."

I was a little embarrassed. "That sucks. Sorry."

"Bah, no problem. I'm on disability; it's allowed me to meet a lot of good folks between here and Houston over the last few months."

"It must not be hard to meet new people." I smiled. "I mean, with all your great pickup lines."

He laughed and wiped sweat off his brow. "I know. It's weird walking up to you like that. By the way, what's your name?" He sat cross-legged, facing me.

"Katherine Campos." I hesitated. Then I said, "I go by Kat." I surprised myself. But after all those days of isolation, I guess I shouldn't have been surprised at how familiar I was being with him.

"Well, Kat, your art is unassuming. I like it."

"If you're calling my sketches art, you must be crazier than I thought."

"Maybe." He scratched his chin thoughtfully. "Don't you hate museums?"

"I don't go to museums." I didn't know how else to respond to his random question.

"I don't blame you. They're boring. They're boring because curation controls the way we experience and learn."

"What I meant to say is no one ever took me to a museum."

"Whoa. So you're a blank slate."

"I wouldn't say that. It's just that my parents didn't have time for things like museums."

"Your parents were genius."

"Ha." I shook my head.

"Well, they kept you from culture's cheap way to achieve an agenda."

"Hmm," I said. "What's your agenda?"

We both laughed.

"No, really," Berlin went on. "What you're doing—practicing, developing, choosing to do it here in this park—is more honest than what we can see in a gallery. In a museum, I can't help wanting to see what's happening outside the frame. I mean, think about your family photo album."

"We didn't have one." I looked away, expecting some incredulous exclamation. But none came.

"Okay, well, the family photo album my parents curated over the years sure as hell doesn't represent much truth. We weren't as happy as the photos show."

"I get what you're saying, but we have to tell stories with frames and curation. Otherwise, the story goes on forever."

"What does it matter if there's no truth in the thing? Or a fraction of truth? All I'm saying is that the 'final product' of a photo or anything else in a gallery is always decontextualized. Most people don't consider this once they figure out how a picture or some other artifact makes them feel."

We sat quietly for a bit. Fountain water blew, and I wiped my forehead. Berlin had said something that sparked a vague idea. His view that my stubborn childhood habit constituted "art" was absurd. But the thought that anything I do—crappy sketches or otherwise—would be contextualized by anyone was either terrifying or comforting. Before I could decide, my brother's stories nudged and elbowed into my mind. And, as if mindlessly preparing for a ritual—or routine—to begin, I waited to hear Berlin brag about the great and horrible things he'd done as a boy in Houston and as a young man shooting a gun in Iraq, like that would somehow explain how he had become a person with opinions about art and its contexts.

No boasting, though. In fact, I didn't learn much about Berlin except that he had a sharp ear for details and wasn't afraid to ask questions. Over the week we spent wandering the streets and parks of Manhattan, Berlin pried my stories in two, scraping out their insides, holding them up to me, trying to get me to look at them for what they were. One time, Berlin and I were wandering Midtown, trying to find an uptown subway back to our hostel and get away from the tourist mobs. It was a couple days after we'd met, and I'd just finished telling the story my brother told about my dad as a boy.

Berlin stopped in the middle of the sidewalk and said, "All you're doing is telling someone else's stories." He paused. "What's your story?" He frequently made comments like this. And each time, it sent fear and exhilaration pulsing into my gut, like I'd been caught staring at a stranger.

As if it answered his question, I said, "Most of my life, I've listened to stories my brother told. When I was a kid, he'd tell me stories about my dad as I fell asleep; the only way I know how to tell my story is with his words."

Berlin was quiet for a moment. People streamed around us, jostling us as we stood facing each other. Then he said, "Are you like your brother, reciting the fables—or parables—as though they were literal truth? Or are you more like your dad—like most people with questionable pasts—elaborating on a history you can't be held accountable for?"

He turned and walked into the massive Saint Patrick's Cathedral. I followed in a conflicted daze but then paused. As I stared at the ridiculous bronze Atlas statue across the street, I considered walking away from Berlin right then. I wanted to be around Berlin because he led me to ideas of myself that I'd never considered. But this was the exact thing that scared me to death. I wanted to continue telling him my family history, but I resisted the idea that someone could help me sort out fact from fiction; I felt that I had to do that on my own.

In the church, Berlin walked on the outskirts of the pews, pausing every few steps at the carvings in the wall to study or pray or wonder at context. Maybe all three. I left him alone. It was only my second time in a church, but I had never envisioned anything like this: a priest talked, tourists snapped pictures, someone chanted, two old ladies whispered, chimes rang. Not knowing what to do, I sat near the back. And it wasn't long before all the sounds wrapped me in one unified, humming thread. Then I saw my father floating. He was the faded scents of melting wax, frankincense, and moldy sponges soaked in holy water; he was among the royal stained-glass colors and the lofty intricate ceiling. Whether this place was a tribute to man's magnificence or to something far larger, I can't say. But I believed, if only for a few moments, in that immense unknown. Lonely among the mass of people and empty space, I cried. Kneeling, I laced my fingers together and pushed my knuckles into my eyes to drive back the tears. I saw animated, undulating green clouds. Then shoes scuffed. A baby cried. A woman laughed. Perfume permeated. A camera clicked, flashed. I had to get out of there.

Berlin caught up with me, saw my puffy red eyes, and put his arm around my shoulders.

"I understand what you're going through. Believe me, I do. You're trying to untangle yourself from an entire lifetime of digressions and distractions."

Looking back, it was just about the only thing he said to me that revealed much of anything about who he was. But at the time, I took it as permission to recite more family histories and to relate, as Berlin called it, a version of my own story. Even though—or maybe because—he knew I was still struggling in the swirling eddies and rapids of truth and lie, he became more assuring with his touch. After we left the church, it was an arm around my shoulders, the next day it was his big, gentle hand on the back of my neck, and the day after that it was his hand on mine, in mine.

And even if you think his affection was all part of a long seduction, his touch assured me that he had not abandoned me despite my problematic stories.

Berlin was the first man I slept with. Right in the hostel at 103rd and Amsterdam, twenty-three international women slept, dreamed. Or maybe they watched and listened and smelled. Or maybe they shut their eyes and buried their ears in pillows and clapped their hands over their noses. Maybe all of these things, but it didn't matter to me. My insides felt a little sore for days afterward; that didn't matter, either. Berlin hadn't been rough at all. It could have been worse. Alma wasn't even kissed until her third time.

The next morning, Berlin left town.

After he left, I sat smoking at a picnic table in front of the hostel with a familiar feeling. And I wondered why the traffic tones and grinds and honks differed from San José's. And it got me thinking about how the flow of people in and out of my life had changed. I mean, people are always leaving, have always left. But in my hometown, it seems that where one person left off, another picked up. There is some satisfaction in that. Here in New York, though, I was suddenly alone again. That's not such a bad thing, either. Like when a long, profound symphony is finally over: the silence—the relative silence mingling with the sound of traffic—is a relief. Berlin was gone. I was sad that I'd never see him again. He just had to move on. But there was satisfaction that I could now sit in relative silence.

In my life, I've often sat with this "melancholy satisfaction"—a phrase I once heard in an American literature course at State. Some goateed blond guy said it about the ending of Kate Chopin's *The Awakening*. The professor asked what he meant. The guy fiddled with his orange-and-black cap, defining a term with its own words: "You know. Like, um, a melancholy satisfaction that you get when things are sad and you feel this, um, happiness that you feel sad . . . like a melancholy satisfaction . . . that she died, that she lived a life, that she finally had some sort of . . . um. . . I don't know . . . I just feel a melancholy satisfaction that she died . . ." It was as if the guy believed repeating the same phrase three times could magically clarify its meaning. He could have said that he felt sad and contented because the heroine, although she died, had finally taken control of her life. But I didn't say anything; I was too caught up by the fact that she'd drowned herself. The ending is implausible. But nothing was said about that. Certainly not by me.

Anyway, I sat there on Amsterdam Avenue, thousands of miles from that classroom and my hometown, with melancholy satisfaction. When it comes to Alma, I'll only be satisfied if she is doing what she needs to do. But now all that remains is me. Melancholy.

A taxi honked. A truck's gears shifted. German backpackers laughed. I lit another cigarette and reminded myself not to expect the vanished to reappear. Except in my dreams. Recently, a silhouetted figure has been speaking from the far side of a brightly lit, symmetrical room. There are the screams and hollers of drunken college kids, sirens, and one long drone of idling engines. Most often, the silhouette says to me, "Katherine, it's okay. You can go now."

These dreams comfort. And torment. I wonder whose dreams I'm in and if the dead have dreams.

I thought I heard a whisper. But it was a street sweeper.

*S*ay no.

"Whaddya want then?"

Don't answer. Push by her and throw open the curtains. Stand at the window in the fading sunlight and white streetlamp. Run fingers on flesh.

"That skin. Beautiful." *She reaches out.*

Jump away from her. Tell her to get dressed.

"Okay."

Give her a lit cigarette.

"I don't smoke."

Disrobe.

Walk to the wall and place hands on it.

"Oh. One of those, huh?" *She walks over.* "Want a drink first?"

Say no.

She presses the cigarette tip onto the ridge of backbone.

Realize that there are great ideas in the warmth and stench of wounds.

2.

AFTER YOU LEFT ME here in bed yesterday morning, I grabbed some cash and wandered the streets. Why? I don't know. Then I rode the subway to evade the rain, sweaty hands jammed in my pockets, clutching the damp money. It was almost dark when I got out somewhere to escape the press of people incessantly yammering about the Yankees, Braves, World Series, Game 1, rainout. Out of the growing gloom, a young woman approached me. Next I know, it's morning on our front steps, and you're looking at the burn mark on my back and asking what happened to my keys and how I got around without money. I still don't know.

Wherever I had been, I knew I needed to come back to you. Who else can treat my wound?

———————————

It's stupid for me to believe I came here to New York to find or be found by Berlin. It's as silly as your saying I was "compelled by some cosmic force" into your life.

I don't mean to make light of your spirituality; the mystery of it draws me to you. In fact, I wish I could thank your ex-girlfriend. Gloria's unshakable faith lives on in you. If it's possible to love someone I've never met, it would be your Gloria. But it's her passion—your passion—that I love, not her belief in fate. It seems dangerous to pair zeal for a cause with faith in destiny. At the very least, the two seem to cancel each other out.

What I'm asking is this: Would Gloria—that woman of strong feminist ideals and woman of great belief in fate—think a woman like me was destined to meet Berlin? If so, would she admire me for choosing to sleep with him, for allowing myself to say "I'm in charge of my body"? Or would she see me going to bed with him as a necessary failure of my feminine spirit, a predetermined encounter that was meant to show me what I'm up against as a woman in a man's world, a world of subtle but insidious occupation? Would Gloria think I am pathetic for interpreting his interest in my story as anything other than a long, self-serving seduction? Would she think I was just a story of conquest for Berlin to tell his war buddies, a story about an ugly homeless girl that he fucked?

You think I'm projecting?

Maybe you're right: I don't really know who Gloria was. But if you think she would hear my story and say that I am an "exceptional beauty," all I can ask is, who the hell talks like that? Did her parents teach her of her own exceptionalism, or did she have to go to Vassar to learn that? Until recently, I didn't give that much thought to the contexts of suburban white women from wealthy families, not to mention my *own* context. If I'd ever in my life had the time to interpret these kinds of things, maybe I wouldn't have ended up here, guessing why I'm in New York, hoping I'm not here to tell other people's stories for eternity. I've managed not to do that with you. Yet.

You see, I don't want to lie to you, but I might.

Here's the thing: With Berlin, I was trying honestly to weave my recent history with my distant past. But it became a colorful, tangled mass of thread. So I want to be careful here. Otherwise, my story—the tapestry I am trying to create—may again become entangled or come undone.

Yes, I know. I've got weaving on the mind. Alice in Chains' "Got Me Wrong" is the last song I listened to. But in a couple other songs on the EP, a wailing woman makes me shudder. I can't stop listening, can't stop wondering why—in a band of all men—certain lyrics are highlighted by her voice, what the songs would mean without her. It's you who helped me to wonder about the presence of things like this, to consider what their absence would mean.

Anyhow, I just couldn't untangle the mess of my youth while in California. I know that still doesn't fully explain why I'm here. But the ghosts back home shrouded me, bound me to immortalize them. And no one living, at least not in San José, could help me cut the threads.

Since we're talking ghosts, we might as well start with my dad.

I never actually heard Dad tell his own story. You may not believe this, but I never picked up much Spanish. Dad didn't talk to me all that often anyway. So up until a certain point, I only ever heard Oso's ornate, historical translations, beginning with "Papá was born in the southern San Joaquin Valley, where the majestic Sierra Nevada greets her old friend the Pacific Coast Range with a handshake agreement to always protect the vast, fertile God's country from the hole of vice and misery that was Los Angeles."

And when I told the story to Berlin, I told it word for word as Oso did:

"When Papá was born in mid-August 1945, in a town called Bakersfield, he smiled before anything else. Shortly after his birth, he smiled at his mother when he was laid on her bosom for the first and last time. His mother was so surprised and overjoyed by her son's toothless, dimpled greeting that she died with a giggle trapped in her throat and a faint smile frozen on her lips. That same night, Dad smiled up at our abuelo as our six tías wept over the body of their dead mother, our abuela. Early the following morning, the entirety of Papá's immediate family was dead.

"Papá's tío, Juan—who had, upon hearing the news that his sister-in-law had died, traveled all night from San Diego—discovered our abuela and our six tías in restful poses around the family room, the girls with the same soft, mortal smile as their mother. Our abuelo was curled in a ball, facing the wall. Papá giggled as he lay on his back next to his dead father, looking into the lifeless eyes. Juan crossed himself. He called a priest both for last rites and to ask if the laughter was evil, if it was natural for a baby to be making this kind of racket. The priest could only say that crying was much more common."

You get the idea. I don't want to make the same mistake I made with Berlin and end up with you asking whose story this is.

Dad's aunt, Gabriella, moved up from San Diego. It was bad enough that they had to live in the same house where all that death had happened, so Juan, superstitious as he was, kept his distance from the newborn by working long hours clearing brush and weeds around oil derricks and roaming the streets. As the boy grew, he laughed for increasingly longer periods. By the time Dad was six, Oso would say, "Papá was known to laugh every day for two straight hours, as if it were as natural as breathing."

The routines and rituals Juan and Gabriella enacted around the boy were very different. For years, Juan—fearful asshole that he was—walked the streets, looking for silence rather than helping to raise the orphan. When he was at home, he placed cotton in his ears and held it in place with Jacob Marley gauze wrapped around his head to guard against the "unnatural" boy. But Gabriella took up her knitting while the boy laughed and played. And she would fall asleep listening to the boy chuckle like he was sharing secret jokes with his dead siblings.

Dad had been kicked out of all the schools in Bakersfield by the time he should have started high school. Though all the kids loved him and "his laughter broke up fights," teachers were made uneasy by his uncontrollable and unaccountable laughter. So when the boy was thirteen, he went to work in the fields; Juan demanded that he help provide for the family. And with his "lyrical laughter," Dad enchanted the men and women who worked the cotton fields with him, just as he had with his friends in the classroom.

Juan must have been jealous or, like I said earlier, a scared dick.

Despite protests from Gabriella, he insisted that the boy work the off-season as a landscaper's assistant on the farmers' private residences. Juan succeeded in tiring the boy so much that he would come home and go straight to bed. Gabriella took to sitting in the house, shades drawn, housework undone, foolishly waiting to hear her nephew's laughter during the daylight hours. She would stay awake late into the night—a little ghoulishly, if you ask me—to listen to the boy chuckle with his dead siblings. She was so exhausted in the mornings that the boy would be out of the house before she woke.

Dad worked in the farmers' fields and yards for four years. He grew taller and more handsome than most men. The people of Bakersfield were, as Oso said, "in love with him and his laughter. They didn't know how to be happy without him." (Oso could lay it on pretty thick.) Juan couldn't go anywhere without hearing of his nephew. And at home, he couldn't escape the "icy depression that had made his wife and marriage brittle."

One Sunday, Juan asked the boy why he continued to laugh all these years. "Don't you know it upsets me?"

The boy laughed softly. "Laughter is like a sneeze for the soul."

That Dad said something like that seems implausible. But whatever he said got him kicked out of the house. The night before he left, the boy laughed, Gabriella sobbed, and Juan walked the streets. When the boy went to bed, Gabriella lay alone, listening for the night chuckles. All she heard was the silence of the dead. The next morning, the boy left without a sound.

Over the next decade, Dad—the boy, Papá, José, whatever—moved mostly north along stretches of Highway 99 and the rail lines that ran the length of the Central Valley "like lonely tear streaks." In Delano, he broke bread with César Chávez and Bobby Kennedy after a day of picketing grape growers. No, I don't believe the part about Chávez. I can't say anything about the timing of his visit to Delano, much less his being there with RFK for the breaking of Chávez's hunger strike, but Dad surely would have been a scab rather than a picketer: he needed the money.

Besides, he was, for the most part, a selfish bastard. Oso, on the other hand, must have done some reading; though never a picker, he idolized Chávez. I can't say how I felt about Chávez. Maybe I was too young. I certainly didn't know or care about the farm workers or their unions. Maybe that makes me an asshole, but I wasn't taught about Chávez in school. Then again, people have to be dead for a while before they make it into a history book, right?

"In the shadows of the southern Sierra Nevada foothills," Dad picked up a job as a freight loader in the train yard in the small town of Hanford. After a year or so, he hopped a freight north to where the tracks met with Highway 99 in Fresno, where he worked in a dried apricot plant. But something had disappeared: his laughter. So he wandered north until his money ran out; he settled for a job at a poultry slaughterhouse in Merced.

After a few months of beheading and quartering chickens, Dad woke early one morning in a field of tomatoes with both his pinkies sliced clean off. Oso said it was goons hired by "those goddamned growers in Delano." It seems doubtful that they could have lopped off his fingers while he slept. But what is true is after the wounds healed, his hands looked like chicken feet. Dad left Merced and traveled north a hundred miles to the middle of the Central Valley. The Garden of the Sun was "a tight-knit farming community blessed by God with the richest soil in the world."

I'll spare you Oso's lavish details. Let's just say the Garden has three rivers that used to be named something ancient, but they were renamed El Jardín, the Muddville, and the Ralston, in homage to the three small cities nearby. At the risk of getting too sidetracked, Berlin was adamant that these places—El Jardín, Muddville, and Ralston—weren't real, saying he had been through the Central Valley. I'm still not sure why he called me out on this particular detail. At the time, I told him I had never even left the Bay Area until recently.

"I can show you on a map."

"It doesn't matter," I almost yelled.

"What would your teachers say?"

"That doesn't make a difference to me, either." My voice rose. "Names and places and dates aren't important. Only the events themselves."

Maybe it was my insistence about this—and so many other details of my story—that convinced him to leave a few days later. I really have no idea why I defended my ignorance. But now I think I understand his obsession with "context." In a way, though, I think I understood it before I met Berlin. You remember that American literature course I told you about, the one with the blond guy that was all melancholy and satisfied? I can't help but think about the pallid old professor lecturing head down, reading from his curled and yellowed handwritten notes. On the first day of class, he told us we were going to learn to accurately interpret any piece of fiction by knowing only where and when the author grew up.

Even then, I remember thinking there has to be more, that his theory was a bullshit oversimplification—or maybe just too inflexible. Yet the crusty old man—the gold, feather-helmeted mascot staring at me sideways from his blue university polo—returned to his theory every week. His droning got tiring, so I began creating a theory that went further: we might accurately interpret an *individual* by how he or she interprets or retells a story. With only five minutes of discussion at the end of each meeting, there was no time to share my thoughts—not that I would have anyway. So I thought about writing an essay about it. But after interpreting the old prof himself, I was convinced he'd make a stink about it. So I stopped going to class. I mean, what was the point?

———————

Dad found work in Ralston. Picking tomatoes, Dad began to laugh again. The people he worked with came and went with the seasons, but they all appreciated Dad's "melodious laughter," which helped pass the days of hard labor and fueled the nights of eating and drinking. When picking season was over, the temporary help disappeared to various winter jobs in the cities. Dad hated cities and was too tired from his decade on the move. So he kept the grounds on nearby farm homes and was around early in the season to help plant the new crops. He loved those years on the delta where "man's needs and his ambitions converged gracefully with God's bounty."

It was at this point in the story that Oso would editorialize, railing against the farm owners: men who believed their small farming operation: were respectable, that the Garden towns had sprung from the soil due to blood, sweat, and sacrifice. "Yes. But the blood, sweat, and sacrifice were not necessarily their own." According to Oso, it was these owners who had, for over 130 years, "exploited" Native, Chinese, Mexican, Filipino, and Oakie laborers with "endless hours, poor living conditions, and meager pay." These same "respectable" families ended up selling their farms some years later to a few big businesses that might be able to stand up to Chávez's and Itliong's United Farm Workers.

I know I'm telling other people's stories again. I can't help it. These stories might explain something about me. But I don't know how or why any of the details matter. Why does it matter to me that Dad, not yet thirty years old, had seen the entire Central Valley change so drastically? Why do I care that by the spring of 1972, the entire valley was owned and controlled by ten or twelve families, corporations, and land developers? What does it matter that houses began to "sprout up like weeds all over the rich soil"? That the borders of towns like Ralston continued to spill over themselves "in waves of cement"? That everyone wanted their own yard, their own headroom, their own sky unobstructed by neighbors?

On a biological level, who I am seems to derive from Dad catching up with his estranged laughter in Ralston, where he met my mother.

Dad was out of a job after the owner sold his tomato plantation to a land developer. In turn, the developer "cultivated Vintage Faire, complete with five thousand parking spots and seventy-five stores to feed and clothe and entertain the increasing mass of people." But Dad easily got work picking, planting, cutting, and maintaining grapevines year-round with the Giordano family, who had built a viticulture empire that was expanding despite the skyrocketing land values. The Giordanos had, ever since the Great Depression, "capitalized on the dispossessed with cheap fortified wines."

Supposedly, the seasonal and full-time workers fell in love with Dad, both men and women, who "swooned" over him. And Dad, for the first time in his life, had "enough love to keep him happy well into the night." And the men were happy, too. Since the women who didn't sleep with Dad still felt at ease and amorous, there was plenty of love to go around.

I agree with you: it sounds like some horny male fantasy. And kind of nasty to think of your dad laying all those señoritas. Anyway . . .

A year and a half after he started at the vineyard, Dad met my mom, Clara Flanagan, an assistant to Giordano Sr. Apparently, Dad was alone and barefoot among the boundless rows of vines, giggling to himself as he surveyed the young leaves and unripe grapes. He soon realized that he was no longer alone. A few rows over, "a pair of white legs walked beneath the hem of a green skirt." Dad went about his work in silence. When he looked over again, the pair of legs gleamed in the next row over. He turned his back, pretending to inspect a leaf for imperfection. He tried to hear where she was. Then he turned to see a skinny woman with bobbed, sandy-blond hair standing nearby. Dad had never seen her before. She was as geometrically sound as a rectangle. She sniffed, wiping her nose with the back of her hand.

Oso would have me believe she said something goofy like, "So, you're the one they call Happy José?" and Dad laughed and said, "No, señorita. At least not to my face. But you can call me that if you want." She walked closer, and Dad saw crow's-feet curling from the corners of her eyes.

She introduced herself, shaking his hand. Dad was "somewhat lost between humor, admiration, and fear." Mom was "endearing in her attempts at flirtatious posturing and her misplacement there in the middle of the vineyard." Though she was angular and self-conscious, she "carried determination in her eyes." But Dad knew he had to be careful, that even the handshake was dangerous. He'd had friends run off the land or arrested or killed for "little more than a long gaze at a white woman."

Over the next couple months, they met secretly in the vineyards, Dad practicing his English by telling his California odyssey and Mom correcting his grammar and getting an occasional word in about her own life. She was seven years older than him and had lived in Ralston her entire life. Eventually, she told Dad she wanted children with him, but she knew that couldn't happen in that little farming community. She wanted him to move with her to San José, a place she believed they would be accepted as a couple, a place she also thought "was bound to be as great as its famous cousin to the north." Dad said his place was in Ralston at Giordano Estates, tending to what he felt were his vines and grapes. But when Mom became pregnant with Oso three months after they met, moving became crucial. Dad's laughter slowly slipped away from him again. In its place was a constant sneezing.

That's funny. I've never interpreted the sneezing to be an allergic reaction to fatherhood. After all these years and endless tellings, it's damn near impossible to know which details or turns of phrase were Dad's. What I can say is Oso would have me believe his birth on March 9, 1973, saved their marriage. As I found out later, though, Oso's very existence in Ralston likely put them in some danger.

When Oso came into the world, he "roared." And Dad giggled for the first time in months. He held Oso and gazed at Mom; he put Oso on her breast and kissed her. She smiled warmly even though the labor had drained her pregnancy glow and had "trodden a deep groove on her brow." Oso "roared" again and fell ravenously to his first meal. They were going to name him Segundo, but they agreed to name him Oso.

Dad's sneezing became so intense that he often passed out in the middle of the fits. The Giordanos' family doctor discovered that Dad had a heart arrhythmia that was aggravated by the sneezing fits. But the doctor was not sure how to prevent the sneezing. He fitted Dad with dark sunglasses just in case he was a photic sneezer—the kind who sneezes because of sun sensitivity—and prescribed powerful antihistamines. When the antihistamines didn't work, Mom told Dad that they should move to San José for the better climate and less pollen. Reluctantly, Dad conceded. And for the rest of his life, Dad would observe the world this way—with "a thin layer of tinted glass between him and the explosion of his heart."

I'm not kidding you. I believed this absurd story about their migration to San José until I was in middle school and Dad himself told me the truth. Or a different version of the truth. But I don't want to get tangled up by jumping ahead.

Dad's "connection to the vineyard" was soon replaced by Oso. Father and son would sit on the floor and giggle for hours, their laughter "intertwined, like new and old growth in a vineyard." If you believe everything, the kid was feeding himself at six months and speaking in complete sentences before the age of one. And he could walk even before he could talk.

Until he found better work, Dad helped Mr. Henry at his furniture store. Eventually, Dad convinced Mr. Henry, an impeccably dressed German American with neat black hair and a trimmed goatee, to let us stay permanently in the apartment above the store. Obviously, it was convenient to his job at the time, but Dad fell in love with the little rounded dining room above the street corner: "So much to watch out of all those tall windows." Dad would sit there after a meal, gazing east, "imagining San José's rich agricultural history." But he'd usually end up a little depressed since "the valley's fields and orchards were rapidly being covered by houses and concrete."

Now, I've seen enough of that valley—Santa Clara Valley—to know the exaggerations. There's even a huge swath of land in south San José that still produces healthy crops; the farmer refuses to give up to developers. But I think Dad—or Oso—wanted to make clear that the love of his livelihood was sacrificed for the family. In any case, Dad soon got a job at one of the seven major fruit canneries. He learned to like the job well enough. Mom had no problem getting a job doing the same kind of thing she had done for Giordano Sr.

Oso in tow, Dad and Mom got married in a simple ceremony at city hall, across from Saint James Park, on a Monday afternoon. Afterward, they walked the two blocks back to our run-down third-story apartment and sat in candlelight at a small table in the circular room. Watching a panorama of activity on Santa Clara and Third Streets through the open eight-foot windows that surrounded them, "they were wrapped in the sounds of the city." As daylight faded, they shared a nice bottle of wine—a wedding gift from Mr. Henry. With Oso asleep in her arms, Mom dreamed out loud about refinishing the tattered hardwood floors, painting sea green over the random white roller-stroke patch jobs on the walls and soaring ceilings; she thought white would make the crown molding shine like a light. None of this ever happened. Over the years, the only thing that changed was the amount of mismatched furniture in the apartment, sold at discount or given to us by Mr. Henry.

I'm sure Mom wasn't the first to make plans for improvement in the old building. A hundred years and thousands of people had come and gone, passing beneath the motto of that onetime men's lodge still visible from the street: FRIENDSHIP, LOVE AND TRUTH. Oso said he could smell sweat and iron from the boxing gym that'd been on the second floor ten years earlier. Maybe Mom would have said she smelled fresh blooms from the first-floor florist that'd been there forty years before. And perhaps Dad would have smelled fresh produce and horse poop as farmers pulled their crops to market down Santa Clara Street eighty years ago. But Alma and I never smelled any of that. We just smelled dirt and dried lead paint.

Nine months after they were married, Mom gave birth to me.

Mom was an office assistant before I was born and worked for a socialite, Gretchen Wagner, who was also pregnant at the time.

Less than a month after Alma was born, Gretchen returned to work. She and her husband, Martin Abernathy, were in some sort of business—defense contractors, maybe. This, along with their political aspirations, kept them away from home, located in the wealthy Naglee Park neighborhood just outside downtown. Since Mom didn't go back to work after I was born, she took in Alma during the day for a small fee. Every morning before I woke up, Gretchen would drop off the still-sleeping Alma. During the weekdays, and often on weekends, I woke with Alma next to me, her pale pink arm draped over my body, her long, stringy blond hair scattered on the pillow, her morning breath intruding my nose, her big black eyes staring at me. With some obvious exceptions, we could have been twins. At night, we would be put to bed long before Gretchen picked Alma up.

In the mornings, Oso always found some way to torment me and Alma, sometimes slipping from his chair and tugging at our tiny feet, trying to drag us under the table with his oversized hands. Other times, he would wake us by jumping on our bed, a flurry of dark-brown skin and wild, curly black hair, screaming and yelling, in a too-small teddy-bear-print pajama top and tighty-whities. Alma and I would be in tears before Mom came in, always ready for the day, prepared to do battle, a determined look in her light-gray eyes. Earth-toned sundresses were Mom's uniform, minimal black eyeliner and rouge her war paint, her gray-streaked, sandy-blond hair always in a high, tight bun, no jewelry to avoid entanglements. Her hair and neck were sprinkled with an herby, floral oil—a calming agent for me, likely for Alma, and perhaps even for her. But Oso was impervious.

Patiently, Mom would tell Oso to get off the bed. Most of the time, he would tooth-smile, keep his eyes on her, and get off the bed in slow motion. Sometimes Oso just continued to jump as he smiled at her. Mom would try to grab him by the arm while wrestling with a dress strap slipping off her shoulder. For a big kid, Oso was nimble, squirming away from her grasp. Mom usually left it at that. But my mother could sometimes exact a wordless yet resounding punishment that brought any room to a standstill—maybe that's what you have to do with boys sometimes. One morning when he was being a particularly ripe piece of shit, Oso slipped on the sheets when skirting away from Mom. He bounced off the bed onto the hardwood. And before Oso could stand, Mom slapped him so hard it rearranged his floppy black bed head instantly. Our crying stopped, and we watched Oso for his next move. Oso sat stunned at Mom's feet, rubbing his cheek. Then he cackled in a deep tone uncommon for a boy that age. He stood, kept laughing, stripped off all his clothes. He strutted to the bathroom, and Mom folded her skinny arms. When she heard Oso peeing, she started getting us ready for the day.

In those early years, Mom would run errands with all us kids. On the city bus, she'd sit with Alma and me and try to wrangle Oso. But she had no choice but to stay with her wobbly toddlers while Oso wandered around and talked to other passengers. "What's yer name? I'm Oso. It means 'bear' cuz I roar like one. Raar!" When Mom tried to gather him up, he would scream and run from her, somehow staying on his feet as the bus lurched. Eventually, she gave up for good.

One day when Oso was four or five, he approached a bearded man with sun-weathered skin who was sitting a few seats away. The man had ratty gray hair, a tattered black overcoat, and a maroon beanie. He was probably one of the residents of Saint James Park, one of the many who would accent much of our youth.

"What's yer name?" Oso asked the old man, pushing his bangs out of his face.

"I'm Joe. And you must be Oso. I've heard about you."

Oso glanced at Mom and then back at the old man. He hiked up his khaki shorts and said, "Really?"

The old man nodded slowly and smiled. He cast a look from under his bushy eyebrows at Mom and whispered something into Oso's ear. Oso took a few shaky steps back as the bus jerked along; he nodded to the man, knelt down, pulled up his rainbow-topped tube socks, tightened the shoelaces on his blue Zips, and sat quietly next to Mom. Mom raised her eyebrows at Oso, who tooth-grinned back at her. When she turned to the man, he was stepping off the bus. We never saw him again.

From then on, Oso sat quietly in his seat on the bus. But at our stops, he'd tear down the steps and into Relics, a run-down two-block area of pawnshops, secondhand stores, a fabric store called In Stitches, and a pizza joint called Pizza Jacques. By the time Mom entered In Stitches with Alma and me in a side-by-side stroller, Oso was nowhere to be found. But he always appeared when it was time to check out. One time, after Mom'd picked out some cheap fabric so she could make us new blouses, the clerk at the register told her it was the last time she would be allowed into the store. She asked why.

"Well"—the clerk nodded as she frowned past Mom—"there's one reason."

Mom turned to see Oso lying on the floor, wrapped in an expensive shock of purple cloth. With a sigh, she paid the balance and wheeled the stroller toward the inert Oso. When we got near the lifeless mass, Oso sprang toward Alma and me, bellowing loud enough to stop all the shoppers in midbrowse. While Alma and I cried, Mom spun Oso out of the fabric. He reeled, tripped over his untied shoes, and fell to the ground, his dark curls covering his eyes. Mom piled the fabric on the clerk's counter, grabbed Oso by the arm, and steered us out the door. Soon after, Mom stopped making our clothes.

We would go by bus to the massive grocery store a couple miles from home. Why Mom took us that far when there were good, cheap Vietnamese and Mexican markets nearer to downtown, I can't be sure. People really are so obsessed with skin color, and maybe Mom got fed up with the many sideways glances at the little markets. She was, after all, an older white lady wheeling a light-brown baby next to a bright-white baby in that side-by-side stroller. Maybe too many old ladies curiously, innocently, invasively asked, "Is that one yours?" pointing at me. "Is she adopted? She doesn't look like you and she doesn't quite look like the rest of us here." Maybe Mom thought the neon glow of the huge chain store would whiten all of our skin, or that the sheer size of the store would swallow us up, or that we would better blend into the crush of all sorts of people hunting for coupon-buy-one-get-one-free-price-decline-clearance cans, jars, and bags of food.

More likely, though, is that we were kicked out of the Mexican and Vietnamese marts because of Oso's madness. Mom would wheel the cart through the wide aisles of that large chain grocery store, maneuvering us around the destruction that Oso left in his wake: toppled pyramids of fruit, dented cans of vegetables, emptied boxes of cereal, gouged milk cartons, dropped yellow-white eggs. Mom did her best to clean up the mess as she filled the cart with our food. By the time we got to the checkout line, Oso would appear and snatch at Alma's and my tiny feet dangling outside the cart. Bellowing, he would send us into hysterics. When Mom swatted his hands, Oso would scream as if he had been stabbed.

On one occasion, though, he didn't appear at the checkout stand. Mom had the manager call Oso on the PA. When he appeared, he had a saucepan on his head and a plastic tablecloth around his waist, cheeks covered with heavy rouge, eyes with smeared eyeliner, and lips with neon-pink lipstick.

"Ha! Ha!" he cackled, lipstick glowing on his teeth.

Mom sighed, stripped the checkered skirt and cookery hard hat from Oso, and seized him by the wrist. Head bowed, she handed the goods to the manager, and Oso sank his teeth into the back of her hand. Mom yanked her hand from his jaws and whacked Oso so hard that a strap of her brown dress fell off her shoulder. She put the strap back in place, smoothed her neat, dingy hair, and led us out of the store. The customers collectively gaped in silence.

For the most part, the way that Mom put up with the crap my dad dished out was much different from the way she dealt with Oso. She was quiet and communicated with the family almost entirely in how she did things. Maybe the effect on me was not a positive one.

When I was two, Oso started school. It was the only time I remember seeing total relief in Mom's eyes.

How could I possibly remember this detail? My memories, until long after kindergarten, are only brief snippets, vignettes really. I'm sure it's the same for you. But I wonder who it was—which adult—that filled in the gaps for you. For me, it definitely wasn't my mom. Like I've said, she didn't talk much. And she sure wasn't going to relive those days. It was Oso, of course, who filled—or, as you and Gloria might say, colonized or cultivated—my mind with the details of the terror he forced on us.

I don't know why Oso shared this part of the story. It's not like he was a shithead all his life. But maybe you would agree with me that men, in general, seem to need to talk about what awful things they've done. What a strange way to make a connection with another person. You wouldn't believe the kinds of things I overheard down at the Cavalcade. The Cav was a crappy little dive bar—the only bar I could get into at my age— where all sorts of guys just out of prison came straight from a Greyhound bus that stopped next door, cashing their walking-money checks to have their first drink of freedom. While sipping vodka cranberries and smoking, I listened to the ex-cons boast to the bartenders about beating up homeless guys in Saint James Park, cheating on girlfriends, not paying child support, and punching police horses. And the bartenders also boasted about stupid shit. A cute blond college boy—one of the many guys who worked there and flirted with me and fed me free drinks and never checked my ID—bragged all the time to his buddies about the many things he should have been arrested for: DUIs, throwing a bale of hay in the middle of Tenth Street, having sex on top of the university event center, possession of weed.

But that was child's play. I once heard an old, rotund, Scotch-drinking mestizo man tell a couple college kids that he, in exchange for US citizenship and a UC Berkeley education, was trained in the 1960s by the CIA to kill communists and their families in the Yucatán jungles. Why would anyone admit to such things? All those boozehounds, young and old, talked so much. And maybe it was just talk, a way to justify spending their lives on barstools. Maybe you think they're not much different from most men, telling stories of their wickedness and violence so you know not to mess with them, as if to say, *You fuck with me, I'll kill you like a communist cockroach.* But I don't think that's what Oso was doing. It's possible he told me what a dick he was as a kid so I could see how much he had changed, like saying, *Look what a good guy I became despite what I've done.*

Other stories were just downright weird for Oso to tell. I suppose that was Dad's influence. I mean, Oso told the stories as if he were able to hear conversations from inside the womb, as if he had a heightened consciousness upon his own birth. But certain things he conveniently forgot, like his first day of kindergarten: the day his supernatural ferocity left him. You'd think that my own first day of kindergarten would be the first vividly terrifying or exciting moment in my life, but the memory is somehow cut into little pieces, not to be remembered in its entirety. It seems like the first memory I can call my own is of Oso's reluctant induction into the ranks of school. Oso's knees buckled underneath him, and he sank to the ground in front of the school. He hugged Mom's calf and was unable to speak through his quivering lips. Mom tried for five minutes to pry him from her leg, the strap from her yellow sundress sliding down. Finally, with the weight of her six-year-old son and his fear, she just limped to the classroom, pressing a few stray hairs on her head back into place.

—————————

Around the same time that Oso went reluctantly into kindergarten, Dad began working double shifts at the cannery and walking the streets with Oso whenever he had off days. When he came home from work in the evenings, Dad would tousle Oso's floppy curls with his chicken-footed hand, flop on the floor, kick off his boots, lean up on his elbow, cushioned by his smelly, balled-up work flannel, and tell the stories of his boyhood in the Central Valley. At least I assume that's what he talked about: it was all in Spanish. Then Oso would share the adventures of his own day at school. Oddly, he told these in English, perhaps a sign of his future generosity, a way to let Alma and me into the fold. Maybe it was just a way to piss Mom off with his stories of terrorizing the school, but she never said anything.

So far as anyone could tell, the classroom capers and playground misadventures were his own, given the reputation he had made for himself as a hell-raiser in his early years—I can still picture him pulling at my toes and running rampant through those stores. It's hard to believe he got away with the things he told us about, but he had such a gifted way of telling a story, embellishing with adjectives when facts became questionable and dramatically changing the pitch and tempo of his voice when escapes became improbable.

Dad never showed skepticism. Oso said he had put gum on a teacher's chair, turned over all the trash cans in the lunch yard, and slapped a glue-covered construction-paper hand cutout on the butt of a young girl. But Dad was in a state of suspended disbelief, enthralled by the renditions of these high-flown stories. Truth took a back seat to entertainment.

Mom also lived in a state of suspended disbelief. She quietly made fresh tortillas, black and red bean soup garnished with cilantro, onions, and jalapeños. But as she chopped and spiced, she never called into question the validity or the lack of punishment of Oso's so-called misbehavior. Besides, Dad's presence—much less his occasional angry outbursts—demanded that everyone listen, as if the males were sharing with us the discovery of fire or of God.

Once, while Alma and I went about our usual play beneath the kitchen table, we laughed or talked too loud; the next thing we knew, Dad was bellowing at us in Spanish to shut up—something that needed no translation. Mom stood scowling at the back of Dad's head. Alma clutched my shaking hands. Dad and Oso started talking again as if nothing had happened. I started to leave the kitchen, but Alma wouldn't let go of my hand. So we stayed there under the table. It was the first time I remember Dad acknowledging my presence.

Lost in all this was my first day of kindergarten. My introduction to thirty new people—when I had, up to that point, really known only a total of four—was not the same terror it was for Oso. If anything, I found relief from the chaos at home. Fragmented relief. Riding trikes at recess, wind in our faces. A show-and-tell puppy pooping yellow on the teacher's shoe—such giggling. Greek and Roman gods I came across while browsing the library—what amazing pictures.

Even before we started going to school, Mom would sometimes take us to Santa Cruz. Clambering onto the bus just as the doors were about to shut, she would find us a seat in the middle, always sitting next to me; more often than not, Alma would get the two seats across the aisle to herself, keeping in the seat closest to Mom until we got into the mountainous pass, at which point she would slide to the vacant seat next to the window. I was petrified during those bus rides. It always seemed we were going too fast for that dark, twisting road, where the enormous trees stretched forever upward to blot out the sun and the blackness below obscured all else. But Alma welcomed its unknowable quality. I often stole glances at her, her forehead glued to the window, and the white sunlight—if there was any—strobing through the trees and onto her pale skin and blond hair. Mom would glance over at her and then close her eyes and smile. I'd curl up in a ball, lie on Mom's lap, and try to wrap myself in her comforting warm-flower scent. Yet my shallow naps were always twisted, jostled, infused with suffocating, substanceless terrors as we wound our way over the hill.

What can be simultaneously without substance and full of terror? I don't know. I used to think that those namelessly asphyxiating dreams from childhood—and all the other dreams I've had since then—were the only things that were genuinely mine. Now I'm not so sure.

The routines and rituals of the trips to the secluded clothing-optional cove in Santa Cruz almost never changed. City bus rides to Diridon Station. Bus rides through the heavily wooded pass. A city bus to the cliffs above the water. Mom would put our hair in ponytails to keep it out of our faces on the often windy beach. In the spring and summer, Alma and I would mingle with the locals and strut around with the roaming, sand-matted mutts while Mom sat on the rocks for hours and sunned her stark, skinny body. Shortly before we left, each time, Mom would walk into the foamy surf and swim about fifty yards offshore; she always tried to coax us into the water.

Alma would say, "It's like magic, the way she floats out there. Let's go in."

"No way. She's gonna get swallowed up. Besides, we're still too little."

In the autumn and winter, with the whipping winds and the shorter days, the cove was nearly empty. But Alma and I contented ourselves to build cities of sand near the crashing waves. Mom would sit nearby, smiling, loosely wrapped in a blanket. Shortly before heading back to San José, Mom would, just as in the spring and summer, go into the water.

She would rise, let the blanket fall from her glowing white shoulders, and slide without pause or word into the surf.

These images have implanted themselves in my mind because they happened the same way every time we went to the seaside. Though these excursions happened for years, they exist in my memory as a singular trip. But one day, late in October when I was five, a separate memory of the coast rests in another, deeper region of my brain. And it was the exact same incident that Alma talked about the last time we saw each other. Mom levitated from her warm huddle on the gusty beach as the sun sank toward the hazy horizon. She glided toward the turbulent water but then hesitated. As a wave flattened and spread over her feet, she put her hands out to either side, palms facing us. Alma and I looked at each other. Then Alma went to Mom's side and with her two hands grasped Mom's hand. The two stood there, facing the orange-gray water. Mom's empty hand waited for my grasp. But I didn't move. Neither of them turned around.

After many long moments, Mom's empty hand dropped to her side; she entered the water, Alma clutching with both of her tiny hands. Alma squealed at the shock of cold water, but they waded out until a wave as high as Mom's shoulders yawned toward them. And in one instant, just before the wave crashed over them, the two vanished beneath the surface. They were gone. I gasped. The wave that had swallowed them dissipated on the shore and receded back to its source. I ran to the water's edge to search, as if I'd find particles of their disappeared bodies. But when the next swell grew, crested, and broke on the shore, I turned and screamed as I fled to the dry sand. When I turned back to the water, the heads of Mom and Alma floated beyond the breakers. Mom's bun had come out completely, and her hair covered her eyes. The two laughed and urged me to join them. I shook my head and sank to my knees to await their return. The sun dipped below the horizon.

The newness and excitement of that time—and, in a way, of most of my formal school experiences through the years, come to think of it—were stifled by Dad's and Oso's evening storytelling in the kitchen. Also, the possibility of Dad erupting in a flail of his chicken-feet hands and flare of his eyes behind those tinted glasses squashed any enthusiasm for school or friends I may have talked about. Dad took no notice that my activities under his kitchen table had changed. No longer did Alma and I play with paper dolls and Matchbox cars. Now we colored the alphabet and our numbers brought home from school, or we sketched ears in little notepads that Mom had given us.

Dad would also ignore Mom and the dinner she made. He talked and laughed with Oso while Mom cooked; when the meal was ready, he disappeared out the front door until long after we had gone to bed. Mom would cover Oso up on the couch where he'd fall asleep waiting for Dad to return. Until Oso was fourteen, Mom slept alone in her own room. That changed—along with so many other things—when Grandpa moved in.

The silver snake stops and opens its translucent jaws to inhale the people. The inside wraps in a warmth that smells of dirt and urine and sweat. The snake closes its jaws and burrows on.

A language with no voice says, "Click here, get anywhere."

Say: Where else would I want to be?

Thousands of faces are indifferent and talk in a language not understood.

"Deal," states the language with no voice.

Say: Deal? For what? With what?

The language with no voice glares. "If you see something, say something."

The thousands of faces—all sorts—turn away. From out of their backs emerges a man with white hair. He raises a sheet of plain white paper above his head. It says, in a language with no voice:

"Forgive the sins, resurrect the flesh!"

Say: What are you hoping to accomplish?

"Forgive the sins, resurrect the flesh!"

Say: Is that a statement of fact?

"Forgive the sins, resurrect the flesh!"

Say: Isn't that what we all want to do? Wait. Grandpa?

The man with white hair melts into the dirt and urine and sweat.

3.

EVEN IF I HAD FRIENDS, none of them would have wanted to hike with me from Inwood to South Ferry. They would rather spend this beautiful day buying their last-minute gifts than being outside. Here I was expecting a white Christmas, but it was just like the ones back home. It's probably lucky, too. Who knows what would have happened if there were snow—my first snow. I got all turned around in those crowds of shopping madness at Times Square. I must have gotten on a train. And then I was here.

I think your doctor friend overdid it with all the tests. It's only a couple little scrapes and a bruise.

No. No overnight observations. I'm fine. Just take me home.

———————

When I think of Grandpa Jonah, I can't help but think of you as a kid, making annual visits to your grandpa in Scotland. It's not that I can relate to your long walks in the countryside together, or what it was like to have a little time, space, and quiet all at once. Those things are as impossible to fathom as the idea of your fully functioning family, your suburban Providence childhood, and your Cornell education. What I do sympathize with, though, is how you conjure up your grandpa so you can walk with him, and how you like to imagine that he is messing with the people who took over his land, that he's tipping over their teacups, rattling their doorknobs, and whispering in their ears. But that's the thing about ghosts: envisioning them as quiet hiking partners or rascally, pissed-off poltergeists doesn't help with the intrusive, never-ending pursuit of a dream, a dream of your own father—long dead, long gone—walking with kids you don't have—can't have, won't have. Yes, I can certainly relate to those kinds of ghosts, the ghosts of unfulfilled happiness.

When I was ten, Grandpa Jonah and his LPs came to live with us. For almost sixty years, Grandpa had lived in a modest home on a vineyard. He wasn't accustomed to excessive comfort, even when he had money, so he had no complaints about staying in that apartment with us.

Mom's love for her dad was boundless. And after the time I spent with him, I could understand why. Sadness was never far from him. He was recently poor, and despite his brilliance and self-sacrifice through most of his life, the treads of failure had worn heavy grooves on his tanned, leathery face. But the burden of sorrow hadn't diminished his sturdy, lanky frame; he stood tall. And his white beard gave an aura of distinction. Besides, his willingness to talk about his life gave the impression that he was fine with the disappointments as long as he had his family.

I got to know Mom's family through Grandpa's stories, which I heard a lot since Grandpa slept in Oso's vacant bed, Oso still camping out on the couch. Piercing the dark ceiling was a sickle of dim hallway light cast through the partially closed door. Sounds that you would think competed seemed to work together in some mysterious tapestry. The faint sound of the jukebox in the Mission, the bar across the street, would waft through the door as carousers came and went, jukebox and carousers would waft and linger, linger with car engines and the air brakes of buses and mingle and dance with a moan or a conversation or a laugh of a bum. Alma's occasionally loud sleeping breaths beside me danced and embraced, embraced and wove throughout the deep tones of Grandpa's voice and dwelled among the classical notes on vinyl, notes of symphonies, sonatas, and concertos—some bold, others sweet, yet others odd, all of it baffling, that such sound could be created by people . . .

In that din almost every night, Grandpa's narrative was different from Oso's, yet somehow similar. I don't know. You tell me. Listen to how he would open his story:

"I was born among the refugees and beneath the smoke of San Francisco. My father, William Flanagan, was an ambitious man raised in Dubuque, Iowa, who had, in mid-May 1905, moved with his new bride—Bertha Flanagan, née Shaffer—from Cleveland to San Francisco to expand on his investments, putting large amounts of money into an import–export venture with companies from Asia. The venture was successful, and in early April of 1906, the young father-to-be caught wind of a business opportunity, but he had to act quickly. So two weeks later, he pulled all his money from his investments in the Port of San Francisco and went with his eight-months-pregnant wife—my mother, Bertha—to Oakland to take a final walk-through of his new waterfront property. The doctor had advised bed rest for the twenty-year-old mother-to-be. But my father was insistent that she come with him; he didn't want to be apart from her if her labor pains started.

"My mother would say that her labor began shortly before the ground started shaking across the bay. Twenty-seven hours after the shaking had stopped, I was born. She would say it was divine providence that she was robust enough to go on the ferry ride to Oakland. It was God's will, according to her, that they were not at home; the entire block of buildings in San Francisco where they resided was decimated by the quake and ensuing fires that April. And to have a healthy baby amid such chaos and destruction was not to be ignored as the work of God: the hospitals in Oakland were overcrowded, the doctors overworked, but I was somehow delivered by a young nurse in training. Surely, in my mother's mind,

Joe—as she would call me—was delivered by an angel. And to be ushered into the world in such a way meant that I was bound for great things: I made the ground shake."

While Grandpa didn't inherit much of his mother's biblical mythmaking, he did seem to have picked up her eloquence and sensitivity. That's probably what made him good at what I can only describe as epic parable. But as Berlin would have preferred, I'll try to stay at the heart of why Grandpa's stories matter to me, to figure out what he might have been trying to teach me.

And maybe he was just trying to give a history lesson about how his strict Protestant family suffered and sacrificed for the good of the country. William Flanagan must have thought patriotism was grooming Grandpa to one day inherit the family business. Whatever he was, William was a savvy—and lucky—capitalist. He started Flanagan Far East Shipping in Oakland and employed refugees from the ruins of San Francisco to help him import handmade furniture from China and Japan while exporting canned tomatoes and cherries.

As Grandpa played on the waterfront, he saw the city across the bay grow a skyline and a population once again. Artists, writers, businessmen, and politicians alike "found the charm of the city irresistible, despite the violent fault that still—and forever—lurked beneath it." His mother would again praise God in April 1917 because Grandpa was too young to go "Halt the Hun" in Europe. But he was not shielded from watching his father's young workers ship off to European trenches, some never to return, and others only to return less than whole. Before the war, Grandpa did his homework in the entrance of the warehouse so he could listen to the longshoremen and merchant marines. He loved them for their tall tales about drinking, women, and travel. Even then, though, he did not understand why these men had "no desire for a steady home and family," and wondered incessantly about the "underlying sadness of their existence" and why they could not find a way to be content. So when the young men who did return from fighting had trouble finding work and suffered from "unseen wounds," Grandpa became even more "fascinated with the unrooted."

Grandpa never left Northern California. There may have been a lesson in that for me, but I'll be damned if I can figure out what it is. I think it has something to do with his three brothers who volunteered for the Army and never came back from their posts in the Philippines; three other brothers who went east for school and didn't return even when their mother was gravely ill; or his youngest brother, who drowned a few months before his mother died while surfing a big wave off Pillar Point. After walking with the ghosts in his own family, and seeing how people returned to the shores of Oakland ground up, mangled, and torn down by their adventures, he must have thought that enough terror and uncertainty comes to our doorstep without having to go looking for it. Or maybe he was telling me that the rootless were running from some unnamed horror or discontent. Why did Grandpa tell me that Charles Lindbergh attended the dedication ceremony for the new Oakland airport? Was he saying that the famous pilot's "incessant quest for glory" masked some deep fear?

Whatever the case may be, Grandma Irene Coglin makes her appearance at this point, striking up a conversation with Grandpa on an April day in 1927 as they watched Lindbergh's plane rise from the runway.

"Do you like to travel?" she asked. Because her dad, C. E. Coglin, was a Navy supply officer, Grandma had moved from Annapolis to Charleston to Pensacola before the age of ten. At the outbreak of World War I, her family was shipped back northeast to Newport. Because of US "incursions in Latin America—Dominican Republic, Haiti, Cuba, Mexico, Panama, Honduras," Grandma and her family were relocated several more times to various bases on the Gulf Coast before moving to San Diego in 1925. She was nearly eighteen when her family moved to the Oakland Naval Supply Station in spring of 1927.

They watched Lindbergh and the *Spirit of St. Louis* disappear over the horizon. And Grandpa said, "I have no interest in seeing the world. There are those who are put on the earth to tell stories of their own lives. And there are others who just think they're put on the earth to tell the stories of their own lives. Most of us, though, are put here to listen and to tell other people's stories."

The security entailed by Grandpa's answer was enough for Grandma. She fell in love with him. She had seen much of the country and was tired of traveling. Of course, it didn't hurt that Grandpa was set to inherit his father's fortune.

Grandpa and Grandma got married in the spring of 1928, a week before Grandma's father and mother shipped out for C. E.'s new post in Seattle. In the fall, Grandpa's dad died. With his young wife pregnant with my aunt Mabel, Grandpa sold Flanagan Far East Shipping to spend time with her. After finishing his business degree at Berkeley, he pulled all his money out of the stock market. Smart enough to see the dangers of buying on the margin, he wasn't immediately harmed by the crash of October 1929. Instead, he got by on building-project investments near the bay. He did well enough to pursue his interest in making wine. After reading a few books on grafting and dry farming, he bought land in Napa and the Central Valley.

One particular day in 1938, the growing family was bumping along the dirt roads in their two cars to various investment sites. Grandma hit a pothole and blew a tire somewhere on a back road between farm plots. Before Grandpa realized Grandma was no longer driving behind him, Grandma had jacked up the car, pulled the inner tube off the radial, and patched it—and then realized her water had broken, one month earlier than expected. Squatting over that dusty road beside a disabled Model T with her husband looking on dumbly and four excited kids dancing around, Grandma gave birth to my mother.

If she hadn't have died a year before, Grandpa's mother would have believed Mom's birth on that dusty road had some biblical significance. In the dripping, melodramatic self-pity that you describe in your own family, I imagine Grandpa's mother would have interpreted Mom as some sort of blessèd cherub given to her son by God to help him through all the hardships that would be imposed by his own children.

I can only guess how Grandma felt; she's only ever been alive in the details Grandpa shared with me. Incidentally—and you may say sadly—that's how I got to know my mother. It's odd, now that I think about it, that the people in my family—both the ones I've known and the ones who were dead long before I was born—exist in the same way: one foot in this world, the other in a world that itself appears and disappears like a weary adventurer. It makes me wonder where people choose to draw the line when they give the details of a story. Like, I wonder why Grandpa told me, with tears in his eyes, that he saw Amelia Earhart's *Electra* plane leaving Oakland Airport in 1937, always emphasizing that it vanished exactly eight months before Mom was born. Why did he choose to tell me that detail? Or any of the details, for that matter? What difference does any of it make to me? Did he believe in omens more than he let on? Did he believe that his daughter was bound to be an adventurer, an explorer, a pioneer? Or did he believe that the proximity of my mother's conception to the disappearance of Earhart and Noonan meant that Mom's own final moments would also be made up of confusion, terror, and helplessness?

Maybe it is like you say: he wanted to direct my attention to the significance of those details as they intertwined with and determined the events of my life. But that seems too heavy handed for him; in the stories of his early days, he always seemed so passive with his family. It does make me wonder, though, if he told my brother the same stories with the same details.

Grandpa was paralyzed by a tightness in his chest as he watched Grandma's feat of solo labor on the dusty road. He was convinced he was going to lose the baby and his wife in one day. He thought he was going to die, too. Frightened that he almost made his kids orphans that day, he stopped traveling for business. They settled right there in the Garden of the Sun. He didn't travel any real distances until he came to live with us in San José near the end of my fifth-grade year.

———————

Gifts at Christmastime were sparse. And despite Grandpa's offers to give what little money he had to help out, Dad wouldn't accept much from him. Oso would probably say that Dad would never bow and scrape to a farm owner. You know, out of respect for the work that César Chávez was doing.

At that point, Oso was too young to know or care about Chávez, so he happily took the bit of secret money Grandpa gave us. I spent my money on fishing supplies: a rod for Grandpa, bait for Oso, lures for Alma, a net for Mom. Who knows what we would have pulled out of the Guadalupe River or Coyote Creek. A tire? A tarp? A sleeping bag? A flannel? A shopping cart? A beanie? And none of us even knew how to fish. But it didn't matter to me. I thought we could all figure it out together. Grandpa later asked why I didn't get anything for Dad. I thought for a little, trying to answer truthfully. "He can't even sit still," I said. "How's he gonna catch anything?" Grandpa smiled.

That Christmas Day—like all Christmases I've experienced—didn't go the way it could've.

After a morning filled with small gifts and smaller sentiments, Dad could have done what he usually did on any other off day: leave with Oso to walk until well after dark, to talk to the shopping-cart pushers who roamed the streets or the homeless friends and strangers who rested in Saint James Park at the foot of monuments commemorating the scandalous Colonel Naglee and the speeches given in the park by McKinley and RFK. My mother could have done what she normally did in the kitchen, preparing this snack or that meal, content to talk with her dad. I could have read that well-worn abridged copy of *A Christmas Carol* (what a crap story, by the way) under the kitchen table. It would have been that much quieter because Alma was gone, Martin and Gretchen treating parenthood like they treated their religion, devoting Christmas week to novelty. There could have been that new (to me) music on the record player, music that gave glory in grand fashion. Hosanna in the highest and Counselor and forever and ever and all that.

That Christmas with Grandpa defined the following few years.

Grandpa had yet to put on the grandiose music he'd been playing nightly through the month of December. When Dad came into the kitchen, Mom stopped chopping, Grandpa stopped talking, and I stopped reading. Dad said nothing, searching around the three people in the kitchen, looking in the pantry and under the table. He even looked behind the refrigerator before giving up.

Then Mom was standing in the doorway, Christmas-green sundress glowing against her skin. She said, "Why can't you just stay with us this time?"

"Tradition," Dad said, rubbing his eight calloused fingers together so they sounded like sandpaper.

Mom said, "I'm starting a new tradition: my boy will eat dinner with us."

"Clara," Dad said in a low voice, "you know how I feel about my time with Oso."

"Yes." Mom's voice rose. "Well, go walk the streets with your vagrants. But my boy stays here."

Dad grabbed her by the arm with those chicken-feet hands and dragged her toward a corner, shaking her by the shoulders; the tie holding her hair back came loose. He pulled her close and whispered, "Oso will come with me. He doesn't want to sit around with crazy Grandpa and these silent ladies."

Oso had appeared and stood in the doorway, wearing a green-and-red-checkered flannel that matched Dad's.

"Right?" Dad asked Oso, smoothing his thick hair.

Oso pushed his curly bangs behind his ears.

"All right, then," Dad said. Walking toward the door, he ruffled Oso's hair.

Mom smiled faintly at Oso as she pulled her hair back into its usual tight bun. Then she sank to the kitchen floor, rubbing the back of her neck. Oso hung his head and walked out the front door behind his father, hair obscuring his face. I crept out from underneath the kitchen table and stepped toward Mom. Her folded legs under the green dress made her look like half a person. Head down, she rubbed the fingerprint bruises already forming on her arms. Grandpa knelt next to her and took over massaging her neck.

And the tension escalated over the following days, Mom ferociously attempting to keep her son in the house, Dad reacting violently to Mom's attempts. Dishes broken, walls punched and kicked, arms squeezed. Husband storming. Son taken. Wife bruised. Grandpa comforting. Me watching and stuck with that image of Mom being shaken.

One day, after about a week of this, Mom stood barefoot in our dining room. She was rubbing her right hand in pain. She had just struck Dad with a closed fist on his cheek, the sound magnified by the small room. I was startled from my reading, a tattered copy of *The Indian in the Cupboard*. Oso froze at the table, holding a half-finished model car. Grandpa led his daughter to the other side of the kitchen, keeping his eye on the silent, fuming Dad. Grandpa whispered to his daughter.

"No," she replied, replacing a shoulder strap and smoothing her red dress. "You don't have to do that. It's too cold." She swallowed hard.

Grandpa smiled and said, "I've seen enough."

He turned to Dad, who was still rubbing his cheek. Grandpa took Dad by the arm. I half expected Dad to call him something nasty in Spanish.

"Oso," Grandpa called. "Let's go, nieto."

Oso, then an awkward fourteen-year-old, clomped to the front door. And with that, they were gone.

A little later, Mom and I retreated to our bedrooms. The apartment was void of its regular nightly noises: no record albums, no stories echoing off the high ceilings to accompany me as I tried to fall asleep. Alma was not beside me breathing, sleeping.

As I lay there between sleep and wakefulness, visions threaded. Mom violently shaken by Dad was replaced: In the middle of a white room, a white daisy in a white vase on a white stool. A sickle of dim light on a ceiling. A sickle and an unusually loud hum of traffic. Traffic and music from the Mission across the street. From the Mission a midnight burst of "Happy New Year!" celebratory shouts. Shouts and a laughing young man. A man and rail yards. Yards and headless chickens. Chickens and severed fingers. Fingers and vineyards. Vineyards and vast valleys of concrete. Concrete and unknown soldiers, aunts, uncles, grandparents. Grandparents and warships and container ships and airplanes and bridges and oceans and shores.

The next morning, the typical noise on the street was muted. Across the room, Grandpa's white hair peeked out from under the blue covers. I sat on my bed, waiting for something to happen. I studied the high ceilings and waited for answers. When none came, I opened the door to my parents' room. In the gray of dawn, my mother's entire pale back was exposed, her drab hair unbound, flung on the pillow; her bruised arm was slung across Dad's heaving, dark bare chest. I waited. Nothing happened.

I stood next to Oso's sleeping body on the couch. I wanted to scream, to alert the family that something wasn't right. Instead, I sat in the dining room, my sketchbook laid open among a couple empty dark-green wine bottles and three smudged glass tumblers. The light grew. A bundled figure limped along the nearly deserted streets below, turning up Third Street toward Saint James Park. I sketched vague outlines of my family's profiles, each with detailed drawings of their unique ears. No one talked to me that day. And before I knew it, the light had faded again. It was time to go to sleep.

The next day, Alma told me her own Christmas horror story.

========

Look, I'll be honest. At this point, I don't feel the need to tell you about Alma's harrowing holiday saga. What's the point? When I told Berlin, I intended to show that Alma's dash through the wilderness somehow symbolized my terrified paralysis that holiday week. But I botched it. After I finished, all Berlin could say was that he "failed to see the equivalency."

Yet I could relate to Alma's desire to flee the sinking feeling she always had throughout most of December. We somehow became infused with the same sense that something fantastic was supposed to happen. But the alternately high-spirited and depressing tunes of the season led us to conclude that the hope in the season was all an illusion. Over the years of sad Christmases, we had grown used to the feeling. But that particular Christmas, by the time Alma reached her grandparents' mountain home, Hosanna and "I'll Be Home for Christmas" and "Christmas Eve Can Kill You" were just too much. So she did something I would never have done: she ran into the woods. Before she knew it, night was coming.

And what did I tell Berlin? I told him that Alma was distracted by the fucking branches sighing above her in the cool, faint ocean breeze that drifted over the crest of the hill; I tried to convince him that, as darkness was falling, Alma had stopped to contemplate the first star of the evening peeking through the canopy.

I know you. You would say it was "cosmic intervention" that made her look up at that moment, that the "celestial body" represents hope, inspiration, or assurance. But don't give me that. All she did was look to the sky in frustration like anyone else does when she's lost. If you had it your way, Alma would see the star and remember something wise Mom had said to her as they floated together in the ocean—"It's only a predicament if you make it one," or some bullshit like that. Then Alma would say that, in spite of the deepening gloom, she was unafraid. But it didn't happen that way.

I don't mean to take out my frustration on you. It's just that I feel like a fool for telling Berlin the story like this. I have no idea what the forest was supposed to represent, much less the family of deer she encountered. What about the sound of their eating that barely registered? Their veering off into the underbrush? The ensuing definitive silence? Then the layers of sound that surrounded her: the low growl that wafted down the trail and was overtaken by a crashing of the underbrush, the short, high-pitched cry cut short by a ripping snarl? Am I supposed to have you believe that the undercurrent of frantic, dashing movement that descended on Alma had some parallel with my own drama? And what about the cry falling into a snarl? And what of the silence that rushed in, the violent noise dissolving into the pale light, the trees, the pine needles, the rocks?

If anything, Alma's story shows contrast. I would have been too petrified to move were I placed in that forest. Think about it: I never even so much as whimpered in protest through all of Mom and Dad's fighting. And Alma didn't draw attention to herself by screaming or crying. Instead, she hiked back toward the house, stopping every so often to determine if the sounds in the underbrush were real or imagined. But she continued on.

Somewhere along the way, a broken branch snagged her right ear. By the time she saw lights in front of her and heard the unbearable music, the blood from her ear had turned from slick to sticky. She stood silently in the doorway to the dining room for a few minutes. The drunken adults exchanged insults as they played a card game, and they took no notice of Alma or the thick streak of blood running down the right side of her face.

In that moment, she decided not to complain of her neglect or injury.

In the bathroom, Alma found a half-inch tear just above where the cartilage connects to the head. She pushed at the cartilage and watched the blood ooze in greater amounts down the side of her face and into the ear hole. She watched it bleed until it finally stopped in a crusted and shining blackened crimson. In the fluorescent light of the white-tiled bathroom, she must have looked like a ghoul. Eventually, she put on a hooded sweatshirt and lay on her right side—pain and all—falling asleep in front of the downstairs TV to *The Sound of Music*. The next morning, long before the adults were up with their hangovers, she rigged up a bandage from a paper towel and masking tape.

In the days between Christmas and New Year's Day, Alma was on her own, hiding her wound under a hooded sweater—not that the four adults would have noticed anyway. The Abernathys were connected people, so they spent much of the holidays going to parties in Los Gatos and Cupertino and sleeping off hangovers. I asked Alma why she didn't call us for help; all she said was that she didn't want to be a bother, an excuse so weak that it makes me think she wanted the pain she endured.

Looking in the florescent-lit bathroom mirror, she sketched her deformed ear, filling up a number of pages, tracking how it changed between dressings. And again she went into the forest. I would have been content to lie there alone, watching the old movie over and over again.

But Alma went out unnoticed in the daylight hours, looking for the remains of the dead deer. And pressing on her concealed wound until it throbbed blood. And gazing from the top of a boulder overlooking the valley. And wondering what I was doing.

All I was doing was nothing, nothing but hoping my family wouldn't disintegrate as Mom pushed, Dad pulled, and Grandpa sutured. On that New Year's morning, I didn't sketch the ears of my family members, as I told you before. I crawled back into my bed, everyone still asleep. I lay still, and the brushing whisper of a street sweeper below seemed to make me cry. And I fell asleep. I wish I had sketched instead. It would have, in a way, connected me to Alma, comforted me. Later, though, we connected and I lived Alma's experience, as I have so many times.

Gretchen and Martin dropped Alma off midafternoon New Year's Day. Alma went to the bedroom, hooded sweatshirt up over her head. I followed, asked her what happened. She told me that I couldn't tell anyone, not even Mom. She didn't want to make any problems. I told her I would stay quiet, but when I heard the story of the dead deer and the week's worth of tiresome old movies and tedious Counselor/Bing Crosby/Everly Brothers music, I was half tempted to break my promise. Then when she pushed back her hood and uncovered the wound and her blond hair matted with red, the danger Alma was in became clear.

Honestly, I should have said something long before. Alma had told me on more than one occasion that Gretchen had forgotten her in the car all night. Alma told me Gretchen and Martin's house wasn't set up for children. Even in Alma's bedroom, stacks of paper and a large computer gradually replaced stuffed animals and dolls. Sometimes Gretchen would leave Alma on the couch with nothing but a thin blanket.

When Alma showed me her mangled ear beneath the dark red bandage, I had no idea what I alone could do. So I told Mom.

"My God," Mom gasped. "What happened?"

Alma looked relieved just before she burst into tears. I was startled. Was there something she hadn't told me? If there was something worse than neglect, I didn't know what it was. After calming Alma, my mother became all business. She examined the ear. In the bathroom, Mom helped Alma out of the sweatshirt. Both Mom and I covered our noses and mouths. A pungent, bitter smell came from her.

Mom touched the dried blood on Alma's shoulder. "Does that hurt?"

"No."

"Well, let's get you out of that." Beneath the shirt, Alma's right shoulder was stained pink.

"A week without bathing?"

"I washed my face."

Mom frowned, turned on the water, and said, "Get in the shower."

Alma didn't move. Her stringy hair quivered. Her white skin was even paler in the lighting, her arms crossed over her chest. She started to cry. I hugged her, feeling her clammy skin.

"C'mon, honey," Mom said. "You need to get cleaned up."

I let go of the shaking Alma. But she didn't move to undress. I wondered what the problem was; we all had the same parts, after all. They all worked the same way.

Then I learned differently.

"What?" Mom asked.

"I've got blood."

"Where?" my mother said.

"Between my legs."

"Good Christ," whispered Mom in a low rattle. "Was it Martin? Or was it your grandpa?" I'd never seen Mom flip emotions so quickly.

"They didn't do anything," Alma said. "But I've gotten blood three times . . ."

Mom's face was then in her hands. Her shoulders shook, a purple dress strap slipping down her arm. Then she tossed her head back, laughing. "How have you been stopping it?" Mom asked, wiping the tears away.

"Kleenex. Lots of Kleenex."

Mom burst into laughter again. Alma shrank away from Mom, pushing me into a corner of that tiny bathroom.

"Oh, honey, no," Mom said, smiling, looping her dress strap into place. Holding both arms open toward Alma, she said, "It's just that it started so early! It's way earlier than most. It doesn't matter, really. Come here. No more crying."

Mom wrapped Alma in her skinny freckled arms and whispered something. When Alma took out a mass of ripe-plum-colored tissue from between her legs, I was both disgusted and amazed. First Alma and Mom had water between them, floating together without effort on those swells. Now they had blood. I knew on some level that wherever they were, they would always have water and blood to hold them up. I was lonely but never said anything. When I started my own period amid the chaos several years later, I didn't even tell anyone. Maybe for the same reason I never told Alma that my family had almost disappeared that holiday week: it didn't seem that important compared with what Alma had been through.

That's what I'm trying to show you, Lilly. The reason for my "diminished self-worth," as you put it, is somewhere in these stories, these stories that always seem to be about someone else.

The recent events at home, guided by Grandpa's mysterious intervention, transformed the house for a few months. And the changes were immediate. Mom, who had up to this point rarely stood up for anything with any amount of success, seemed to realize that indifference— perceived or otherwise—cuts deeper than any jagged tree branch. Dad, who had survived most of his life on, among other things, the kindness of strangers, must have come to the conclusion that food and shelter alone weren't enough to support a life. After a few long walks together, Mom and Dad figured the best thing was for Alma to become a permanent member of our family.

Honestly, I have no idea how they pulled it off. Maybe Mom composed a carefully worded letter to Martin and Gretchen, revealing a plan that would keep Alma safe and well cared for, a plan that, most important for the negligent parents, would allow them to pursue political power. As I read the newspaper over the years and caught bits of news on the televisions in Mr. Henry's showroom, I came to realize how most politicians used the defenseless—like children and the homeless—as a way to demonstrate their generosity of spirit. But Gretchen and Martin seemed not to have any interest in such a thing. If anything, they were politicians in another sense: they wanted to pay to have the problem go away. Since this appears to be how things turned out, good riddance to those monsters. Mom must have convinced Martin and Gretchen that if they sent a greater but reasonable monthly payment, entanglements with the law could be avoided. This hint at blackmail was almost as bold as the suggestion she made that Martin and Gretchen never again make contact with Alma. If it had been possible, Mom would have convinced them to feign their own deaths, but not before penning letters to Alma, telling her how much they loved her. That probably would have been easier for Alma to take than the fact that her parents just didn't—and never did—want her.

This is the way it happened, whether you think it's convoluted or not.

———————————

With Gretchen and Martin out of the picture by late January, life resumed and blurred toward the beginning of June like the passage of a few blissful days. Much of this harmony seemed to revolve around Oso, now fifteen and recently sprouted to over six feet tall. As Oso grew, so did his significance for everyone in the house. And sacred routines changed because of it.

Dad and Oso went on walks in the mornings with Grandpa, maybe introducing him to their friends in the park. After school until dinnertime, Oso was on his own, likely loitering with the downtown denizens and the ghosts of the lynched at the foot of monuments to political speeches in Saint James Park. Whether it was because of migrant workers or some old labor activist spouting off, Oso became inspired by César Chávez around this time.

A contentment I had never known came over me in the evenings. Oso, this boy who had tormented me and the adolescent who had ignored me, had overnight been transformed into a being that was essential to the sense of wholeness in our family. After dinner, Oso would join me, Alma, and Grandpa in the bedroom to listen to classical LPs. He would lie down in the middle of the floor and rattle off party lines from Chávez or repeat a story about Dad to put himself to sleep. Alma would fall asleep, too. But I stayed awake to listen to Grandpa tell his stories. When he thought I was asleep, he would cover Oso up right there on the floor. Moments later, there'd be a couple dull pops, a few gurgles, and a clink of glass.

Somehow, I heard these sounds mingle with the sound of traffic, the jukebox, and the Mission below. Dad, Mom, and Grandpa would sit in the kitchen, talking, laughing, listening to a kind of music on the university radio station that I wasn't familiar with. Dad made little effort to quiet his laughter, the legendary laughter that he'd lost and found so many times throughout his life. As I lay in bed, I could almost see his laughter's rich tones and taste its deep, soft, leathery quality. I wondered—I still wonder—what brought those three together after Mom's defiant New Year's Eve.

Whatever it was, I stayed awake to savor it. Both Mom and Dad started coming to the room each night before they went to bed, and I'd pretend to be asleep. I'd sneak a peek as Dad waited at the door, silhouetted by the sickle of light from the bathroom. As Mom kissed the two of us and pulled the covers around our necks, a warm, mild pungency persisted. Though we weren't really all that small anymore, Mom would say, "Time to go home, little ones." Then Grandpa would come in, stepping carefully around Oso sleeping on the floor, stumbling some, and chuckling to himself as he settled into bed. I would hear Dad's laughter in the other bedroom. It resonated as I fell off to sleep. When I woke in the mornings with Oso waking Grandpa to go on their walk with Dad, Alma would be gazing at me with those deep black eyes. She always slept soundly through the comings and goings of the night, a trait that I still can't determine was fortunate or unfortunate.

As far as I could tell, Grandpa and Mom spent our school hours together—maybe talking, maybe reading to each other or to themselves, maybe wandering in their own way. For the last part of my sixth-grade year, Alma and I would walk the dicey streets from school and meet them at a shabby place on First and San Salvador called Café Matisse. The smell of pigeon crap and cigarette smoke outside pushed us inside, where wobbly ceiling fans and brick walls and hardwood floors lived with student art, punk rock and hard bop jazz and Baroque classical, mismatched furniture, and university students. When we would get there, Grandpa and Mom appeared to have been there for hours—newspapers read, old copies of *Harper's* glanced through, books started or in progress or finished, coffee cups empty. They'd talk as Alma and I tried to do our homework. I would look at the weird art and the photos in *Harper's* or watch people or badly draw the things I saw.

A few times, Oso appeared in the open doorway of the café. Each time, he would stop and just look at me, pushing his hair out of his eyes or tightening the flannel tied around his waist. I wanted to wave him over or call his name. But before I could, he would walk out, unnoticed by anyone else. I wanted to have him sit with us or to go walk with him. But none of that ever happened. And I don't know why.

You see, during that year with Grandpa, the details of the world became more colorful to me. Even strangers had a story, and I entertained myself by making up their pasts, pasts that I never wrote down or told anyone. I guess that's pretty normal for a sixth grader. But something changed after Grandpa died: I became overly concerned not only with what other people had done but also with what they were doing, what they might be doing, and what they might do. This seems to explain a lot about my actions—or inactions. It seems I became handcuffed by imagination. And I still am.

Knowing you, you're wondering how someone my age gets to thinking and talking like this, especially with my background, which, believe me, you know nothing about. You're worried that what I've done—or failed to do—are not the things that a nineteen-year-old should worry about.

Maybe you're right; maybe I'm projecting again. But every time you say that, I get the sense that you're deflecting.

Anyway, I ask you this: Did you have a dad, a brother, or a grandpa like mine? Have you lived a century of vicarious life like me? A century of vicarious love, hate, wars, births, deaths, adventures, misadventures, family, no family? You see, for me, it's like these stories I'm telling you are all mine and not mine simultaneously. So does that mean, as you say, that my "systematic regurgitation of everyone else's stories" drives people away because they can't figure out who I am? If that's true, I wonder if it would be so terrifying to be alone. At least with no one to hear my stories—the small bit of history that is solely mine, completely untouched by others— there would be no one there to make me explain myself.

In the end, I'll be completely alone. It seems necessary. But you say it's impossible. Impossible?

———————

I've never watched much TV, but I look back on the day Grandpa died and it was like I was a lonely paraplegic watching the news. No remote control, no wheelchair. Unable to change the channel when I saw despair in distant lands: the walking wounded, starving children, suffocating seabirds. I saw what was happening: a severed limb, an emaciated body, a gull covered in thick black soup. And I think I understood that nothing I did could stop the endless flow of blood, famine, disaster. Perhaps some of it could have been avoided by yelling or crying, dragging myself across the floor toward someone. Anyone.

The previous night—the first day after I finished sixth grade—was like any other over the previous harmonious months, except that I'd actually fallen asleep before the adults made their ritual visit, lulled by Dad's melodious laughter echoing off the lofty crown molding, mingling with Mom's giggles and Grandpa's chuckles. I don't remember any sounds from down on the street.

The next morning, I woke to Oso leaving the room. Grandpa lay in the bed. Alma was still asleep. Then Mom burst into the room, weeping, her hair wild. She felt Grandpa's skin and wailed. Next thing I knew, Alma was sitting on the floor with Mom, brushing Mom's graying hair and tears away, rubbing her back, bearing Mom's clutches of her hand in wincing silence. Only "Hush, hush. Shh, shh." For what seemed like hours, it continued like that. "Hush, hush. Shh, shh." Dad appeared for a bit, his mouth open, his eight fingers holding his head. He left the apartment, banging the door behind him. Oso talked on the phone in the front room. A while later—Mom still wailing, Alma still soothing her—two men came and took Grandpa away. Mom struck the men in the arms and legs as they loaded the body onto the gurney. Oso and Alma wrapped their arms around Mom—to restrain her, to comfort her, to keep her together. They led her to her bed.

The wailing subsided, and Mom whimpered in her sleep in the next room. I was still sitting on the bed a couple hours later when Oso came into the room and threw on a pair of jeans, his usual flannel, and army boots. He mumbled something to me; I got off the bed and went to the other bedroom. Alma was sitting on the double bed next to Mom, rubbing her back amid the occasional sobs. Oso went out the front door and clomped down the stairs to Third Street. I squatted with my back on the wall near the bedroom door.

Both Alma and I kept our places through the afternoon and into the deepening evening shadows. Though far more faint in that room, the sound of traffic went about its usual patterns, the music and the voices from the bar rose and fell and changed as the day-drinkers gave way to university students who had just finished final exams. Mom slept the sleep of the possessed as Alma and I kept vigil over her fitful body.

*A*n old pregnant Asian woman sits across the aisle and smiles.

   Say: I am bored on this train, ma'am.

   "I was born on a train of thought that was boring."

   Say: Sometimes I just want to stand on the tracks as the snake bears down.

   "It's as big as a bear and woolly as a mammoth."

   Say: Do you think the mammoth stress of poverty is as monumental as the stress of property?

   "What kind of priority is property if property is the priority?"

   Say: I found a room for eighty-five dollars a week, but I'm almost never there.

   "Where are you then?" the old woman asks.

   Say: Here.

   "Then it appears that you have a clean slate in a dirty city."

   Say: But I am in a broken state with a fixed direction.

   "That's true north for the misguided."

   Yes. Huh? Mother? Mother! Wait! Don't go! Don't go! Don't go!

   The pregnant woman exhales a moist stench of dirt and urine and sweat. She lies down, turns a pale gray, and dies.

4.

I'VE NOTHING VISIBLE from my mother, aside from my pale skin, and even my father's complexion influenced that.

I'm not changing the subject. You asked me about the last thing I remembered. On the train to Chinatown to find you something for Valentine's Day, I got distracted from my book and started picking at the skin on my hand and musing about it. And now here we are again in a hospital, treating mysterious injuries. Though I don't know if you can call the patches of frostbite mysterious. What I can't figure is where or why I would have stripped off that old parka of yours . . . oh, damn. It was Gloria's. That makes this even worse.

No, I get it. You're far more concerned about your lunatic girlfriend pacing in front of a shop window and screaming at it. But even if the cops could tell us what I was shouting, even if that would somehow explain why I'm here in New York, aren't you afraid the answers would destroy your romantic idea of cosmic predestiny?

Look, I can't talk about this anymore right now. Can we go? I just want to crawl under the covers with you.

———————————

I'm starting to think that my skin color—and the shape of my eyes, for that matter—has as much to do with my story as the scar on my back and all the other scrapes and bruises and cuts and burns that have started to appear. The real problem is that I become more unsure about everything the more I talk. So what's the point?

Well, for months now I've been debating how to tell you more about Mom. The details about her early life—her life on the vineyard—either confuse or clear up a whole lot. Besides, I've been embarrassed. Berlin's voice keeps suggesting I wait until I figure out how to interpret what Grandpa told me; only then can I determine what it means to who I am now. But I don't know how to do it, especially now that I'm trying to tell you. Think about it. Mom's story is like every other story I've told you so far. It's, as you say—as Gloria said—"packaged in male perspective." To make matters worse, I find myself comparing your nurturing, strong, intelligent mother with my own mom, this woman I'd known as bottled up, that you know as oppressed; this woman who stood up against Dad's tyranny only once; this woman who was too weak to hold on to what she had achieved; this woman who couldn't—wouldn't?—guide me with explicit purpose.

A mom like this, and you still wonder where my madness comes from?

All joking aside, you might say that Grandpa "co-opted" his daughter's story. But I've begun to think of it as him grafting her story onto his. In either case, though, does Grandpa's co-opting/grafting make Mom's story less true? It's not that I don't trust what Grandpa told me about her. But it does make me think of his suggestion that Mom was conceived on the day Earhart and Noonan flew out of Oakland. When, where, why, how Grandpa chose to share details of Mom's history, Dad's history, his own history, my history . . . why Grandpa chose—or, as Berlin might say, "curated"—those details, I'm not sure.

About a month before he died, Grandpa and I were listening to Rachmaninov's piano sonatas and the street and Alma's sleep-breathing, as we usually did. I thought about how Mom entered the world.

"What did Mom do when she was born?"

"Your brother would say she entered the world in silence." Grandpa chuckled. "But no. She cried like most newborns do."

"Why is Mom so quiet? She hardly ever talks to me. Just today I told her about the new art teacher at school, her paisley skirts, her accent, the Matisse paintings she showed us, how she told me she liked my eyes—Mom hardly even nodded. Would she notice if I screamed? Does she think I'm ugly?"

Grandpa said, "She thinks no such thing. It's just that she thinks you're so much like her that it scares her."

"Why would she say that?"

"I'm not sure. Probably has something to do with how smart you are. Or how loyal."

"I don't understand. And why doesn't she tell me any of this?"

"I know it hurts you. But you can't change people."

"Why don't people change?"

"Well, they do. Don't get me wrong. But it usually takes a tragedy. Some people change for the better, others for the worse. And most of the time, you can't even see the change at first."

"Then how do you know they change?"

"It's easier to see over a long period of time and with knowledge of history."

Why wouldn't you believe he talked to me like this? Aren't you always telling me how smart, insightful, and articulate you think I am? Well, if any or all of that is true, where do you think that came from? Dad, who didn't really talk to me until I was in middle school? Oso and his rote myths? Mom and her one act of rebellion against Dad and her one manipulation of Gretchen and Martin to get Alma?

Maybe you're right. It probably is a combination of all these things that made me who I am. As Grandpa said, it's easier to see over time and with knowledge of history.

"Did Mom ever change?"

"Sometimes I think I see something in her change, but then it goes away and I wonder if I really saw it."

"I should ask her if she's changed."

"I think you can't—shouldn't—ask those kinds of questions. It has to be something you yourself see and then tell her what you have seen changed. But you also have to allow people space to have realizations on their own."

Now bear with me. All of a sudden, even as I'm trying to tell you the story of Mom, I find myself reliving this decade-old conversation with Grandpa. And I wonder if he really believed it was the best course to "allow people space to have realizations on their own." It occurs to me that this sort of faith led to the disintegration of his family. Near the end, he must have seen the error of his ways. Living in a crappy apartment, sleeping in a twin bed annexed from his grandson, and telling his failures to an eleven-year-old, he attempted to create a legacy, a legacy that is bound to haunt me forever. After he died, the shattering of the fragile peace he negotiated between his daughter and her husband only served to show me that the idea—the ideal—of family is a dream at best. It makes me wonder if Grandpa knew his story would live on in my head, that someday, "with knowledge of history," it would occur to me that the very dream of family is really no better than the myths or fables or parables on which we are raised.

Of course, you wouldn't agree that this is what family really is. It's true what you say: all families have their problems. But that your parents always fought about how to raise you and your siblings—that they could never even inspire the "appearance of unity" at public functions—is not the same as what I went through. And let me stop you before you play the age and wisdom card, saying some bullshit like I might see things differently when I reach your age a decade from now, that if I ever see all the death you saw in the years before opening your clinic, I might change my mind because I'll then understand how family pulls together in desperate times. But I don't see how you can have that faith after your mother died and your siblings moved to the West Coast. When was the last time you talked to them?

If you still have to ask me what made me look at things this way, then I really have been doing a crappy job. Or maybe it's just incomplete. But if you believe one thing that I tell you, believe me when I say that what you know will always be incomplete.

I don't know what I mean by that. Maybe it's that there is no story of my birth. Or the knowledge that what Oso told me about Dad's life before he met Mom has gaps that will never be filled and inconsistencies that will never be called into question. Or maybe it's that my mother disappeared without a trace and there is no clear reason for it. It could be that the answers are in Grandpa's details—missing or otherwise obscured—of Mom's youth.

According to Grandpa, Mom had always been quiet, like she was "living another life in another land" other than the sixty-acre family-owned vineyard where she was the youngest of five kids. It doesn't matter that the five years or so that all of Grandpa's children were in school at the same time were the happiest time in his life. It doesn't have any bearing on Mom's story that Grandpa loved when all his kids came home with new information, a welcome distraction from those grafting and dry-farming books he was reading at the time. What does seem to matter is that every night, while Grandma finished up the cleaning and drew baths, Grandpa sat one-on-one with each kid to hear about what he or she learned. During Mom's turn, instead of talking about science, history, or literature, she recounted what she had heard about the people in her classes. She learned with disbelief about those who lived in rickety housing, which was all they could afford even though they worked for the largest landowner in the greater Modesto area, Giordano Estates.

I don't know. Berlin asked me the same question. I guess Modesto is "Ralston" in the story Oso told me about Dad. I'm trying to keep it with Mom's story, about how she didn't so much talk to these kids at school as she did linger on the fringes of groups, too shy to speak but wanting to hear about their lives.

To his credit, at least Grandpa didn't insist that she talk about a school subject. But he did end every one-on-one with the same question: "Why's this important to know?" While all the others told him exactly where we use trigonometry, how important it is to medical research that primates and humans are similar, what we can learn from the Battle of Waterloo, what we can learn from a character like Pip, Mom always replied, "Because people don't write books about them."

That she said this seems a little too neat. And maybe you groaned on the inside, thinking that Grandpa was full of it, that kids don't talk like that. But even if he did take some license, it does seem in line with how, shortly after World War II ended and she'd started her second year of school, Mom came home talking about how she heard that some people didn't get to go to school and didn't even have a house or a car. Up to that point, she'd never imagined life without a home or car; she hadn't known that the people she was talking about worked for Grandpa every autumn, picking his small grape crop. She was very concerned, so Grandpa explained that this was what America was all about: allowing people to come to the country to earn enough to raise their families in this land of plenty. But they had to earn it, like everyone else. Oh, you and Gloria would *love* this: Grandpa said, "Your mom was just a little girl. She didn't understand how the world worked. She never even bothered to ask what had happened to our Japanese American neighbors during the war."

Exactly. She was only seven. And terribly shy. But it's not like Grandma would have allowed a friendship with "those people" anyway. Hell, Grandma demanded that the family be so tight that no friends were allowed to visit. Again, this detail seems a bit extreme, yet it is consistent with what I learned about Grandma. Whatever the case, Mom and her oldest sister, Mabel, were really close. They would walk in the vineyards, and Mabel would talk to Mom, pointing to the buds on the vines, the stealthy tracks of the feral cats, the secluded holes of field mice, the partially hidden nests of sparrows, the patient, deadly concentric circles of hawks. Apparently, Mom took to picking up springtime baby sparrows and putting them in the nearest nest, not caring if it was the right nest. Was this anecdote meant to show me how wrong Mom was for what she had done? Or to inspire in me the tenacity she showed in her younger years? Or maybe it was Grandpa demonstrating how terrible his extreme belief in natural selection was and to show how far he had come as a man, as a human. Hell if I know.

Whatever his intent with me years later, Grandpa asked Mom all those years ago, "Can you think of a reason you shouldn't help the fallen babies? Don't you think you're upsetting the balance of things by saving the baby sparrows? Hawks need to eat, too."

Mom replied with something like, "There's tons of grapes for everyone," or "Won't other sparrows just fly in from somewhere else?"

Even then, if what Grandpa was telling me was true, Mom's "hidden indignation came out in the most surprising ways." A few years later when she found her father destroying a nest and its eggs, she asked why.

"The birds peck at my grapes, cost the family food on our table, cost the pickers food on their tables."

She nodded and stared at the smashed eggs beneath his work boots. Something in that "youthful heart understood the brutality of survival and truth." Mom stopped saving the little birds, and Grandpa stopped destroying the nests. But he didn't tell her then because of the "stupid ideal of fatherly superiority." It wasn't until years later, after Mom had Oso, that Grandpa told his daughter how letting the baby sparrows hatch hadn't decreased the grapes' quantity or quality. He didn't know why he took so long to tell her this, telling me, "What is it about men—like those tramps on the docks in Oakland—and their need to talk about what terrible things they have done? I just wanted to connect with my daughter, the last daughter to leave the vineyard. I told her—maybe too late—that she had made a difference in my thinking."

Mom forgave him. Grandpa said she always was the forgiving type, but he couldn't say where she got that. Maybe Mom's forgiving nature was in reality, as you have said, simply "meek and passive." Or maybe she was more like how Grandpa saw her: "a kind soul who had great capacity to endure the deep flaws of humanity." But he also said, "It seems the quality of mercy can skip generations."

You're right: it does sound like fatalism. In hindsight, it was strange for him to speak as though personality traits were inherited like big protruding ears or pale-brown skin or light-yellow skin or dull-white skin or straight black hair. Grandpa's sense of guilt was much deeper than the smashing of unborn birds. And it made him fall back on heredity for explanations, like someone who retreats to religion for comfort in times of uncertainty. It was also at odds with the stories he told, in which people succeeded or failed because of how they reacted to their circumstances and how the circumstances reacted to them. In retreating from uncertainty and the full effect of his own culpability in how his family turned out, Grandpa oversimplified and distorted who Mom was, how she became that way, and how it somehow meant that she would stay the same person her whole life. And now I wonder: if he reduced his own daughter's essence down to one imaginary genetic trait, what single trait defined who I was in his eyes?

Ironically, I can't help but think about a sort of birth story Grandpa told, a birth story of his own wife's personality traits. And it sure as hell didn't have anything to do with heredity. Grandma Irene's own mother, my great-grandma Agnes, was "a silent soldier," as Grandpa put it—a dutiful wife. But my great-grandpa C. E. was a "big, strapping, confident, opinionated" father. He was also a fearful man, though "he would never admit to being afraid of losing his status and reputation." In the place of fear, C. E. had an air of superiority and was proud of his role in "supplying the rapidly growing military for its exploits all over the world." This kind of pride gave young Grandma Irene "an inflated sense of importance."

And C. E.'s influence extended well into her adult life. Even after he retired from the military and opened an army surplus store in Seattle, C. E. wrote letters to Grandma about the essential service his store served in the neighborhood where it was based. He also wrote about conflicted feelings. On one hand, he believed that wars in places like Korea were important to keep communism from spreading. But on the other hand,

C. E. would say it was a shame so many people had to come here to the US after leaving the "shitty countries that were susceptible to Bolshevism." Excited and anxious, Grandma read aloud to her husband and their kids such C. E. diatribes as

> *We have endeavored to make this nation great. But refugee traffic has grown to a flood reminiscent of a stampede of animals with packs of wolves, jackals, and other beasts of prey worrying the flying herds. It is natural for us to respond to the victims of persecution wherever they may be. But why not permit charity to begin at home? Why shut our eyes to the pleas of twelve million jobless working men?*

Yes. These are the kinds of things Grandpa talked to me about. A lot of it I didn't understand or care about. For instance, I didn't care why the military was growing and getting into early-twentieth-century misadventures. And I sure as hell didn't care about the plight of the migrant worker. And I still don't. It has nothing to do with me.

Who? Dolores Huerta? No, I've never heard of her.

Well, maybe if Grandpa—or Oso, for that matter—had told me what she meant to César Chávez and the UFW, I might have cared more about what they were fighting for. Hell, I might have developed a different personality altogether.

Even though he was deeply flawed, I love Grandpa for how he talked to me. Regardless of his possible reductive view of me, I think Grandpa understood the same thing you do: I "lacked a strong woman's presence." If in fact this is what he wanted me to know, Grandpa would never have been so blunt. But he can't have expected me to draw any conclusions back then. What was a young girl like me supposed to do with a detail like "When your mom was twelve, America was prosperous at home and continuing to grow in global influence"? Whether it was Grandpa's intent or not, I'm now starting to see a sort of imperfect metaphorical cautionary tale: the oversized influence C. E. had on Grandma Irene—and the silent consent of Agnes to this influence—seemed to have poisoned Grandma for life. And even though I'm still sifting through all the little details of the stories Grandpa told me, I get the sense that the subtle specifics will someday add up to something significant.

What is clear to me now, though, is that Grandpa knew he himself was guilty of timidity. He worried, for example, that his kids might confuse migrants for flying herds and beasts of prey and become needlessly frightened. Having raised his kids in harmony with migrant workers and their children, Grandpa felt great shame for never speaking up, for silently forgiving C. E.'s and Grandma's rhetoric. It makes me wonder if he died in a state of lament, never able to determine at what point forgiveness—the personal attribute of "great capacity to endure the deep flaws of humanity"—is perceived merely as meek and passive consent.

But Grandpa must have found at least some melancholy satisfaction in the fact that the ideas in C. E.'s letters may have had the opposite effect on Mom's siblings. Years later, her brother became a doctor in East LA, one sister became a schoolteacher in Saint Louis, another became a producer for a small acting group in Montana, and Mabel went off to South America, never to return. And Mom felt responsible for all of it: Mabel's departure and the rest of the family peeling slowly away and scattering over the following years. Mom's silent shame—and, in a way, her sense of duty—came from her own brief disappearance.

The ideas of status, honor, and superiority—not to mention the fear of losing all that—had a lasting effect on Grandma, whom Grandpa saw as "a beautiful, caring woman with a strong heart when she wasn't exposed to public opinion. But when the outside world imposed itself on her, she would revert to certain defensive—or offensive—positions." It didn't help that a homeless young Black veteran just back from Korea robbed, shot, and killed C. E. and his wife at their surplus store in 1951.

After her parents' funerals in Seattle, Grandma returned sleep deprived and in a state of panic. Her son was entering his final year of high school and was intent on premed at UCLA the following fall. Soon Grandma's "nest would become much less populated." Then Grandma had her first stroke.

"Come away from those books," Grandma once said to Mabel from her sickbed. "I need you to wash me and get me some tea. Besides, how are those books supposed to get you a good husband?"

As usual, Mabel washed Grandma and brought her tea. But almost every day, Mabel and Mom would bring food and drink to Grandpa and the workers in the vineyard. They would also sit in the vineyard while Mabel read out loud to Mom—Dickens, Austen, Brontë, Twain, Steinbeck. Mom was "silenced by fascination rather than the mysterious stifling ghost that had bound and gagged her for most of her life."

As she taught English and learned Spanish, Mabel got to know the migrant families, the ordeals and triumphs of their travels. But all the time in the vineyard drew the attention of the ailing Grandma.

"You cannot let her stay out there so long," she complained to Grandpa. "Today, I wet the bed and she wasn't here to help me."

"You know she always brings us a little snack in the afternoon," he replied.

"Us? We're feeding the Mexicans, too? God in heaven! Mabel? Mabel! Come in here. You are to come directly home after your father is done eating."

Mabel responded, "No, Mamá. Aprendo—"

"What? Are you speaking Spanish to me? What's really going on out there? Jonah? Mabel?"

The idea of keeping her bloodline alive—not to mention pure—became an obsession. Grandma confided in her husband and scolded him, saying that Mabel speaking Spanish would be the beginning of the end.

"Next thing you know, she'll run off with one of those poor brown boys. What good would that be for our family?"

In order to "protect" the family, Grandma began to rouse herself on the weekends following the Spanish-speaking incident. Unwilling to go against her mother—at least in any obvious way—Mabel went into town every week to be paraded around. Starched dresses, light makeup, forced smiles. But Mabel made herself "impervious to the potential suitors."

When out of earshot of her mother, Mabel would sometimes use Spanish phrases to talk of books rather than the crops, of migrant working conditions instead of profits, of the benefits of selling land to Giordano Estates instead of trying to maintain the smaller family farms. If the boys were able to get through her discussions on literature and labor, "the last suggestion always sent them running."

Mabel also believed in the importance of family, but her desire to see the world and keep her mind open "ran a divergent course with marriage and family." The migrants had opened Mabel's—and therefore Mom's—eyes to more than books ever had. The two sisters talked quietly about the "burgeoning, eclectic scene" in San Francisco.

Mabel's reputation around town began to take its toll on Grandma.

"With the way people think of you in town, you might as well marry a Mexican. Why not a black? God help us if there were any Jews around here."

No sooner had Grandma said this than Mabel packed a small bag and kept it ready to go under her bed. But she didn't leave then, perhaps because she was sympathetic to her mother's wrath toward all things foreign. Grandpa said, "You might think that I, too, was sympathetic. If anything, a sensitive observer. But what good is a witness who doesn't speak up? My apathy seemed to set a good example for my kids, at least. They all went off to make a difference in the world."

I think you're right: what a strange way to spin his own failure. But I think it's statements like this that reveal Grandpa's intent: to sacrifice his own reputation—a reputation he could have enhanced any way he wanted—in order to steer me away from committing the same sin of inaction. I don't know how successful he was.

Grandma's insistence on marriage and family, among other things, drove Mabel to the brink of running away. But she dreamed instead of acting on those impulses, held in place by her devotion to—or fear of—her mother. Mabel stayed in the house "night and day in silent armistice, doing Grandma's bidding." She hoped her mother would see devotion in her domestic efforts, take all this as a sort of peace offering. At first, though, Mabel's dutiful silence did nothing but embolden Grandma with the idea that she had finally gotten through to her eldest daughter, that she had subjugated Mabel's defiant spirit that had peeked out in the recent months. But Mabel's mute conduct extended to the weekends in town as she was displayed to potential suitors. Mabel the statue. The stoic. The dummy. Grandpa remarked, "They may as well have called her 'indifferent,' 'passive,' 'bovine.' They would have been just as wrong."

And that was true. Mabel was still just as engaged with Mom, talking during their afternoon walks in the vineyard and late into the night after the lights were out in their bedroom. Mabel and Mom dreamed of San Francisco, its people, arts, schools, languages, ocean. They "animated the darkness; the loud whispers infused the night—and Mom's mind—with fascinating questions."

But the silent war raged on, silence itself a weapon Mabel wielded deftly. Soon Grandma was stirred to worry, fear, and sickness yet again. She became so ill that she, too, was unable to speak. She'd had another stroke, and her fingers and toes "curled as a hawk's talons, her face gnarled as an old oak's trunk." Everyone in the family pitched in to help out a little more around the house, to make Grandma comfortable as she ailed. A sense of uncertainty hung around husband, daughters, son. All seemed to "hedge between looming grief and potential reprieve," Grandpa said. "True grief is to admit there will be imminent relief in the eventual death of a family member; everyone felt it because all that was good about Grandma—her strength of spirit and her belief in the importance of family—was mashed by the grief at the loss of her parents."

Grandma's sadness turned only to anger. When the sheets needed to be changed or a sponge bath given, the entire family was involved. One of them would always be gripped on the forearm by her functioning right hand and pulled in close to the twisted, silent face. None of them could pull away, like she was demanding that each take the time to figure out what her gaze meant. Sadness. Rage. Tenderness. Disappointment. Grandpa never knew what to make of the stare. Mabel was stoic. Mom would leave the room every time in tears.

In midsummer 1952, Mom, all of fourteen years old, disappeared.

The police asked Mabel, "You didn't notice a packed bag?"

Mabel shook her head.

"Did she talk about going anywhere?"

"No."

"Was there a boy? What kind of a boy was he?"

She said nothing. Everyone saw the sadness in her eyes and assumed she was just too upset to help with the search.

Grandma, however, regained her speech, and she would shower her doubts and confused conspiracy on Mabel. "You know where she is. I know how close you two were. She told you everything. She hated taking her share of the responsibility. She's a coward. She's a fool."

Grandma soon regained her ability to move all of her limbs, and with that came more ferocity than ever, still inspiring enough fear to keep her adult and nearly-adult kids in line. At night, she disparaged her absent youngest daughter. She brutally scoured her other daughters' skin and tugged their hair clear of tangles after bath time, alerting them to all the terrible things that were likely happening to Mom out there by herself in the world. One of her daughters once complained that she wanted privacy to clean herself and brush her own hair. Grandma told her she knew nothing and swatted her rear with the brush. That same night, Mabel was scalded by hot water and later had a clump of hair torn out during the ruthless brushing. Grandpa confessed to me, "Of course I knew how Grandma talked to the kids, but I never knew about the burns and bruises until years later."

A whole year passed with no sign of Mom. Several of Grandpa's experimental vine grafts failed, migrants came and went, "mice were poisoned and came back for more, sparrows were born and died." The only son went off to UCLA premed. All the adjacent vineyards had been bought up by the Giordano family; Don Giordano himself came and offered a deal for Grandpa's small plot of land. During that year, Grandma swung violently from depression to brutality, silence to censure. And when she found out her husband had turned down Don Giordano, she berated him viciously until he persuaded her that he was "close to producing a new, dynamic blend of varietals that could make a lot of money. Besides, we should stay here in case Clara comes back after realizing her mistakes."

Grandpa didn't really believe Mom had made a mistake. And he remained calm, believing that nothing bad had happened to his little girl. He knew she would come back. After all, he was used to people "leaving to find a place in the world." Though most of the longshoremen from his father's docks and all his siblings had disappeared—"many of them in distressing, even lonely circumstances"—Grandpa knew they'd lived a life that was their own. And that somehow extended to his missing fourteen-year-old daughter.

You're exactly right. Grandpa's delusion and neglect were spectacular.

One night, Grandpa heard inconsolable crying coming from Mabel's room. Grandpa said it sounded as though Mabel had had a dream of her own death; he went to comfort her. What he found was Mom sobbing in Mabel's arms. Mabel was whispering and smoothing Mom's hair. Mom stopped crying, glanced through her tears to see her father standing in the doorway. She extended an arm toward him before her face crumpled again into sobs. He knelt on the floor and embraced his eldest and youngest. "There was a nameless loss, and words would never define it." When Grandpa told me this, I wondered if Mom's tears weren't the relief of being with her sister again or the devastation of something awful happening to her out there. Now I wonder if she was utterly saddened that she had ended up back in Grandma's home.

The three of them held one another, but no sooner had Mom's weeping subsided than Grandma gasped from the doorway, her two other daughters standing behind her. Mom cringed as her mother walked toward her. Grandma said nothing and drew her youngest daughter to her, holding Mom's head against her chest. "The kind of silence in that room was unique: even Grandma quit raging against what she couldn't change, stopped pushing for what she wanted. And she was just a mother relieved to have her child unharmed."

There was, in fact, no visible physical harm. Over the following days, as the household adjusted to the "prodigal daughter's return," Grandma did her best to care for a catatonic Mom. She imposed a peace on the rest of the house as Mom slept for most of every day. When Mom was awake, Grandma sat on the front porch with her. The questions that Grandma asked as they looked out over the vines were the same that everyone—family, cops, doctors—asked of Mom.

"Are you okay?"

"Where have you been?"

"Did someone take you?"

"Where did you stay?"

"What did you eat? How did you eat?"

"Did something . . . happen . . . to you?"

But all of it seemed just as much a mystery to Mom, who stared past dreams of education in books and back out into the world. Mom herself, it seemed, could only speculate about what had happened to her—"speculations," Grandpa hypothesized, "that ran nightly in the muted circles of her mind."

After only a couple weeks of trying to nurse her daughter back to health, Grandma grew frustrated.

"This is what happens," she lashed out. "If she'd never left, she wouldn't be this way."

Grandma tried to bind what remained of her family together by sacrificing her youngest, using her daughter's despair as a cautionary tale for her other three daughters, young women who would obviously become just as wounded—if not just as profoundly broken—as their sister, should they escape the family.

Mabel felt she should have at least tried to stem the flow of Grandma's causticity. But Grandma had imposed silence on all the girls while Grandpa was in the vineyards during the day. As for Grandpa, he was not oblivious to his daughters' muted behavior. But he was, perhaps, selectively oblivious to the tyranny of his wife. "To be selectively oblivious or indifferent is what people call 'passivity.' It is the worst cowardice." Here, again, it seems Grandpa was highlighting his own failures to shoulder the blame for others' shortcomings. Or he could have been making all this up as a dramatic way to warn me against oblivion and apathy; if this was his intent, he failed utterly at that, too.

At night, Grandma went to great lengths to keep a gentle decorum, playing the piano or reading Bible verses with her daughters. And Grandpa "foolishly took that as fatigue from their long day of ironing, scrubbing, washing, wiping." Mom didn't do much of anything but glance through the headlines in the evening paper. Grandpa wrote to his son down in Los Angeles, paid bills, and enjoyed the calm.

Eventually, Mom started talking to Grandpa, making Grandma both glad and jealous. But Mom's quiet talk wasn't about the different people in the community, as it had been when she was younger. Nor was there any clue as to where she had been or what she had done while she was gone. Her eyes following the movements of a wounded and unpredictable mother, she expressed guilt, indicating she wanted to make things up to Grandma and the family.

———————————

When I told Berlin this story, he thought certain details unbelievable and certain themes too perfect. But for Berlin, the most unsettling thing was the way Grandpa seemed to have taken over my voice, mind, and soul—how the dead old man seemed insistent that his story must be told in his exact words. "Catechism" is the word Berlin used. You might use the word "doctrine."

Whatever you want to call it, it's clear to me now why I must not recite the story word for word. It's the same reason I had to stop repeating Oso's myths. There's an implied acceptance in an exact retelling of someone else's story, and, as you yourself have said, it's "devoid of individuality." Well, I couldn't agree more. But the more I toil against the catechism/doctrine/myth I was raised on, the more lost I get, the closer I get to my own disappearance. Won't I vanish if I continue slogging to tear down every bit of the family history? Yet here I am, questioning Grandpa's motives for telling me how Grandma's commitment to family could make her do such terrible things to keep it together, or how Grandpa could have been so blind to Grandma's abuses. Or, more to the point in the story now, how Mom recovered.

Grandpa could never figure how Mom found out that a laborer's young daughter had become pregnant. The girl was so scared of her parents' expected reaction that she had come to Mom, who then turned to Grandpa. Mom saw an opportunity to rekindle her compassionate spirit, as well as her beloved sister's. Mabel had been silenced by some culpability in what happened to her youngest sister, whatever that may have been. Grandpa, easy to persuade because he loved seeing his daughters animated with possibilities again, was convinced by Clara to allow Mabel to escort the girl back to La Cruz in her native state of Sinaloa, where she had a sympathetic aunt. And Mabel lit up at the chance to travel, her first time out of Modesto. None of them could have known that the fire reignited in Mabel would take her away, never to return when the six-month retreat was supposed to end.

Grandpa's desire to see his daughters happy outweighed all other factors. So he decided it best to keep this plan secret. Certainly, Grandpa didn't want his workers to think he had anything to do with the sudden disappearance of the worker's daughter. And Grandma's wrathful opposition had to be considered. When Mabel returned, Grandpa would deal with the fallout then. As it happened, Mabel's disappearance "clamped down on the ire that had typified your grandma's nature for the previous year." The same mother who had at one time been "mummified by stroke and had come back stronger and more vitriolic was now gone, deep inside herself, paralyzed by disappointment" as she sat on the front porch. Waiting for Mabel. The one who might still set an example for her other daughters. Mabel. The one who might still "model the benefits of a tight-knit family." Mabel. The one that all others might follow. Mabel.

Grandpa, with typical poetic embellishment, speculated that "it probably occurred to your grandma it was inevitable that all her daughters would follow Mabel into that dark, unknown, unstable world." And that's exactly how it turned out. As if Mabel's disappearance weren't enough, my uncle wrote nothing to Grandma in his letters. He never returned for a visit on school holidays, and though he sent letters and pictures, they were addressed only to his father.

Grandma almost found a way out of her despair when she heard of her middle daughters' engagements, which happened at nearly the same time—and quickly; Grandma seemed to forget all about Mabel. But one week in August 1954, the other two daughters were gone, to live in houses of their own in Missouri and Montana. All without more than a week of warning. All without emotion. Or regret. All done with calculation, as some sort of nameless vengeance. When her son didn't return after graduation in 1959, Grandma once again lost the use of her left side, and her ability to do anything around the house. With no prospects of even a visit from any of her children—or grandchildren—Grandma sat on the porch for years.

So, her sense of responsibility and guilt renewed, Mom took over the household. And she was once again silenced. Any chance at finding out what Mom had done—or what had been done to her—would forever remain hidden, like she had been sleeping when she walked away and had woken up a year later, weeping from some nightmare. The only thing remaining from the horrifying dream was the pain, the pain that would not allow her to forget the unnamed, unknown terror that she forever carried in silence among the awake, the living.

No. You couldn't be more wrong. I can't tell you where my "episodes," as you call them, are from. I can tell you, though, with complete certainty that I didn't inherit the "episodes" from Mom. And you'll question my conviction about this, too. You'll just have to accept it. I have.

What I have a harder time accepting is that I never asked Mom what happened to her and where she went that year. But Grandpa's words have stuck with me: you can't—shouldn't—ask those kinds of questions. People have to come to realizations on their own. It occurs to me now that I may have misunderstood what he was saying. In any case, when Grandpa told me about her year-long disappearance, the apartment was the calmest it had ever been, and I had never seen Mom at such peace.

I waited too long for her to come tell me about any revelations she may have had. A few weeks later, Grandpa died, and our house descended back into chaos. And then Mom was gone forever.

Anyway, Mom kept the house clean and brought Grandpa's lunch to him every day in the vineyard, staying only long enough to exchange a few quiet, cordial words of Spanish with the workers. Grandpa went alone to her graduation, offered to take her into town for dinner. She refused, saying that Grandma needed her. And that's how it was for the next ten years: a sole daughter possessed by the obligation to her mother, an obligation that, until years later, "was as nameless as the reasons for the others fleeing the family."

It seems that Grandpa was that naïve. Or maybe just wrapped up in grafting vines, creating a healthier varietal so he could keep the vineyard for the rapidly diminishing family. I don't know. Maybe people only hear what they want to hear, see what they want to see. Just as likely, they only say what they want to say.

Grandpa spent longer and longer hours in the vineyard, tending his crop and experimenting with new growth in the greenhouse, like the extra work would somehow improve his chances of surviving the decreasing profits of his small piece of land. It became more difficult to defend against Don Giordano's regular, increasingly smaller bids, bids that were still more than Grandpa could make in five seasons. But he loved the land. The vines. The people. The ritual. He worked each day as long as light permitted while "the gloom in the house became intolerable."

That's when Grandpa finally bought his famous record player and as many classical LPs as he could. That same evening, Grandpa played Beethoven's Piano Concerto no. 5. From his little plot of land, from his modest house "encumbered with the weight of loss," he was "taken to a place of regality and pride." He turned the volume up and sat on the porch, staring above the vines into darkness that was "soon animated with grand possibilities." Beethoven transplanted Grandpa, the most deep-rooted person I've ever known—transplanted him to Venice, Prague, Paris. "Loss and its universal nearness were made unimportant by that piece." In those forty minutes or so, the quiet suggestions in the notes that came before explosiveness allowed him to understand his "long-lost children." Beethoven's "temperamental, strident outbursts that responded to those quiet moments in the concerto" even permitted Grandpa to grasp some of his wife's suffering.

The piece ended. Mom was sitting next to him, staring into the night. But the music clearly had a different effect on her. Something "flickered or whispered repeatedly in her." He let her alone.

Until Grandma's death, Mom cared for her, taking her through the routine. Wake. Eat. Defecate. Urinate. Bathe. Mom somehow helped Grandma with all these tasks by herself. At Mom's insistence, Grandpa had long ago moved out of the master bedroom; she said Grandma seemed less agitated when her husband wasn't around. "Her sense of duty was becoming more than just a penance. I don't think she believed the responsibilities she took on could only be undertaken by a woman, though it certainly seemed as such."

Sometimes paraphrasing just won't do. I had to tell that last part in his own words. Whether he, as you or Gloria might say, was a "patriarchal whitewasher" or a coward doesn't really matter. Don't try to define me with your agenda. Who in the hell do you think you are?

You can say you're just trying to understand me better. Would it make you feel better if I admit that I'm from a family of cowards? There, I admit it! But don't you think your story—or anyone's, for that matter—could be seen as cowardly? I have a hard time believing that every human life is not defined by what they should have done.

No. Absolutely not! It's much bigger than you trying to understand me or me trying to understand you. And the further I get into this story, the more I'm coming to believe that none of us ever really did what was best for the family. Cowardice or selfishness. Call it what you want, but it's only about self-preservation.

I don't know. I don't know what I'm talking about! And I may be just too young. But I came to these beliefs somehow, didn't I?

I'm going for a walk. Alone.

I got to thinking about what you asked. Maybe I thought using some of Grandpa's words was a way to keep him alive. But I don't need to do that anymore.

In '67, Grandma finally died. Mom sent out letters to the last known addresses of her sisters and brother, but only three people were at the funeral: Grandpa, Mom, and Don Giordano. No one visited after the funeral, and only a couple cards from Mom's sisters came in the mail.

This is the point when Grandpa would try to expand on the details of grafting vines and dry farming. Looking back, I'm sure it was some sort of metaphor. But it was a weak one; I'm still not sure what it meant. And I'm sure you have Gloria's women's-lib take on all of it. No matter how it's interpreted, Grandpa probably never finished the books he had started reading about the subjects. He likely never put any of the knowledge to work. Even if he had, he showed himself to be a fool, continuing to use his ever-smaller profits grafting grapevines so they'd stay healthy above the soil, the soil where the healthy roots went deep, deep for nutrients through rock and minerals, minerals that added dimensions to the grapes' flavor, flavor heightened by the depths the roots had to go for water. Grandpa said he knew—he was utterly faithful—that dry farming was the key to making the best wine, wine from roots that were not overfed with irrigation.

Whatever he meant by this—or if he ever really tried the methods—it was clear he didn't know what he was doing. Grandpa sold his land to Don Giordano in '71, finally reaching an agreement on money—far less than what he'd first been offered almost two decades before. But included in the agreement with the don was that Grandpa could keep working the land and maintain his home on the land. It was difficult to tell what was more disappointing to Grandpa: tearing down the greenhouse where he'd supposedly worked for years on his experiments or tearing out his entire crop. Giordano had Grandpa plow up the soil. Grandpa couldn't protest. He had nowhere to go.

Yes, he stayed on to work for the man who'd threatened him all those years. It reminds me of that story you told me of your friend, the one who continued to sleep on the couch while her ex-girlfriend slept with someone else in the next room. I wouldn't care if it was the only warm place I had to live. I'd rather be homeless.

Anyway, Mom took a job with Giordano, too, doing low-key administrative work in his main office. The land that used to be Grandpa's was stripped and planted with young growth. The vines grew quickly and healthily. In near silence, Grandpa worked the land, which now was one massive plot of the big, fat, watery grapes from the same shallow-rooted, irrigation-drenched vines that'd made Giordano his fortune. Over the next several years, Grandpa and Mom sat on the porch in the evenings, listening to sonatas, concertos, symphonies. Floating music over the new crop. Watching the changes.

In the summer of '72 they received word that Mabel had died in Costa Rica—some hiking accident. Grandpa, perhaps made numb by the remote quality of loss throughout his life, left his daughter alone with her grief. He walked and worked until well after dark, maybe talking to himself, a coworker, the vines, and crying.

I was too young to think to ask why he abandoned his only remaining family at such a time. Besides, his stories always gave me a better sense of belonging to a family. Mostly, his stories were just an escape, an escape from all the chaos that went on around me. To my mind, the missing details didn't register a presence. But it may have been Grandpa's intention all along to show me that absence has as great a presence as presence itself.

Well, anyway, I think that Grandpa's leaving my mom alone with her grief about Mabel and his attempts to escape through the music of the classical greats altered her mind forever. In the days and weeks following the news of Mabel's death—alone on the porch, her father roaming the vineyards—she must have felt the full force of all those years of his vanishing acts. Her father had not been there for her during the most crucial and difficult times. To make matters worse, he didn't go recover Mabel's remains, claiming it was best for Mabel's spirit to lie in the soil where she was most at home, in another land. Alone with the distant death of a once very near sister, Mom turned elsewhere for comfort. That's when she met Dad. That's a story you've already heard.

I'm starting to see now why my normally quiet mom had such an extreme response to her father's death: the year he lived at the apartment with us was like a reunion, a forgiveness, a move into the present, a fulfillment of an obligation to the future.

In the week that followed Grandpa's death I began to understand— or, I try to convince myself I understood—Alma's place on that bed next to my mother's grieving body. Orphan with orphan, in a way. I didn't approach until much later when Alma motioned to me. I crawled into the bed, my mother lying on her back. Alma reached over and took my forearm, draping it over the murmuring, moaning, trembling, rising, falling breast of my mother. Alma put her own arm on top of mine, patting my shoulder until we fell asleep.

*F*lickering, leaping beams of light with voices go up from the darkness.
    "Follow me," says a woman's voice.

Feel along a grimy wall. Go up stairs where monoliths are dark except for small trembling flames and more leaping lights in the windows. Taxis unavailable. Buses packed.

"Let's walk home," the woman says, her long black hair surging in the breeze.

Go north with her. Walk past stores where shadowy figures drink warm beer beyond the light of barrels of flame. Kids smoke cigarettes and melting ice cream drips down their fists.

"Come away from them," the woman orders. She's short but authoritative.

A few gunshots. The woman is gone.

Break into a run, leading or following masses of people fleeing from the crackle of gunfire—or firecrackers.

Stumble and fall, shoved aside by the woman. Then alone.

5.

I UNDERSTAND. I NEVER THOUGHT anyone else's experience of loss could come close to my own. And the way you care for me and hold me like you're afraid I'll disappear forever . . . well, I admire you for it. I'm inspired by it. And I love you for it. But we don't need to call your psychiatrist friend.

Yes, it is strange that I was under the impression the power went out last night. I clearly remember finishing my walk from home to Battery Park right as the sun was setting. A woman on the train struck up a conversation with me. Her two sleeping kids, under the illusion that spring break was the beginning of summer break, had run ragged at the Statue of Liberty. She said she had lived here for ten years but had never been; her parents in Los Angeles wanted pictures, had always wanted to visit but were "too busy working their asses off to keep up with the Chois," she said with a chuckle. She said that maybe because her parents built up the statue in her head too much over the years, it was bound to be a disappointment. Either that or she was just too distracted keeping her crazy kids from falling into the harbor.

No. No doctors, either. My scrapes and bruises aren't like frostbite, after all. Besides, we need to open these clinic doors so you can help people who really need it.

━━━━━━━━━━

I know you think all my talk is a diversion of some sort, given the influences that men have had on my life, my story, my sleep. Oddly enough, when I'm lying here in our room, I often try to imagine the music of my youth to help me sleep. But neighborhood sounds don't comingle. I hear the train clacking across the 225th Street bridge, the sporadic sirens. But it's quieter here than I'd expected. Grandpa's old classical LPs don't come through the silence.

Recently, though, as you fall off to sleep in my arms and your breath becomes regular, I've been thinking about Lincoln Center a couple months ago, you dozing beside me despite the money you spent on our tickets, the dimmed yellow light around us, the brilliant glow of the unified movements onstage, your breathing, the rustling sheet music, a cough or two that accompanied the notes. I had never seen a live orchestra, so all of it was exciting.

Even though I hadn't listened to any classical music in over two years, I was on the edge of my seat from the very beginning, the strident low and high piano notes of Rachmaninov's Piano Concerto no. 2 building a sense of peril until the strings join in their romantic sweep, the hint of bass drum a reminder of foreboding. It's always been a favorite—it helps me traverse the imagined or real episodes in my life. And you already know that. But I wondered if the music a person listens to can tell you all you need to know about her. I mean, I already know what you think about my obsession with music by men in Seattle. In that moment, as you snored ever so slightly, I wondered what you thought about me growing up on the classical music of men. I guess it couldn't be all bad. After all, there we were, listening to the music of dead white guys on your dime.

The piece after intermission—Shostakovich's Symphony no. 7, *Leningrad*—was new to me. The menacing undercurrents in the second and first half of the third movements gave their jarring counterpoint to the patriotic, militaristic drive of the first movement, and I wondered if the music a person creates can tell us all we need to know about that person. Without the biography in a symphony concert program, could you listen to the music and figure the content of a composer's character? I nudged you to ask what you thought. You grimaced, and your chin slumped again to your chest.

I should have let you sleep; you run ragged at the clinic all day, then you get home and come to bed with me. It's a wonder that I myself didn't fall into some fitful sleep, not from working at the clinic but from all my wandering. Maybe I was kept awake in the concert hall by the scrapes and bruises and cuts and burns. But they alone cannot tell a story. They only call for speculation.

And there were plenty of injuries to speculate on in the weeks after Grandpa's death. Early the next morning after spending the night with Mom, I heard the front door open. I stared at the ceiling, wondering who'd come in. A few minutes later, Alma sighed and sat up. She smiled sadly as she put her hair in a ponytail. Taking me by the hand, she led me out to the front room. We smelled him before we saw him. On the couch, fast asleep and gamier than usual, was Oso.

She told me to take off his muddy boots. So I did. She got a pillow from his bed and put his matted head on it. She told me to get a blanket from the closet. When I came back from the closet, Alma had gotten a warm, damp washcloth and was wiping his scratched hands clean of grime. "Where did you look for him?" she muttered. Oso snored. She took the blanket from me and spread it over him, leaving only his face uncovered. I backed up to the wall and squatted, wondering who this person was that cared for my mom and my brother. It was as if Alma'd woken up that morning two or three times her age. As Alma dabbed Oso's muddy face, a faint noise come from the other room.

"José." It was my mother's voice, sounding as if it were about to break. "José!" she said again, then broke into sobs. Alma shot me annoyed glance and went to Mom's room. I wondered why she gave me that look as I squatted near my brother's sleeping body. The activity of the morning settled. I stared at the assorted ancient paint-roller strokes on the walls, crown molding, ceiling, and tried to make sense of them, imagining why someone had left them like that. And for the entire day, the ebb and flow of the city outside went on in the gray light. Day-drinkers. Car engines and bus air brakes. Moans. A conversation. A laugh. Breaths. I missed Grandpa's voice, his music—how they would weave and dwell with the racket outside, taming it, making some sense of it. My brother slept. Alma spoke in quiet tones and slept next to Mom.

I was waiting, waiting for a large, invisible hand. To scoop me up. To push me. To shove me. To slap me. But the firm grasp of time did not touch me directly that day. Nor did its rage toss me headlong into any motion. Instead, I waited. I stayed where I was, my back to the wall in the front room. I didn't dare move. If I did, things would have gotten worse. A calm settled on the apartment, and I didn't want to unsettle it. I squatted in the fading light. Above the din from the street below, the sound of Alma talking to my mom came and went. I never knew what was said.

Darkness fell, and the voice in the other room had stopped. In the yellow of the streetlamp lighting the front room, Oso rose. He seemed to have gotten even bigger since that morning. His massive fifteen-year-old frame rose, and he looked at me—or in my direction—and pulled on his shoes. And he was gone. Mom groaned in the other room. Dark and wispy, her words floated: "José" and "Oso." Each uttered once and then silence. I shivered.

Later, Alma came into the room.

"Where's Oso?" she asked.

"I don't know. He got up and left a while ago."

"He didn't say anything to you?"

"No. I guess he went to look for Dad."

"What's with you?"

I didn't say anything. Alma mumbled something, and I found

myself walking to my mother's room. I sat next to her, saying nothing. Smells of food entered my nose. Muffled yelling and struggling steps up the stairwell assaulted my ears. A doorknob slamming against the wall. Tumbling bodies. A lamp smashing. Furniture dragging along the hardwood floor.

"Kat!" Alma screamed. "Goddammit! Get out here!"

I went.

Odors of sweat and iron and wet fur met me, as did the sight of a boy manhandling his father. Dad was limp as Oso pummeled him. Alma grabbed me, and we ran arm in arm toward the swinging Oso. We tackled him off Dad, but not before I caught a glancing blow. Oso lay on the hardwood in a dirty white T-shirt, sweat-wet hair flung back, his signature flannel nowhere to be seen. Her white skin pink and glistening, Alma sat beside him, patting his heaving chest. I rubbed my left temple as a headache grew. Dad was on his back, unconscious. His face was a mass of gushing blood, with broken teeth, a split lip, swollen eyes and ears. His ever-present sunglasses lay twisted.

It got stuffy, so Alma opened those big windows, letting in the breeze and fumes and sounds from the street.

━━━━━━━━

We all handled Grandpa's absence differently over the next year or so. For me, it was simple: I just did what others told me to do, helping with little things around the house, cleaning here and there, washing dishes. I didn't even have the self-direction to be resentful of Alma's time with Mom, her convalescence yet another shared experience between them. Oso came home directly after school to prepare meals out of the same few ingredients, the way Mom had always done. Other than school hours, the only time Oso left the house was when he sleepwalked—something he started doing after Grandpa's death. After their brawl, Dad and Oso didn't talk. They couldn't even be in the same room together. Dad was up to his old tricks, working late and staying out even later, sometimes not coming home for days.

Mom became unable to do much of anything. She'd mostly sleep, rarely shower, wear the same dress for days, and let her hair—almost completely gray now—stay untied. From time to time, though, she'd put herself together a little and take me and Alma over to the ocean after school or on the weekends. And if she was quiet before Grandpa died, she became positively mute afterward—except when talking to Oso to get him to go to sleep in his bed. The way that Alma took care of Mom in the days and weeks following Grandpa's death made Mom seem like something other than a mother.

Though she was practically nonexistent as a mother to Oso, she did look after him when he started walking in his sleep. Up to that point, she'd been distant from him, only involved with the early punishments of his crazy behavior many years before. But for the year before she disappeared forever, she slept on the couch, trying to keep Oso from leaving the house in his sleep. It seemed this was her small contribution to keeping the family together. After all, Oso was the one keeping the family together now.

At night, we all ate in our dining room, the table angled so that each of us could watch the street activity in a different direction; that was our version of TV. Then we'd do our homework at the table while Mom stared out the window, maybe waiting for her husband, maybe guarding against him. Oso would invoke Grandpa by putting on his old classical LPs, and later we'd fall asleep as we had so many times before, wrapped in the weavings of the city sounds and the music. Often, though, Oso would wake Alma and me in the middle of the night with his rambling. When we told him of his odd nighttime behavior, he refused to believe that he'd talked nonsense to us or that he'd sung Sinatra to the carousers below.

One night, Mom mumbled something as she got up from the couch and went downstairs. When she led Oso into our bedroom, Mom tried to get Oso to lie down.

"How am I supposed to get home?" Oso said.

"I don't know, Oso, honey," she said in her quiet voice. "But here is your mooring. Now lie down."

He sat on the edge of the bed and said, "I have found it more or less disconcerting to find that a large portion of the workforce is up at this hour."

"Yes, I understand."

"I've seen such a haste of time and a pack of reduction."

"Never such a better reason to a rhyme and place for reflection," Mom concluded as she gently pushed him into his bed.

This kind of nonsense always made me wonder if Mom herself was sleepwalking. In all honesty, it was one of those rare times she fit my idea of what a mother should be. After coaxing Oso back in bed, she'd come over to the bed where Alma and I were. She'd touch my face. Kiss me. Cover me. Whisper to me the soft sound of sand moving against itself. Then she'd leave, the slight smell of sweat hanging in the air long after she had shuffled out the door. As always, she'd leave the door slightly open. The night-light in the bathroom slipping through, the sickle-shaped luminescence on the ceiling. A pleasant dream before sleep. Oso would hum a tune for a few minutes as I nodded off.

You're right to wonder how Mom could be so delicate and patient in caring for restless men. For the most part, I saw her quietly—you might say meekly—deal with all their varying, questionable states of consciousness over the years. What Mom ever saw in Dad—what drove her to put up with him—will forever remain a mystery. Her patience— you might say passivity—with her husband and her tenderness with Oso the sleepwalker had an impact on me. Later I would have some success in gently prodding him back to bed. To this day, when roaming Manhattan, I can't keep from trying to soothe the men gibbering on the street corners and in parks. Yes, it's Mom's example that dictates I soothe crazy men. But is there something about being a woman that compels me to do this?

I knew you would hate that I asked this. It may, as you say, "reinforce a stereotype." And I understand your concern about the "outsized influence" men and their versions of history have played in my life. But doesn't feminism mean striving for equality? If that's true, I think I've been trying to achieve that very balance in myself ever since I left

California. Sometimes I think you get so angry about men's historical oppression of women that you forget their influence can also be positive. Think of it this way: Had I not spent time with Berlin—allowed him to talk to me, to listen to my flawed family epic, or to sleep with me—I wouldn't have come to some pretty fucking important realizations. And all I would have been to you is another angry or passive stereotype. Would that have made it easier for you to love me? easier for you to shape the way I think and act?

As it stands, I am angry but passive. I guess what infuriates me or scares me the most is when other people's perspectives—yours, Berlin's, professors', writers'—demand so much of me that it paralyzes me. Looking at myself honestly and knowing what I stand for seems like such an impossible task.

In contrast, Oso seemed to be in constant movement when trying to figure out things like this. When he started high school, it seemed that all his meandering among the people on the streets and in the parks throughout his childhood required that he become an organizer, a very unfocused one. He organized hunger strikes in solidarity with César Chávez, walkouts in support of the Chinese students of Tiananmen Square and, later, the striking Boeing machinists, and a march against the Gulf War his senior year. The only protest that ever made sense was when he went out in support of the homeless—his friends—in Saint James Park and against the police sweeps that sent them wandering each day to William Street Park. In any case, the causes he's always been involved in have been larger than any one person, larger than he was—is. He approached all causes with a fierceness of obligation, even in trying to keep our family together as it slowly splintered, shrank, and disappeared after Grandpa's passing.

Where was my ferocity? I have the growing sense that I did great injustice to my family.

You're right. I was young, but it seems my youth should have given way to necessity, the ferocious necessity that emerged from Alma during the progression of disaster that unfolded over the coming years. It should have been me who was tenacious in times of peace, militant in times of crisis. I've recently wondered how things would have turned out if I'd been more like her. But no matter how it plays out in my head, I always find myself alone on a beach, the waves at my feet. Drawing portraits in the sand.

———————————

As I said before, on the occasional days when she felt well enough, Mom would keep up the tradition of day trips to the ocean. She changed the tradition only two times. Changed it so much, in fact, that I should have known something was really wrong. But I was excited by the newness of the experience.

Besides, I was happy to get out of that unbearable apartment, the routines and rituals forever altered from the calm of the previous year. When he wasn't protesting or marching, Oso stayed home to provide some stability and protection from Dad's unpredictability. But when he sleepwalked, Oso often came home with fresh bruises or cuts or swollen knuckles, the wounds and blood unsettling whatever sense of security we had felt in his conscious hours. I don't know if he and Dad were battling each other in the park, but whenever Dad did show up at home, cuts and bruises on his face were evidence of a run-in with some hulking individual.

Through all this, Alma kept her vigil at Mom's bedside, taking to her sketchpad or homework. Mom's melancholy was a persistent toxic cloud that no amount of her floral-herb oil could have scattered. I don't know how I passed my classes that year. I'd try to do my homework at the dining room table, hoping the natural light and sounds of the street filtering through the big windows that surrounded me would help. They didn't. So at least once a day, I'd go alone down to the sidewalk and lean against the wall of Mr. Henry's furniture store. I'd try to draw ears as well as Alma drew them. It never occurred to me to sketch the townies, businessmen, and university students coming from and going to the Mission or the other nearby businesses: Đất Của Chúng Tôi Bahn

Mi, Mía Taqueria, News & Smoke. It's just that I didn't want to be where I was. And drawing those ears over and over again somehow transported me.

By the spring, I had quite a collection of ears, varying in size and shape and degree of deformity. I knew that I was no good, but if I'd stopped drawing, I would have gone nuts, never knowing if Dad would come home or, if he did, what state he would be in: scraped, bruised, covered in mud, dog tired, or rabid like a dog. He could be any combination of these, and together it made some foul cocktail in his brain where all his traits were exaggerated. It's sure lucky he didn't drink much.

The first time Mom took us to San Francisco, everything went as it normally did. Mom pulled Alma and me out of school. It was a Thursday in early June just before Grandpa died; I remember because we missed an in-class review that I desperately needed for my sixth-grade math final. My grades were pretty bad my first year of middle school, but our weekday escapes from San José were sacred and secret. That morning, like every adventure day, Mom packed a fuchsia shoulder bag of necessities. On the short bus trip to Diridon Station, she would put a couple stray hairs back in place, smooth down her thick gray dress, and peer out to the sidewalk.

When we got to Diridon, we'd get on the bus headed for Santa Cruz. But on that day, Mom pulled us toward the train terminal. As she bought our tickets, a thrill ran through me. I hated the bus ride to Santa Cruz. From the moment Mom pushed our way through the doors and the people into the train station, I was confronted by the wonder of infinite destinations. Below the station's gold-faced clock and a large mural showing the Santa Clara Valley before orchards and grazing took over, showing the land that city officials wanted visitors to believe was rooted in harmony—indigenous folks walking side by side with white folks—below all of this, the homeless slept on the benches, and traveling families built fortresses around themselves with luggage, as if that would protect them from the odor and the sight of the destitute. Everywhere I looked, journeys were beginning and ending.

As we rushed through the causeway under the northbound track, everything shook. We emerged onto the platform and into the smell of diesel as the air tousled my hair into a subtle frenzy. I found myself wanting to stow away on the Amtrak trains waiting on other tracks to depart to their mysterious destinations. But I clung to Mom's hand as the train to San Francisco ground to a squeaky stop. The doors slid open, and a smell of body odor, booze, and plastic upholstery invaded my nose. Mom found two pairs of seats facing each other, taking up a spot at the window across from me. Alma immediately put her head down in Mom's lap. Mom stroked Alma's thin blond hair. I couldn't understand how Alma could go to sleep; the journey had endless possibilities, including the opportunity to look, if only briefly, into the lives of new groups of people.

As the train crawled out of the station and wound through the rail yard, people closed their eyes or bent to their work for the hour-and-a-half ride. But I saw the tracks multiply and divide, some lines heading east, silvered by recent use, and others rusted, dead-ending elsewhere, nowhere, a graffitied brick wall, a patch of weeds.

We twisted our way between small metal and auto body shops and scrapyards. A narrow footpath emerged alongside the track, winding by pieces of garbage, burned-out campfires, lean-tos constructed of discarded two-by-fours and tattered blue tarps. I instantly imagined Oso wandering that footpath in the direction of the city, stopping along the way to talk with the nomadic and the displaced to find out if they, too, were headed to San Francisco, a place that seemed to beckon all types of people looking for a fresh start.

When the train slowed and stopped in each town, people tended to look up, coming briefly out of their motion-induced dozing or work. But not me. Sure, I saw the angular, indistinguishable buildings of sterile downtown Sunnyvale or Mountain View—I couldn't tell one from the other. And I saw the cliffhanger houses in the nearby hills of Menlo Park and Redwood City. But aside from the hygienic downtowns, I saw what the sleeping or working people on the train missed. Plight and blight between the towns were kept company by the footpath, the footpath I pondered, its existence brought about by people I never saw on the trail itself. What I did see between the towns were run-down apartments and ancient houses shutting out the world with old quilts and faded cartoon-character sheets as window shades.

Just south of Burlingame, the footpath had some startling deviations. For most of the way up the peninsula, the footpath had roved to various distances from the track, sometimes precariously close, other times straying to shrubs that would obscure it until it emerged once again to weave alongside the rails. And I kept imagining Oso hiking this footpath up to San Francisco. North of Burlingame and on toward the city, the footpath jogged into a grove of trees and reappeared at a sharp angle. The footpath, which had had such nice, soft curves and meanderings, all of a sudden made a harsh, hurried, perpendicular intersection with the tracks. I imagined a lurking monster that lived atop the cedar trees. When the footpath flew out of the trees and toward the track, I dashed to the other side of the train as if I'd seen Oso, wounded from battling the monster, bolt out of the grove and in front of the speeding train. It terrified me to think of what was in that grove that made people bolt across the tracks. And when I got to the other side of the train, the footpath scattered in three directions, none of them heavily worn. They were simply trails of trampled-down brown grass that stopped abruptly.

I remember thinking that these footpaths didn't have as much wear on them because many of the people who had run for their lives out of the grove had been hit by a speeding train. I had that melancholy satisfaction, thinking that at least their terror was short-lived. One of the three footpaths continued north with many lesser-traveled footpaths shooting off like twigs on a branch. The main footpath itself—looking now like poorly recorded Morse code—dotted and dashed in and out of existence, disappearing into stagnant water on the right side of the track, skirting through a series of swampy marsh areas, sometimes disappearing beneath a weeping willow whose branches bent to touch a refuse-choked cesspool.

I was near tears when the footpath ceased to exist about five minutes from the train depot at Fourth and King Streets. I returned to Mom and slumped into my seat, thinking about the clandestine footpath as if I'd just finished reading a book where the main character dies at the end for no apparent reason. As we got closer to downtown San Francisco, I ran through everything I'd seen like I was trying to find a sentence or a paragraph that would somehow explain the death of the main character. But then everything vanished.

We went into darkness, and I reached across to Mom's hands and gripped and released them as we reemerged into sunlight and I saw cesspools but no footpath averting them. I gripped her hand once more as we entered the black of another tunnel. Flash. One second out and then plunged back into darkness and then out again. My grip on Mom's hand like an irregular heartbeat. Then into San Francisco. Downtown monoliths stood at a distance, their wind-torn American flags fluttering. Alma woke up, looked out the window, pushing her hair out of her face and rubbing her eyes. We were in a new world.

For Mom, though, it seemed she was familiar. The possibility didn't occur to me at the time that she had come to the city at fourteen when she disappeared from Grandpa's vineyard. But all the clues were there, strange as some of them were. Mom pulled us from the swarm of commuters and across the street to an abandoned RV park. She bowed her head for a moment and then, from her big ugly bag, unloaded a smaller bag with a few bottles of water, some snacks, and a couple of sandwiches that she placed under some bushes. We were too excited to think anything of the strange deposit. Mom pointed at the approaching Embarcadero tram, so Alma and I ran to catch it. But we missed it, Mom strolling to the platform, taking in the warm breeze. While we waited for the next tram, I gazed across the bay at the massive port cranes of Oakland and imagined Grandpa was with us that day in the city.

Under the Bay Bridge and beyond, the tram moved through rich neighborhoods where panhandlers walked the same sidewalks as homeowners along the waterfront. Alma didn't like the city as much as the ocean, but she was just as absorbed as I was. We exchanged glances and pointed things out to each other, all the while never exchanging more than a giggle or a "wow" or an "ah." Mom watched us, smiling. I never thought to ask her about the tears in her eyes.

When we got to the wharf area, we bypassed all the tourists and street performers—the clumsy guys juggling burning torches and burning their hands; the man who acted like a coin-operated robot, moving only if he got some money; the man who hid behind a bush and scared the oblivious Europeans and Asians—to a lesser-known crab shack. Mom ordered our food without looking at the menu. Mom ate a whole Dungeness crab; her fingers moved and picked with ease, cracking, peeling, undressing the pink-and-white flesh with fluency. And she laughed a little as Alma and I grossed each other out, sucking clam chowder off strands of our hair that had blown into the bread bowl. Again, I glimpsed tears in Mom's eyes. But I was so swept up in the city, too young to think to ask about it. Certainly too naïve to ask where she got the money for that day of wandering.

After lunch, we sat in a small park near Ghirardelli Square. Alma and I could have sat there all day, enjoying the sun and the smell of chocolate in the air. But just as we were starting to doze, we noticed Mom walking away. We followed her to North Beach. We gawked at the tourists eating lunch in the restaurants and bars. But Mom walked on. We trailed her through City Lights Books, where a trumpet riffed with a drum over the speakers. Mom pulled a book, turned to a specific page, and dragged her finger under the words. I was about to flip through a magazine when she glided out the door. We scrambled after her, jazz wrenching the air.

We followed Mom up an alleyway and out to a main street just as a bus pulled up, and we climbed on. Staring blankly out the window, I was in a daze from all I had seen. Alma yanked my arm, and we were off the bus. We tried to keep up with Mom but found ourselves looking in the windows of tattoo parlors, head shops, Eastern rug emporiums, and little restaurants. Patchouli hung in the air with the long, drawn-out guitar solos blaring from tape decks in apartment windows. Young men with metal-pierced faces subtly pushed weed or acid. Girls a little older than me and women about Mom's age swayed in doorways, their bright, swirling dresses and clinking bracelets mesmerizing, both peaceful and exhilarating.

We stopped to talk to a young dreadlocked woman, and Mom waited patiently half a block down. The woman had a half-moon tattoo on one shoulder and a blazing sun on the other. Her German shepherd puppy was tied to a standpipe with some hempen rope. I talked with the woman about her jewelry from places as far away as the Congo. Alma played with the puppy, and the woman told us about some of her travels. She invited me to feel the hand-carved wooden pendant she'd gotten from the south island of New Zealand. When I reached toward her, the puppy suddenly lunged and snapped at me, the length of the rope saving my calf from a bite. The puppy barked wildly, baring her teeth. The woman said sorry and tried to calm the little dog, but it nipped her forearm. Without a word, the woman stared serenely at the trickling blood. The pup sat looking remorseful until the woman scratched her behind the ear. All the while, Mom watched the scene like she had all the others throughout our first visit to the city. Even when foolish drug dealers approached us, two poor-looking youngsters, Mom was both distant in her own thoughts and just close enough to keep an eye on us.

Late in the afternoon, we were back at Fourth and King, visiting the RV park. Mom examined the bushes and smiled, looking like a worshipper whose gifts had been accepted. We scanned the hundreds of people streaming in and out of the train station like we might catch a glimpse of who had taken the bag. On the train, I wolfed down a couple steaming dumplings Mom had gotten from a vendor at the station. I didn't give the bush bag much thought at the time, and I still don't understand it. Its significance was lost between my hunger at the end of that adventure and her disappearance a few months later.

One day, I was reading *Hatchet* in the front room; the plane the main character was on had just crashed in a lake. And Dad shuffled through the front door. He tracked in mud. But it hadn't rained in a couple months, so I told myself I would follow him someday, as if doing so would somehow explain his dripping flannel that night or where he had been any of the other times he vanished from the apartment. I never did tail him. "Apathy" is the only word for it. Or maybe it was fear of what I would learn. Anyway, Dad was somehow different that particular night: his head hung low and his pace was slow, the old hardwood floor creaking under his dirty boots as he shambled to his room. Quiet talk, a series of questions, and silence. And then he screamed.

"Get up, get up, get up! Wake up! Jonah's dead, but you're not!"

A pause.

"Jonah's dead!" He choked on tears.

The traffic outside hummed.

"Ahhh! Wake up!"

And then I heard a couple quick, heavy steps and the squeak of the bedsprings.

"Jesus! Kat, get in here!" Alma yelled.

I found myself going down the hall, the sounds of slapping and the words "Wake up!" rushing to me. Dad flung Alma to the ground. He was straddling bare-shouldered Mom, whose dress straps always seemed to fail her.

"Leave her alone!" Alma cried, hair in her face, her skin pink with rage. The stretched V-neck of her blue YMCA T-shirt hung and exposed her shoulder.

Through his tinted glasses, Dad gaped across the room at Alma. "Who the hell are you?"

Mom's face was swelling. Her eyes—and the fatigue that'd always been there—were the only thing I recognized. I was drawn to those eyes. As if there were no dirty, soaking man on top of her, I neared the bed to touch her face, but she looked up at the ceiling just in time to catch a backhand from Dad. Then I found myself on the ground, Dad's follow-through having struck me square in the nose.

Through watery eyes I saw Alma pick something up. On the foot of the bed, she lined herself up and swung her history book. Dad thudded to the ground on the other side of the bed. It was quiet for a moment. Mom's graying hair was flung on the pillow, and she looked like she was sleeping. A trickle of blood ran from a scratch on her cheek across the bridge of her nose and soaked into the sheet. Alma stood ready to strike again.

"Who the hell are you?" Dad held his ear, blood seeping between his chicken-claw fingers. And he staggered down to the street.

A hush descended on the oddly lit room. Ever-drawn curtains puddled on the floor, and indirect afternoon sunlight streamed through the windows. A fallen reading lamp spotlighted cracked white paint on the crown molding. Alma and I gaped at each other and then at the book. The bottom of the spine was crushed like it'd been dropped from a great height.

"Go get some ice and a towel."

When I came back from the kitchen, the pain in my nose had spread to my ears, inverting my sense of depth. Rush hour on the streets, each engine distinct from the next. Happy hour in the Mission, each voice a cadence of its own. Music floating, each note a separate entity with its own life. Yet only a few yards away, I heard nothing of what Alma was whispering to Mom. And Mom nodded. After my hearing returned to normal that night, and over that week and a half or two, I found relief in the soft drone of Alma's voice.

The incredible thing, you may be thinking, is that the cops didn't show up. Until Mom disappeared, the cops were never involved in anything that happened in the apartment. Mr. Henry used the rest of the building to store his extra furniture, so no neighbor could have called the cops. Maybe that would have changed the course of things for Alma and me. Whether it would have changed things for the better, I'm not sure.

Oso later heard about what happened and took to the streets, no doubt to find Dad. Dad wouldn't show up again until after his wife disappeared. What I found remarkable at the time was Oso's dedication to finding Dad. He definitely could have killed Dad, but it seemed that walking and searching almost nonstop depleted his anger. Finally, one night, he came to our bedroom where I slept alone and collapsed into the other bed, maybe sleeping long before he came home. Maybe not. He mumbled, "Some men see things as they are and say, 'Why?' I dream of things that never were and say, 'Why not?'" Looking back on it, it sounds like something a politician would say. I was going to ask him what he meant. But Alma came in from her observation post in Mom's room, took off his muddy boots, and tucked him in. He was snoring before Alma left the room.

Mom disappeared in mid-July, six weeks before our seventh-grade year.

It was a Monday. Mom packed her big ugly bag as she always did with water and sandwiches and Dad's smelly old flannels. I kept trying to catch Alma's eye, but she looked straight ahead, her hair pulled in a tight bun like Mom's. The three of us made our way down Santa Clara Street to Diridon Station, our reflections in shop windows disjointed by angled panes and linear frames.

Alma led the way to the station and directly to the rails. As we pulled away, half a dozen people came screaming up the causeway, pounding on the side of the car. We pulled in and out of those towns along the way up the peninsula, traveled parallel to the worn footpath, then into and out of the tunnels of darkness and finally into downtown San Francisco. Neither word nor glance was shared. Alma looked out the window the entire time, maybe tracing the footpath, maybe not. Mom closed her eyes. I tried to follow the footpath as a way to calm myself. But when we reached the grove of trees north of Burlingame where the footpath bolted across the rails, I had to shut my eyes until we got off at Fourth and King.

I hoped we would do something like we'd done the first time. Instead, Mom and I followed Alma directly to the tram, which we took to the end of the line. By that time, a certain resignation had set in, though I'd no understanding of why Alma was leading the way.

We got off the tram, and it had gotten quite a bit cooler. Mom set her bag down on the sidewalk; while she dug out our flannels, a thick black parka and a dark-green beanie fell onto the sidewalk. Mom glanced at me and stuffed them back in the bag as the bus pulled up. I wondered where the coat and hat had come from, when she'd gotten them. Then I started to wonder if we were in the same city, the wind pushing the trees around, fog obscuring signs for the Presidio. We got off the bus and were met with the subtle smell of dirt and cat piss from the eucalyptus trees; we hiked uphill past peaceful houses with Spanish-tile roofs and toward the southern headland of the Golden Gate Bridge.

In the muted silence, we stood apart and looked toward the sea. It was impossible to tell if Mom's silence signaled contentment, sadness, anger, unwillingness. It could have been all of these. But with her subtle smile and her arms folded against the cold, I decided it was contentment. The last image I have of her is in an oversized brown-and-black flannel oddly topping her dark-blue dress, the ugly bag over her shoulder. Her now-unbound gray hair began and ended in the mist.

The next thing I knew, Alma called to me, breaking the morning-long silence. She was playing with a full-grown beagle. The dog yapped and jumped as Alma, whose hair had come out of its bun, pretended to throw a stick. The dog barked playfully, and Alma finally threw the stick into some shrubs. The beagle bounded away, tearing up the dirt and weeds, and didn't come back. We searched for fifteen minutes until Alma said that we should give up. And Mom was gone.

"Mom!" We screamed into the echoless fog, our voices absorbed in an instant. Far below the rusty railing were bloodless beige rocks. Her body had been taken away by the mist, becoming the mist itself. We searched the bushes and trees as if she might be playing an uncharacteristic game with us. No response but the receding call of a lone seagull. That Mom had become vapor or a bird were inventions to combat imaginings of everything violent that might have happened to her. Grief is a fertile land for imagination. Alma and I understood this at an early age.

By the time a man jogged up the path, I was in tears. Alma was soothing me, rubbing my neck and back, already telling me those myths about Mom's disappearance. Had the jogger not asked three times if something was wrong, who knows how long Alma would have let me sit there, crying in the dirt. Alma acted like she had honed her patience over decades of motherhood, a patience that could numb the pain of a situation. Her quiet composure in the face of my inertia over the months since Grandpa's passing seemed to be contemplation of a next step, a meditation on the situation, a movement toward the next event.

Berlin asked the same thing. And I didn't mean to give you that impression. By trying to convince Berlin that Alma had helped Mom vanish that day, I was also trying to convince myself that Mom's end wasn't a pointless accidental death or a flat-out abandonment. Maybe I was trying to create some heroic myth about her, though it's tough to see how her concocting an escape plan with Alma could be interpreted as heroic. But the reality is that nobody knows what happened to Mom.

The cold, fog-shrouded precipice above the bridge soon turned into a chaos of men of varying shapes and sizes, all looking official in their own way, all looking in their own way, all attempting consolation in their own way, swirling in and out, asking for bits and pieces, asking and asking again, asking questions that we were unable to answer.

"When was the last time you saw her?"

"Did she have emotional problems?"

"Was there trouble at home?"

"Where is your dad?"

"Do you have any other family?"

If I had answered any of these questions, it could have led the cops to Mom. But I was following Alma's silent lead. Or maybe I was just waiting for them to ask the right question, which, of course, would have been "Did you notice anything strange throughout the day?" Yes! Yes! Every goddamned thing was strange! Mom seeming to take direction from Alma, Alma's composure throughout the day. And even her odd silence at the cops' questions didn't seem to come from shock. Rather, her reticence seemed purposeful. But it could have meant contentment, sadness, anger, or unwillingness. It could have been all of these. But with her eyes brimming with tears and her arms folded against the cold, I decided it was utter despair.

It seemed the cops were looking for answers in our words instead of searching the water, the headlands on the other side of the bridge, the bushes, the trees, the sky, the mist.

Where is she? I wanted to scream.

We are doing the best we can, they would have replied.

Why aren't you looking for her? My rage should have bubbled.

We have men on the job, they would have said.

Men? I would have said. Right.

People. People are on the job.

It was all a show. The only reason so many cops showed up that day was that kids were involved. Do you know how many people disappear off that bridge every year? Well, it's a lot. And Mom was just one. She was insignificant, no connections. She remained just as silent as she was in life. No one to connect her life to anything she did. And there was no body on which I could lay my sadness. Or my anger. I never got a chance to bury all this melancholy and rage with my mother.

Instead, I dropped it inside, like a stone in a deep pool of stagnant water. And then calm resumed. It resumed until the next stone dropped.

A large man is inhaled by the snake, his cup clinking with small pieces *of metal. He sits down across the aisle, jingling the contents of the cup.*

Say: I have nothing to give, man.

"Neither do I. All I need is conversation."

Say: I have nothing to say.

"Neither do I. All I need is conversation."

Say: Well?

"Skankadoople is jargon full of nothingness."

Say: I suppose. But it's unique jargon, unlike the cliché "full of nothingness."

"Actually, it's an oxymoron," the man says. "Like 'numb feeling.'"

Say: Better yet, a clichéd oxymoron!

"Aha! Like the strong you!"

Say: Yeah! Like the intelligent me!

"Oho! Like the dedicated you!"

Say: Or maybe like the visible me!

"Like the existent you!"

Say: Me!

"You!"

The large man turns to vapor and the snake exhales.

You! Wait! Oso?

6.

I WOULD TELL YOU. But only if you promise you won't again insist
I see a headshrinker. Something—someone?—tells me I will—I must—
figure this out on my own.

Well, I was pounding on a subway door when I heard myself
screaming, "You! Wait! Oso?" I stopped and rubbed my throbbing
hands—these bruised fists you're so concerned about—and stared at my
outline reflected in the glass. The A train pulled out of the 163rd Street
station, next stop 155th. Slumped on a bench, I cried, shielded my face,
tried to drown out the racket in my head with my Discman. "Forty Six &
2" on repeat—slowly building over and over, striving to push me forward
through my shadow; blasting into my brain: *slough off your skin, pick your
scabs*; driving me toward a bridge, the bridge with life on the other side,
and growth and taking and giving and movement and learning and loving
and crying and killing and dying and paranoia and lying and hatred and
fear. *Clear the way to the other side.*

But nothing could protect me from the commuters' cautious whispering and silent gaping. So I rode on, all the way out to the airport, dreading your inevitable variations on "Does where you were tell us why you're here?"

Okay. But more than eight months together doesn't mean you won't dump me. Can you also promise me you won't put me out on the streets?

Good. I think I'd cease to exist without you.

So here it is: this morning, I was on my way to visit Oso.

No, he got here about a year before I did. I'm not sure why he came in the first place, but I'm pretty sure he stayed because of Camille. They've been living together in Washington Heights—163rd and Amsterdam—for six months or so.

A week or so before Alma disappeared, Camille sent me a note and a plane ticket; she insisted that I come out to "mend fences" with Oso. But once I got here, I knew I wasn't ready to see him. I still don't think I'm ready. No matter how hard I try to make sense out of things, with Berlin's help and yours, the voices of others seem to talk over me, to walk over me. The voices of others—and my apathy—seem to have followed me here.

And I know you'll say that my action, predestined or not, led me here. And you'd be right. That an action I took led me to you . . . well, let's just say that Manhattan would have swallowed me whole had I not met you. But what now?

Adopt? You do remember I've been lying to you for months now, right? That I scream at myself in windows? That I wander, searching for nothing and injuring myself again and again? Then how am I to help, as you say, "redirect a kid's destiny and give purpose" to our lives? How is that supposed to improve the world that you yourself say is unforgiving? Isn't it enough that we help women every day down at your clinic?

Not everyone is destined to meet someone who helps them survive the toil and sound of the world, much less help them raise a child. Look at my mother. At the very least, she must have feared she would be snubbed for having a baby without a husband. But she likely had a much deeper dread. She must have quit her job and gone into hiding and gone a little insane with fear. Imagine what her community—or even her own family—would have done if they saw how different the baby was from her.

Yes, of course I'm talking about Mom. Who else would I be talking about?

I try all the time to justify Mom's disappearance, abandonment, suicide. I make up stories that she had to leave the family because Dad was the way he was, that something kept her from getting a job after we were in school, that her marriage and her babies brought on more disapproving looks and whispers in San José than she had expected, that the only person who made it seem all right was dead, that enduring all of these things wore her down until she snapped, driven so insane that the children she had raised didn't seem to matter enough to take with her. But then I think it's as simple as Mom being taken away by the cool Pacific mist. And that somehow makes everything better. At least for a moment.

By the time we were finally taken, shivering, off the hillside to the sunny side of town, roles had somehow reversed. Alma now clung to me, perhaps having realized the full weight of what had happened. She had become inconsolable, having lost yet another mother. The thought of this made me sad, too. But it also made me realize that our survival depended on me. Alma had guided me through my paralysis after Grandpa died. Now that Mom was gone, it was my turn to guide—at least for a while.

A social worker—a large Hispanic woman named Miss B who had come up from San José when no one could get ahold of Oso or Dad—drove us back home. I looked out the window as thick, moonlit vapor clung to the Pacific Coast Range. Alma cried in my lap, and I smoothed her hair and swallowed hard against my own tears. I couldn't stop the images in my head. Not wanting to upset Alma, I bit back whimpers of horror as Mom, over and over, was swallowed by the whitecaps, her body dragged out to sea, drawn and quartered by sharks, becoming bones picked clean, scattering and sinking to the ocean floor. Deep water and deep grief: fertile grounds for the imagination.

No one was at the apartment. I held Alma as we lay in the bed and dropped in and out of sleep and sadness. Miss B stayed and made more calls. Much later, I woke up to a sorrowful and tired Oso sitting on the bed, looking bigger than before. Miss B was on the phone in the front room. Somehow Oso's hulking body fit on that tiny bed with Alma and me. He sniffed, but I don't think he cried after he put his arm over the both of us. I fell asleep somehow, longing for Mom's herby-floral fragrance, enduring the sighing squeak-whines of bus air brakes from the street. And wishing to dream of anything but the horrible things that swam and floated in my head.

When we woke to the voice of Miss B, Oso's arm was still draped over me; Alma's back was nestled into his massive chest.

"No sign of your dad," Miss B said as she sat on the other bed. "The police have a description and they're on the lookout." Then she said something in Spanish. Oso sat bolt upright and translated for us. I was terrified. Why did we have to go with her? Where? What had we done wrong?

"Why can't we just stay here?" Oso's voice was shaking.

She responded in Spanish, pleading.

"English, please. They don't know what you're saying," Oso said.

"Sorry, ladies. I know this must be tough. But your brother's only sixteen; he's too young to look after you by himself."

I almost said that Oso was the only one who ever looked after us. But I decided that would make our situation worse if Dad decided to show up.

She drove us way up Alum Rock Avenue into the East Hills, and I was certain we'd be staying in one of those country-club palaces. But we stopped in front of a weed-choked driveway with a beat-up pickup truck and an old Datsun. Miss B knocked on the scuffed front door, and brown needles fell from the Christmas wreath skeleton that'd been hung months before. A balding, middle-aged white man in an old Hawaiian shirt opened the door and greeted us with a weak smile. His house reeked of cooked hamburger meat, and something told me it was as much a part of the house as the wooden beams that held it up.

The man introduced us to his wife, a skinny Asian woman in an oversized floral nightgown. She waved from the old couch, not getting up, and went back to watching TV. Miss B told us she'd check in with us the next day; then she left. We followed the shuffling man as he led us back to the bedrooms where we'd stay. The other kids were already in bed, so we tried to settle into our rooms by night-light. Oso had a bed in the same room as another boy. Alma and I were in another room with three bunk beds full of girls. I worried about Alma, who had said nothing and didn't even whimper in the strange room. But as I lay down in the bunk above Alma, I had a brief moment of calm, imagining Oso sleeping on the floor next to our bunk. A singular talisman.

But in the utter silence of that house—no engines, carousers, music, or stories—I was soon swallowed by my thoughts. It became clear to me that if we told Miss B anything about Dad's constant vagary, questions would be raised about his ability to care for us. Though I would have liked to expose Dad for who he was, I was sure that the three of us would be split up, especially since Alma was not even a legal member of our family. The next day, I talked to Oso about this. And despite his mounting desire to beat the hell out of Dad yet again, he saw the importance of keeping the three of us kids together.

Good question. I don't know how we pulled it off. Was I really that convincing to Miss B, a person whose job it was to look after children's welfare? How could she have overlooked Alma's own lack of a mother? I suppose that part of the story really doesn't pan out.

Anyhow, back to the story as I know . . . as I remember it.

Dad turned up the next day. We were at home with Miss B, getting some clothes for an indefinite stay at the foster home. Oso took the lead of our little charade. As Oso approached him, Dad cringed. But Oso enfolded Dad in his massive arms, saying it was so good to have him back, that we could now grieve together. Oso even cried and pulled Dad down to the floor. As they kneeled in an embrace, I took Alma's hand and we joined them. And I planned all this.

These theatrics made an impression on Miss B. But she had to call the police. When they arrived, it became clear that Dad was a suspect in Mom's disappearance, given that he was nowhere to be found at the time. The plan to keep us together was suddenly in jeopardy by the age-old interrogation: Where were you during the time in question?

"I was at church—Saint Joseph's—with him most of that day," Oso said before Dad could speak. "We usually go together whenever we can."

Dad glanced up at his son but said nothing. Alma and I had never gotten the sense Dad was religious, so Oso's claim about going to church with Dad seemed doubtful. The detective had the same doubt but for different reasons.

"What about the time between when you showed up and the time he showed up?"

"I went to Saint Joseph's and told him," Oso said. "He was so weak with worry that he couldn't stand. I told him I'd call an ambulance, but he insisted he'd be fine. He asked me to take care of things with the girls, to give him some time."

"This was a pretty big deal. How could he stay there?" The detective looked at Dad. "Your wife was missing. Why didn't you leave with your son?"

Dad hung his head and mumbled.

"He needed to pray," Oso translated.

The detective looked doubtful.

Oso continued. "I don't know why he thought CPS or the cops wouldn't be involved. Or why he would actually be a suspect. He loved . . . loves his wife."

And you're probably skeptical again. Like, why didn't Miss B say anything about Oso not having said he saw Dad before being taken to the foster home? You're just like that detective who followed up with questions at the church. Even though Oso's whereabouts were not in question, the detective came back and said that no one remembered seeing Oso.

"I'm sorry, Detective," Oso said, hanging his head. "I was in the park with my friends. You can ask any one of them. I did know all along, though, that he was at the church. I just don't want you to think he was a bad father. I don't want you to take us away from him. He's just had a rough time of it." If Dad had taught Oso nothing else, he certainly had educated him on bullshitting.

Half a dozen people vouched that Dad was there in church the entire time. He was a daily visitor, an extended-stay guest in the house of God. The priest, Father Khoi, said that Dad had borrowed a blanket from him and curled up on the steps, waiting for the doors to open again. And he sat quietly for those couple of days in contemplation. "Even in my line of work," Father Khoi had said, "you have to learn to let people alone. You can just tell that sometimes talking won't help."

That night, after the detective and Miss B finally left the apartment, Oso must have seen the tired look on Dad's face—he looked genuinely sad—and actually led him to his room. When Oso came out and quietly closed the door, he gave us our first glimpse into any significant part of their time together while Oso was growing up. For years, they'd made appearances at Saint Joseph's. They sat in the back pew, never kneeling or standing. And they were there for every Mass they could attend. Weekday, weekend, Spanish or English. They just sat there and listened to the stories. After the readings and the homily were over, they would slip out, walk the park and the streets nearby, only to return for the next Mass. Once, after leaving the church, Oso asked his father why they didn't stay for the whole Mass.

"The only thing that matters are the stories," Dad said. "Well, that and the priests' interpretations. As you get older, those old men who speak after the Gospel will start to sound different from each other. Sure, you can tell a lot about a man by the way he tells his own story. But you can tell a hell of a lot more by the way he interprets other people's stories."

Yes, it does sound an awful lot like the theory I developed in that college English course all those years later. Jesus. You've got a great memory.

A few weeks later, the cops concluded no foul play, and the case became an unsolved disappearance. Throughout the next few weeks, the frequency of clues decreased to nothing. We were officially without a mother. Then the earth shook.

———————————

In the weeks before the Loma Prieta quake, Oso found a way to reconcile with Dad. My brother stopped wandering the street—consciously and unconsciously—and spent long hours taking care of Dad in his mourning, acting as Alma had with Mom after Grandpa died. Father and son talked, talked in low voices, low voices with no laughter, low voices that I could not distinguish. This reunion sparked, yet again, Oso's retellings of Dad's story, as always translating it into English. You'd think he'd tell something different, or at least tell me in Spanish so I could learn the language. In any case, I didn't learn anything new about Dad's wandering or those cameos at every church service.

I know it's killing you not knowing—or understanding—how I never picked up Spanish. Just like it's tearing you up not to know how I got these scrapes and bruises and cuts and burns. I bet a voice runs in your head saying this story should be told differently, that I must tell it in Spanish just because Dad's people were from Mexico. Would you even understand it if I could? What if I told you in Mandarin or Vietnamese or Korean? You probably think that I have no right to tell this story, that it's not mine, that I've been hiding behind the translations and retellings and details of the men in my life.

I've been trying my damnedest to show you who I am, but I know how your mind works. You think my story is being told wrong, that I'm trying too hard. How would you tell it? You must think I'd be a better storyteller if I'd gone to church, that I could have learned more about Dad before he died, that I could have asked more questions, that I could have learned from the way he died. You probably think that my life would have been better if I had ever gone to church, could tell the difference between the New and the Old Testament, could tell you what it was like to go to the cathedral as a kid—even if just at Christmas or Easter.

And maybe it kills you that I don't have more to say about my school years. There's that voice in your head again saying that teachers should have reached out. That the teachers should have or would have helped me to learn a second language. That the teachers should have or would have known life at home was messed up. That the teachers should have or would have helped me find more friends. Your "should have or would have"—that voice in your head—seems to reflect you, your judgment, your ideal.

The teachers from my youth thought similarly. They tried everything to engage me over the years. Most often they tried to get me to take pride in, among other things, being a Rousseau Raven. I was a Rousseau Raven because I grew up a few blocks from Rousseau Elementary School. And none of us knew or asked or cared who Rousseau was, or what a raven had to do with San José. Raven pride my ass. It's like they pulled a name out of a hat full of different animal names and said, *Oh, Rousseau Ravens! How convenient. They both start with* R*!* They were so proud of their pride. So proud of their effort to make me proud. Cinco de Mayo. Lunar New Year. Columbus Day. And days they made up, like Western Day. And Chicano Culture Day. And Vietnamese Heritage Day. Pride! Pride! Pride in something I have no control over! Pride in something I am not. Pride in something I may not be.

I know you didn't mean to piss me off. You're just trying to understand why I never learned Spanish, why I never went to church, and why I didn't get help from other adults. But I also think that you pity me for not feeling proud of anything and that your idea of pride is the best way to save me from my circumstance. Pride seems like such a stupid, lazy concept. It reminds me of those booze-soaked men at the Cav whose bragging confessions told of how bad or indifferent they'd been. Pride also reminds me of the men in my family who told me how revolutionary or passive they had been. And they were all stories of great significance. Significance to whom, I'm not sure. And I'm not sure they knew, either.

And Oso again filled my head with those images, those goddamned stories of Dad's youth. He was proud of his solution to fight off our sadness. He thought those stories, along with the most raucous of

Grandpa's LPs—Beethoven's Emperor, Schubert's Unfinished, Dvořák's New World—were the only way to deal with Mom's disappearance. It did not work for me, and I should have said something. Most times, wrapped in the texture of the music, I would drift through those images of Dad as a happy baby among dead family; of our happy, nomadic-subversive father; of the severed-headed chickens; of partial, bloodied fingers; of rows of unpicked, overripe skin-split tomatoes and grapes. I'd drift through those images and into a dream of a small, bright-white, symmetrical room; silently, I'd stare at a white wooden stool with a white vase and a white daisy. Gasping for air, I'd wake to the sound of Alma and Oso deep-sleep breathing. I'd fight sleep, my eyes not straying from the ceiling near the door where the sickle of light hung poised to strike down bloody chickens and hands and fruit and slash open sterile rooms.

For a few months, Dad fulfilled his minimum duties. He didn't work any overtime; he came home, ate, and went to his room. He'd leave the three of us just enough money to get through the day. Oso would come home every day with a bag of food and cook up a feast, just as Mom had done. And the house was calm—a quiet acceptance that this meager lifestyle was the way of things. We had never known much different anyway.

The big dinners that Oso made for us were like a daily penance for the small amount of money he'd give me and Alma. Oso must have taken more for himself, feeding that ever-growing burly body, well over six feet five inches by the age of sixteen. Yet he always had clothes that fit: faded flannels, jeans, T-shirts from East Coast and LA colleges—everything in fairly good shape, likely bought at Relics.

But Alma and I wore Oso's old flannels, dwarfed and forever trapped in the wet-fur smell of the cloth. We would change out of our school uniforms into Oso's ancient clothes—baggy jeans or shorts and faded T-shirts from events none of us had ever been to—before going down to the street and sitting unnoticed on the sidewalk. The only new clothes I remember getting around that time was a year before when the rags of our Rousseau Raven blue-polo-and-khaki-pants uniform rags gave way to bright, new Monroe Middle School Mallard green-polo-and-khaki-pants uniforms, two sets for me, two for Alma. They fit relatively well the whole three years of middle school, probably because we were five-foot shorties surviving on a shared breakfast doughnut at the corner store. The school cafeteria reduced-price lunches—corn dogs, poor-boy tacos, turkey-mashed potatoes, canned fruit—went right through us; sometimes we'd skip it, drink milk, and eat a bag of potato chips instead.

The day of the earthquake, Alma and I, ravenous as usual, got home from school to a stuffy apartment. The smell of dirt and lead paint greeted us like the aggressive roommate that it was, so we opened all those big windows. We ate a spoonful of peanut butter and changed into Oso's old clothes. We sprawled on the splintering wood floor, trying to escape the heat. But the usual cross breeze was missing. Other than that, it wasn't different from most days. It's strange what I remember from the moments before the earthquake, especially since I witnessed more kindness between strangers in the hours and days after the earthquake than I had ever witnessed in my own family. To this day, I still find it unbelievable how complete strangers took care of one another after everything shattered.

We sat down in the shade of our building, me with the newspaper, Alma with her sketchpad. It was a slow news day, but I read to Alma about protests in East Germany and Bush's threatened veto of federal abortion financing. As I read, Alma lightly sketched a wall topped with barbed wire in one corner of her pad and an infant in the fetal position in another corner; then she set to drawing an elegant doe's ear beside an earring-laden human ear.

A strange trio milled on the street corner. A young man with parted blond hair in a new blue suit laughed and talked with an old man wearing a faded black parka and an even older, bearded man with wild gray hair in stained green coveralls. Curious about the mismatched group, I drifted closer. They peered in Mr. Henry's showroom, watching TV images of a stadium.

"Pride!" said the man in the parka, pacing, zipping up the coat and pulling the hood over his big black hair. He raised both fists. "Your team's got no pride!"

"What do you want from me, man?" said the young man, loosening his tie and smiling with his perfect teeth. "I grew up in the city. You don't just abandon your team because things are bleak. They're home now. They'll come back. Williams will find his stroke. And you watch: Mitchell will crank one tonight."

"Doesn't matter," the oldest man said, lifting his sunglasses on top of his head to tame the hair out of his face. "Giants got no pitching."

Ugh! Sports. Turning to walk away, I heard what sounded like a rumbling semitruck. Then the intersection in front of me buckled, a huge, invisible fist punching it; then it rebounded like water rushing into a void. The ripple twisted its way up and down Santa Clara and Third Streets. Alma screamed. I swung around, almost falling, to see her braced against the wall where she was sitting. Eyes wide, she pushed her feet and hands against the sidewalk as it bucked. I tried to make my way toward her, my feet wide apart; I squatted, surfing for the first time on the waves of a quake.

A piercing shatter behind me accompanied a man's voice: "Fuck!"

I whirled around again, the road still behaving like the ocean. And I saw the young man in the suit on the ground, the plate glass of Mr. Henry's shop in pieces around him, his head bleeding. The two older men started pulling the young man away from the building, but jagged fragments, shards from our apartment, were raining down, sharp angles slicing the awning and splintering on the cement. The three men huddled together under the awning, which itself seemed as though it would come tumbling down. The man in the faded parka was on his knees, pressing the young man's head into his chest, holding the wound, bright blood seeping between his dirty fingers.

When I finally restarted toward Alma only twenty feet away, it felt like I was walking in place. Glass continued to rain down, and I should have run away from the building. But Alma was frozen, arms covering her tucked head, hair draping over her knees. Above her, a crack in the yellow plaster had emerged; small chunks lay around her. Higher overhead, cracked windows held uncertainly in their frames. The ground's convulsions slowed; I sprinted to Alma's side, unsure how long the glass above Alma would stay in place if the cement started rolling again. I made it to Alma and skinned my knee kneeling next to her. She was weeping, her shoulders shaking. All I could think to do was brush the thin layer of yellow dust off her hair and legs. She reached out and grasped me, driving my scraped knee harder into the pavement. I winced and noticed how quiet and still everything was. Somewhere I heard air escaping. I smelled sewage; I smelled gas. I felt Alma all over, looking for cuts. I found none. Searching my pockets, I found a rubber band and tied Alma's hair back.

Alma still clinging to me, we walked into the street. Up and down Santa Clara Street, people shuffled around in the middle of the road. All the windows of Mr. Henry's store were broken; a few massive plates hung jaggedly from the frames. From the bar across the street, people came flooding out and roamed the sidewalk, drinks in hand. Traffic inched through debris and stalled cars. Sirens wailed near and far. The smell of gas faded. Mr. Henry, only a streak of dust on the lapel of his black three-piece suit, climbed over furniture and through an empty window frame to survey the damage; he disappeared again and came back out with a first aid kit.

The man in the parka had removed his coat. The young man's blood on his yellowed T-shirt made it look as if he'd been gutshot. He took the medical supplies from Mr. Henry. "I was a medic. I'll take care of this youngster."

Mr. Henry rushed over to us. "Let's get you out of the street. Is she okay?"

"She's okay," I said, my voice unsteady. "She . . . we're just a little . . ."

"Shocked," he said. "Yes. Me too. Well, stay close. There'll be more shaking."

"Wha . . . ?" Alma looked as if he'd told her he was going to murder us. She and I dropped to our knees.

"Oh dear," Mr. Henry said as he brushed glass shards away from our legs with his shiny black shoe. He unbuttoned his coat and crouched beside us, putting his hands on our shoulders. "It won't be as much, but the earth will move again soon. Just stay close and you'll be fine. Where's your dad? Where's Oso?"

My knee pulsed from the scrape. "I don't know. I mean, Oso's probably at the park and Dad's at work."

"Okay. Don't worry. I'm sure they'll get here as soon as they can."

Standing up and buttoning his jacket, Mr. Henry went back over to the three baseball fans to talk to them. The young man in the suit was getting to his feet, gauze over his ear, tape wrapped around his head, his hair pinched together above the bandage like a sheaf of wheat. I pulled Alma off the ground and led her toward the men, but then another rumbling came from behind; I whipped around to see Third Street rolling toward us, a wave of asphalt yet again. Cars were lifted and set back down, Styrofoam on an ocean. I pulled Alma to the ground as she whimpered. In a few seconds, the shaking was over.

Mr. Henry smiled and signaled for us to stay calm. He straightened his tie, brushed the dust streak from his jacket, crossed the street, and went into the Mission. He came out with the owner, both carrying bottles of beer. The two businessmen and the baseball fans, now grasping longnecks, pointed up and down the streets. Everyone laughed, and the barman returned to his shattered windows and bottles; the baseball fans took up positions around the intersection. The traffic leading to the intersection had begun to back up: people leaving work and the university were trying to manage the roads to get home, but traffic was at a standstill. Armed with fresh beer and the fresh confidence it can bring, the trio directed traffic and entertained the nervous drivers who inched by. From their cars, people asked the blood-soaked former medic if he was injured. He shook his head every time and asked if they needed to be patched up. The old man in coveralls offered swigs of his beer to almost everyone on foot or behind the wheel. Refusing to take up hospital space for his minor injury, the young man told more than his fair share of knock-knock jokes.

Knowing nobody was going far for a while, Mr. Henry convinced others to help out right where they were stranded at Third and Santa Clara. He inspired the young pregnant Vietnamese manager at Đất Của Chúng Tôi Bahn Mi to offer sandwiches to passersby on foot and stuck in traffic, the old Mexican woman at Mía Taqueria to hand out tacos, and the Indian owner of News & Smoke to give out bottles of water and even the occasional cigarette. Mr. Henry himself gave out cans of Coke from his office fridge, and he would share directions and information, careful to keep the news local; it wasn't useful for him to tell rumors about how the Bay Bridge was completely gone or how hundreds had died on a collapsed freeway in Oakland. Where these claims came from no one was ever able to determine, but the trickling news was incomplete, terrifying. And believable. Fear is a place where monsters are born. I myself began to see images of Oso pinned under a politician's monument at the park. I saw Dad among fallen cathedral arches, killed while praying for deliverance or seeking refuge.

The ground shook several more times as sunlight faded. We were still without power. Alma and I started to feel a little sick there on our street corner: we'd had a taco, so we weren't hungry anymore, but the smell of the broken sewer line mixed with the car exhaust turned our stomachs. A little pale, Mr. Henry flagged down a city worker. They switched on a couple flashlights and walked toward a gaping window frame in his store where the furniture had piled up and pushed the TVs facedown on the sidewalk.

"I want to come with you," I said, wanting a break from the polluted air.

"No. Stay here," he said before climbing the mountain of furniture after the city worker. "Your dad and Oso will be back soon."

So we continued watching the baseball fans direct traffic and accept new bottles of beer from the Mission owner. The vendors had run out of food but stood in their shattered storefronts, giving people advice about their routes home, asking if they needed anything. Mr. Henry had assembled a good crew, and we knew they were looking after us. But

Alma and I waited with guts twisted and turned inside out by the odors and nerves.

About twenty minutes later, Mr. Henry and the city worker climbed back over the furniture in the showroom, and Mr. Henry came to us at the corner and called to the baseball fans.

"The structure is stable for now."

"Glad to hear it!" the old man cried from the opposite corner.

"You can stay here tonight if you need to."

The three men waved. The traffic died down, and the sewer smell retreated. Mr. Henry gave the city worker a Coke and thanked him. We heard the next aftershock before we felt it and were more terrified by the sound than the earth itself moving. Yet we were already beginning to accept that this was the way life would be from now on. I remember thinking—if only for a moment or two—that I would have taken that trade-off, somehow feeling more stable with Mr. Henry and the baseball fans acting as sentries in the dark, staying vigilant against looters. No marauding bandits ever came up the road to rape and pillage, perhaps because of the candlelight and shadowy, half-drunken murmurs from the Mission; from time to time, one or two drunks would come see if any of us needed anything.

"Never underestimate the kindness of drunken strangers," the old man in the coveralls said at one point when all six of us stood watchfully on the corner. Everyone laughed.

Around eleven that night, the tremors became less noticeable. The baseball fans and the faithful drunks were still vigilant, as if they were also waiting for someone to return. Didn't any of them have homes? Didn't they have people?

"You two should go upstairs," Mr. Henry said, shining a flashlight near our faces. "You look tired."

"What about Oso and Dad?"

"I'll let you know when they show up. Go straighten things up a bit so they can go to sleep when they get here."

Where does someone get faith like that?

We were turning to go when up Third Street from the park came Oso and a half dozen denizens helping another half dozen limping denizens along. Alma and I ran to him and buried ourselves in his torso. We both were in tears; my gut unclenched. Over the next hour, as the large group shuffled around in the dark outside of the furniture store, we hung on Oso's arms, wrapping ourselves in his familiar stink as he told Mr. Henry and us about how the park had filled up with people from all over, people of all kinds, people unfamiliar to the regulars.

"Would it be okay if my friends stayed around here tonight?" Oso said.

"You're a good kid, Oso," Mr. Henry said. "I have no problem with it, but wouldn't they feel safer in the park?"

"They're just tired. And they're more nervous about all the new faces than they are about falling buildings."

Then Dad came up Santa Clara Street with his own adopted refugees, a gray-haired couple with three blond girls whose apartment had smoke damage from a small fire that had broken out below their unit. Say what you will about my father and his stories and the way he spent his idle time. But in that moment, I actually felt what some people might refer to as pride, almost as if I could take credit for his uncharacteristic generosity. Oso and Alma must have felt the same; we hugged Dad and introduced ourselves to the newcomers. Mr. Henry shook Dad's hand, grasping his arm with his other hand.

"I think we can make this work," Mr. Henry said. "It may not be the safest, but we all need people right now."

With lit candles stuck in the tops of old wine bottles, we helped people clear glass off the couches where they'd sleep. When we finally got into our own beds, we heard another aftershock coming. Alma and I held each other tight. The blond girls downstairs whined. With the fear of more shaking, none of us slept. Moving headlights and jumping flashlights glided and bounded across the ceiling, showing the occasional crack. I remember thinking about all those newspaper stories about disaster and war I had read; I couldn't recall reading much about people pulling together.

Maybe I did read about the kindness of people in desperate times but for some reason had blocked it all out—like I deemed those details not credible because the world I had experienced to that point did not function like that. And now I wonder: if catastrophe brings people together, why did my family scatter? Maybe if I had done anything after Grandpa died, Mom wouldn't have disappeared. Or maybe if I had done even more than I did to help Alma deal with her grief after Mom vanished, she could have avoided the eventual disaster that was her relationship with Loskie and all the other messed-up shit that happened because of him.

———————————

For the first couple weeks of seventh grade—before the earthquake— things were pretty much the same as they had always been at school. No matter what was going on—a Mallard Pride Day, a pep rally for the flag football team, an assembly with a hypnotist, the mile run in PE, in-class activities, lunchtime—Alma and I were alone. This was nothing new. Oso's reputation protected us too well and followed us through the years, and all it had taken was one incident when we were in first grade: a new third grader, a Vietnamese boy named Stan, called me a half-breed, which by itself didn't mean much at the time; but he also threw a rock that hit me in the forehead, just above my right eye—you can see the scar, all white now. The next day, I fiddled with the bumpy stitches and watched Oso, then in fifth grade, punch Stan a few times in the face and dump a trash can on him.

All that drama aside, I think people still would have kept their distance from me and Alma. It wasn't because Alma was white and I wasn't; those kinds of friendships were unavoidable in San José—for people who grew up downtown, at least. No, people stayed away for other reasons. In the classroom we didn't talk incessantly like other girls. At lunch and recess, we sat quietly. Alma drew in her sketchbook. I would sometimes take to drawing, too. But usually I'd just watch the boys play basketball and the girls play tetherball, musing ever so slightly at what it might be like to have more than one friend.

I had watched others on the fringes throughout my school years and wondered if some sort of friendship could be formed between us and them. In junior high and high school, I even wondered if we could do what other kids did with each other, if we could hold hands at school, go to dances with them or kiss them. There was Anita Vasquez, a frumpy, odd Salvadoran girl who, in sixth grade, people said had been caught masturbating in the locker room with a chalkboard eraser; perpetually dirty Joey Matthews, a freckled blond boy who made daily failed attempts to join the games at recess; Daljeet Mazari, a Pakistani boy who never spoke and considered unknown things from the playground wall where he sat; Pon and Seda Sok, the only Cambodians in town as far as I could tell, a brother and sister who played cards and yelled at each other in Khmer. We knew who each other were, but no alliance or love match was ever attempted. And Anita, Joey, Daljeet, Pon, and Seda caught shit from the other kids from time to time, so I remained vigilant.

But Alma and I were pretty much left alone, aside from the few sneers and comments made behind our backs as we occasionally—more occasionally than most girls, though—walked arm in arm or hand in hand. Hell, if anyone ever had approached us, all Alma or I would have had to do was show the sketchpad collection of our classmates' ears. That would have freaked them out well enough. But we never had to use our headless ears as a method of repellent. No one ever approached us directly. And things probably would have stayed that way after the earthquake.

Then came Marlene.

All the girls wanted to be near Marlene Knopf and her shiny new clothes and china skin. Hordes of girls surrounded her from day one, wanting to help the new girl in school, wanting her to come to their slumber parties, wanting her beauty to brighten their lives in a post-earthquake San José. My desire to be near Marlene was not the same as the other girls. It was jealousy. But not jealousy of the things she had—a whole family in a house in Naglee Park, a mother who picked her up after school in a polished black Ford pickup. To me—and to Alma—it was jealousy for the attentions of a woman. Our English and social studies teacher, Miss Femi, adopted Marlene as her new favorite student. A gracefully independent middle-aged woman of

Egyptian descent, Miss Femi stopped her occasional visits to my desk after the earthquake had flattened part of her home over the hill in Ben Lomond near Santa Cruz. It was Marlene who seemed to lift her up.

Before the quake, attention from Miss Femi was different from the attention from the other adults at the school. News of the disappearance of my mom over the summer seemed to be on everyone's mind when we started school that year; most of the staff had a nasty habit of constantly—however innocently—reminding us of what had happened. "How are you feeling, sweetie?" or "You poor thing." But they were phonies. They were only nice because they were exorcising some guilt about their own mothers' deaths. That, or a fear of the inevitable.

Anyway, Miss Femi would never impose her own issues on us. When she glided to my desk and leaned in to look at my work, I felt like the only one in the world. And that made me want to hold on to her many earrings and bracelets and never let go, to fall asleep in her faint, minty, black-pepper aroma and never wake up. I gazed at her from a distance and stole shy glances when she was by my desk. But I had to be careful: I was protected by the fact that all anybody knew about me was based on rumors, but I certainly didn't want to give people the satisfaction that they were right about me all those years. Well, at least partially right.

Miss Femi would check our schoolwork and then ask to see our sketches. Alma's were obviously better than mine, but Miss Femi would ask me just as many questions about line and shading as she would of Alma. She was trained to evaluate my English skills and history knowledge, but she was my first critic in the sense that she was a woman with an obvious interest in what I was doing. And from that grew a great trust that anything she evaluated—honestly appraising my crappy drawings and my mediocre writing—was done so with kindness. She even wanted to showcase my developing talent.

"Do you want to read your story to the class?" she asked one day.

"No," I said. "I don't think it's any good."

Miss Femi frowned, then looked to Alma. "What about your drawings? Do you want to pin them to the wall?"

"I don't think so," Alma finally said. "I don't really want the attention."

"You two will show the world what you can do when you're ready."

With the wounds of Mom's absence still fresh and all the weird crap happening at home, this kind of attention kept us alive. But when Marlene arrived at the school less than a week after the earthquake and captured the heart and mind of Miss Femi, Alma spoke even less than she had after Mom disappeared. And she almost stopped drawing altogether.

But one day, as we sat in our corner of the lunch yard and doodled in our sketchbooks, Marlene approached. Her chosen entourage of blond girls hovered like seagulls over a beach picnic.

"Alma—that's your name, right? I hear you make some pretty neat drawings."

"Yeah," I said, speaking for Alma. Our refuge in sketching had been betrayed by Miss Femi.

"Well, show me some of your work." It was not a question. We hesitated. Marlene pressed. "Come on. If you're going to draw a picture of me, I need to see if you have any skill like Miss Femi says you've got."

Alma scratched at her palms.

"She's good," I said. "What do you care?"

"Miss Femi said Alma should draw a picture of me for the newspaper. And you—you're Katherine, right?—you could write an article."

"We really have to experience you." Where I came up with that line, I'll never know. "How else are we supposed to capture who you are?"

Marlene scoffed and walked away to confer with her new friends. I felt Alma staring at me. But I just looked across the yard at the girls, willing them to come back. And they did.

"So," Marlene began, "d'you think the school paper will want to print the portrait and an article about me? I mean, I only just got here. Do people care?"

"Of course people care," I said, speaking as if I'd rehearsed. "You're beautiful and smart and people want to be around you. They want to know more."

"Okay." Marlene's green eyes sparkled. She and her girls walked away.

Alma said, "I don't think I can do it. All I draw are ears."

"You'll do fine."

Over the following week, while I was talking with Marlene, Alma couldn't draw anything worthwhile. She tried drawing a profile of Marlene, but nothing felt right: the contours of her face seemed shallow, the lines seeming to drift to purposeless ends, the shadows and lighting inconsistent. Alma tried drawing herself next to Marlene, me listening to Marlene's story, Marlene with her friends like flies around her. Nothing seemed to work. I was having similar problems in writing about Marlene. All she could tell us was about Los Angeles, her family's Newport Beach home and sailboat. Oh, she missed it so much! I couldn't help thinking of how Oso had always described LA as a "hole of vice and misery." So biblical sounding.

Anyhow, Marlene told of how she'd been in a few commercials when she was younger and would have been in movies if her parents didn't also note her intelligence. "Too much of two good things, my parents had to make a choice." And she spoke of her parents disdainfully, mostly surrounding the choice they made. School over the silver screen. She came across as a thankless girl who thought her parents were lucky to have her, as if she had some choice in the matter. How was I supposed to write about that?

We were quickly getting bored of Marlene, who was a cliché if ever there was one. One day at lunch, Alma showed me pages of deformed versions of her.

"What's the deal with the eye patch?" I asked in between fits of laughter.

"I just thought she'd look good as a pirate," she said.

"And the one with the mohawk?"

"Don't you just want to shear her head?"

"I do now. I really like the tribute to the minotaur. I see you're learning a lot in our mythology unit. Oh my God, that's funny. Marlene's face—which, by the way, is the best you've drawn of her—on the body of a pig."

For the rest of lunchtime, we giggled as Alma drew quick sketches of

Marlene, one with Elvis's hair, one with Michael Jackson's nose, another with Alfred E. Neuman's smile. All of them with tiny ears.

"What're you guys laughing at?" Marlene was suddenly there in front of us with her flies. With her translucent skin. With her fiery hair. With her beauty. With her hurt eyes. "Let me see."

She tried to snatch the sketchpad out of Alma's hands. I pulled it out of her fingertips.

"Hey, relax, Marley," I said, putting a hand on Marlene's shoulder. "It's a comic that Alma's been working on. It's not your business."

"Well, when do I get to see my portrait? Shouldn't she be done by now?"

"Soon, okay?" I said.

Marlene nodded and shuffled away.

"I still don't think I can draw her in a good way," Alma said, fingers digging at an itch in her forearm.

"Something's up with that girl," I said. "Make sure you listen when we're talking tomorrow."

The next morning, the three of us went to our customary corner in Miss Femi's English class after our schoolwork was done. I asked different, better questions. And Marlene gave us a more honest version of herself.

She told us about her parents pulling her out of the film industry to come up here and take care of her mother's parents; Marlene's grandpa had come down with a pretty bad case of pneumonia a day or so after the earthquake. She said she didn't even really mind, that it was a pain to try to keep up with schoolwork and friends when regularly being shuttled to and from the auditions. She said it was kind of funny: she got out of a way of life that she didn't really care for, but she still lost all her friends, many that she'd felt were like sisters. She had a connection, though, with her grandma Margaret, a woman that she'd only seen on holidays but who talked on the phone with Marlene every Sunday night. "If anyone could understand how hard this move has been for me, it's her."

But that was not the case.

"Ever since we moved here, she's done nothing but worry about

Grandpa Fred. And when she's home, she'll sit in her nightie in the dark in front of a blank TV. Or she'll make a mess in the kitchen during the day, trying to bake a cake or some cookies. But she either forgets a raw ingredient or wanders off, burning the cookies. She can't take care of herself. And my parents only pick me up on their way to or from the hospital. That's the only time I get with my mom and dad. I know Grandpa's real sick and all, but I . . . never mind. I feel bad for feeling that way." Suddenly, she grabbed for Alma's sketchpad again; this time Alma herself gently pulled it away.

We hadn't expected to feel anything but loathing for Marlene. Our purpose—to get the attentions of Miss Femi—became less important. It was clear that Marlene was disappointed, truly bitter. She was a forlorn girl, forgotten in the scenery behind what was, for all intents and purposes, a disappearing family. I could definitely understand that. And we began to understand why Marlene was the way she was at school. I poured myself into the piece and was very proud of the work I had done.

Yes, proud. It was a feeling that always felt forced on me—whether by teachers or by Oso's stories of Dad. But by getting to know Marlene better and writing something favorable about a person who initially seemed pretty dreadful, I was proud of both getting to know her and of the effort I put into the excellent article.

Alma and I compared our work after we were done. Independently, we both managed to produce the same meek light. We were a little nervous to show Marlene what we had done, worried she would want to mess with the words or say something looked off in the portrait. Even then, I—and maybe Alma—understood how people tend to want absolute control over how others see them.

But we showed Marlene anyway. Again I felt pride swell. Not only had I written something worthwhile, but I had also showed another person that I understood where she was coming from. She thanked Alma and me for what we had done; I even got the feeling that she would one day listen to me tell about my messed-up life. It was amazing how my writing made me feel a connection with another person I thought I had nothing in common with. So I was shocked when Miss Femi said the writing couldn't have been my own.

"The turns of phrase are not something you're capable of," she claimed. "Did someone in your family write this for you?"

The question, as you know, was completely absurd. Mom had always been dead quiet, was probably dead, and was certainly not around to help me plagiarize; Dad was not exactly literate in English; and Oso's ability to tell a story never translated to the page—in fact, I edited some of his high school papers for him. The only person who could have written that piece for me—but never would have in the first fucking place—was Grandpa. He was the articulate one, the one with all the "turns of phrase" that would have laid bare my deception. But he, too, was dead. So when Miss Femi accused me of plagiarizing, I was left with a feeling of guilt for the influences in my life. To this day, that's all I have. Well, that and anger.

The following Monday, I found myself standing in front of the class, pointing at Marlene.

"Miss Femi, I think Marlene stole Alma's sketchbook." Because of what I had learned about Marlene, I certainly expected a reaction. But the degree of Marlene's rage was startling.

"What?" Marlene screeched, looking down at her bag. "Why would I want that stupid thing?" She yanked it out of her bag and flung it against the wall. Then she started screaming, pulled by an unseen force into a trap. Marlene turned bright red, forgetting to breathe. "Don't you see, Miss Femi? They just want me to look bad! They're jealous."

At last, I struck: "What about the newspaper article? I made you look like a saint!"

"You goddamned mulatto!" Marlene shrieked as she leaped toward me, scratching my cheek.

We slammed into the blackboard. Before Miss Femi could stop me, one of my fists was punching Marlene in the side of the head, my other fist closed tightly on a tuft of hair—I must have looked like I was playing the cymbals in the raucous ending of the *1812 Overture*. As Marlene screamed and a few desks were knocked over, Miss Femi tugged and jerked on my right arm, yelling at me to let go. Finally, the tugging stopped with a sound of dead grass being ripped by a dog's teeth. Marlene fell to the ground, a hand on the side of her head. I had scalped Marlene, hundreds, thousands of her orange hairs in my fist.

What became clear is that if you finger a flap of skin—if you hold that flap away from its position over the wound—it'll heal wrong. And we'd lifted that flap and held it, seeing the Marlene that was just under the surface. To make matters worse, Marlene had spun away so fast that we didn't have time to let go of the flap. Standing before us was Marlene in skinless flesh. And in reaching for a robe, she grabbed a saber.

Of course you think it's understandable. But that didn't make what she did okay. I think the biggest disappointment is when we discover that a person has more dimensions than we'd expected. Would it have been better for us—for everyone—to remain with our first impressions of Marlene? I mean, I'd been reading in the newspaper for years about priests and politicians. Their jobs are to keep their flaps of skin from being held back too long, if at all. Then they, too, spin away, flailing for cover or weapons, even knocking over those who intend no harm.

During my suspension from school, Alma reported to me—and Dad—about whisperings: Alma herself had put the sketchbook in Marlene's bag. Of course, I was the one who had put it there. But the idea that people thought Alma had framed Marlene irritated me, almost as if she had gotten credit for something I had written. Alma was, after all, incapable of unguided action after Mom's disappearance. If you think about it, it was me who had authored both the story and Alma's comeback from despondency. Anyway, Alma also reported that kids at school stared, scoffed, sneered, pointed. Clearly Marlene was talking shit, saying that Mom had abandoned us like trash, that I'd made out with Anita Vasquez in the locker room, that Alma had given Joey Matthews a blow job— while he was wearing a condom, no less. Even after I returned to school and we steered clear of each other, Marlene succeeded in making us more noticeable than ever. I was not slow to realize that I preferred—still prefer—people's indifference.

Even though the kids couldn't help spreading Marlene's lies, they could not forget that she had hurled "mulatto" at me. Ill informed as the students were about the slur, they understood the sentiment. In a school of equal parts white and brown and yellow, no one could forget—or forgive. Except for one girl, the mousiest of her entourage, the others steered clear of Marlene. Marlene clung to her little friend for mere existence. What are you, after all, if no one acknowledges that you are there? Maybe that's how it is: people come into and go out of your life so often that you grasp and grapple, trying to hold on to at least one of them so you know you're really alive.

Marlene sat with her mousy friend on the other side of the lunch yard for the remaining time at Monroe Middle School, occasionally looking across at Alma and me. Mostly, though, she huddled with her friend, waiting for the experience to end, to go on to the next group of people to impress. Or to steer clear of. After eighth grade, we never heard of her again.

I wish I could say that things changed at school for me and Alma. I wish I could say that the Marlene incident forced people to see the need for harmony. But people have their own ideas of harmony. After I returned to school and the rumors faded, things were much the same. But Miss Femi kept a distance from us—Alma guilty by association to me, my ugliness.

Even if Miss Femi hadn't betrayed me, her attentions wouldn't have mattered anymore. Home life changed again. And so did my view on the world.

A *small square room, bright and white and without sound.*
    Stand with back to the wall.
On a white wooden stool sits a white vase.
A single white daisy leans right.
Double doors open on the wall opposite.
A backlit female figure beckons.
Go.

7.

A DEATH. LOSS OF VIRGINITY. A fight. A kiss. A rape. A murder. A firstborn. An earthquake. Can we really boil down the result of our individual lives to one particular moment?

Mom probably believed that what shapes us is more like a series of small moments within the larger tidal cycle of moments. And I think that's more accurate. Still, since I so often relive the '89 quake and the weeks and months after it, there must be some significant meaning to me. Whether that meaning was good or bad, I don't know. The meaning to those around me, though, was a positive one, a force for harmony. For a little while, at least.

Trucks rumbled at all hours down Santa Clara Street, loaded with debris. And people were living in their cars and wandering the streets more than usual. So Oso became more focused than ever before on our neighborhood; with the help of Mr. Henry, he gathered food, water, and blankets from local residents and shopkeepers to give to the newly homeless. When he came up short on supplies, Oso even convinced his friends—the permanent residents of Saint James Park—to donate some of their shopping-cart-hoarded supplies to the temporarily homeless folks.

One day, he came home to find us on the street corner, Alma doodling and me nose-deep in the newspaper.

"If you're not going to help," he growled, "the least you could do is show a little respect."

So we put away our pastimes. But we just sat there watching.

It was an urgent time, and people were pulling together. Other than being moody adolescents who didn't give a damn what their brother thought, I'm not sure why Alma and I didn't find a way to get involved. It probably would have helped Alma to get her mind off Mom or the next possible quake. As for me, maybe caring about someone other than myself and Alma would have diverted my general angst or diluted my anger at Miss Femi's betrayal. To me, helping others seemed like a waste of time; I was owed something more than mere survival in this life. But I didn't know what that was or who would provide it. Whatever the reason for our indifference, Alma and I sat there empty-handed and quiet in front of the freshly cracked yellow wall of Mr. Henry's store.

One afternoon as we sat digging dirt from under our fingernails, three bundled people with shopping carts full of their lives approached our intersection. A gray minivan sputtered through a red light on Third, its tailpipe dragging under the weight of a bedroom's worth of stuff. A dump truck traveling on Santa Clara Street blared its horn and swerved, some of the broken glass in the back falling out in the middle of the intersection. Swinging to the left, the minivan hopped the curb and almost hit one of the cart people, who shouted profanities at the minivan, and a couple college kids popped their heads out of the boarded-up Mission. A haggard woman stumbled out of the minivan and toward the cart people. They exchanged some quiet words, laughed a little, and even embraced for a few seconds. Then the woman waved, got back in her van, and drove away.

"That would never have happened before the quake," I said and went back to picking at my nails. Another dump truck full of broken glass clattered by.

Even though I really wanted to believe that it didn't matter what Oso or the rumor-mongers at school thought about me, I sat on our street corner and slowly realized just how much others' interpretations of me shaped who I was, what I thought, what I did. So I was actually forced to care what other people thought of me. And that pissed me off—still pisses me off. It seems my life—my very existence—has always hung in the balance of other people's perceptions of me, my story, my race, my musical tastes, my family life, my reading preferences, and my relationships. And in telling you about the earthquake and its aftermath—even that stupid Marlene incident and the rumors that followed—it's obvious how absurd it is to think that I have ever made decisions on my own.

No, it's not fate, my dear; that's too simple. It's much messier than that. I don't know what the fuck a professor would call it, but it's clear to me that every single thing I do is influenced by what other people—even unknown, unseen people—think and do. As much as I would like to believe in free will, there are too many invisible forces simultaneously pushing me down and pulling me up, laboring hard to control who I am, what I say, and what I do. It's impossible to be free.

Maybe your worldliness—and, for that matter, your upbringing, your education, your experiences, your age—tells you a different story of the way things work. But to me, at that age, in those circumstances, the realizations made the past, present, and future shift.

They still shift. Strike. Slip. Subduct. Liquefy.

Dad's own anger at that unattainability of freedom and what Grandpa might call "the unstable ground of life" drew me to him in the time after the quake. In a very real way, I understood that Dad's rage and insecurity was made worse by the inevitable loss of family.

How could Dad lose something he never had, right? And maybe you're wondering what family means to a man if he never had one growing up, especially since it seems he was repulsed—sometimes violently—by the very idea of family. But the experience of loss was with him from the time he was born. And any sense of refuge he found with his adopted Central Valley families in the 1960s was always lost to some bigger cause and those often unknown, unseen people trying to subdue that cause.

In spite of all the terrible things he'd done as a dad and a husband, I did my best to understand him. After Mom vanished, I studied him. But he didn't give me much to work with; all he did was work, eat, and sleep. We essentially fended for ourselves for months, and I was left with no faith that anything I thought to do would help me understand him better. And when he led that family to safety after the earthquake, I thought it was a sign that things would be better. But it was really the Marlene incident that sped up his recovery from grief. After he found out I was suspended, he actually started smiling at me.

Why had he ignored me all those years? Maybe it's because he thought I was simply an observer. A ghost, rather. This, I think, made Dad uneasy. In his youth he was a doer, an adventurer who'd had his hands in the muck and dirt while trying, in his own small way, to make the world better. But me kicking Marlene's ass changed Dad's view of me, if only briefly. I'd fully materialized before his eyes as someone—in addition to his son—who might carry on his legacy. Maybe that's why Dad ended up telling me his "real" story.

I'm not surprised that you think this is all too convenient: that Dad began to speak to me all of a sudden, that he even acknowledged my presence, that there was any way this could be his real story. I don't blame you for your disbelief. But just listen.

José was born in a blissful time: August 1945. But that was only what history told him; history leeches into you even if you never picked up a book. He was born in Los Angeles, a place he hated though he had never visited in adulthood. It was the place where his mother died giving Dad life and where his father died trying to sustain that life. He lost something he never even remembered having. And I could sympathize with that.

He never knew his mother, Maria. Certainly he hadn't smiled at her at first nursing and made her giggle to death. Nor did he remember any siblings or drive them to their demise in fits of blissfulness in the early moments of his life. He was the first and last offspring of that young couple. And suddenly his father, Miguel, was a single parent at the age of twenty. Before Dad was born, Miguel loved to work the land, enjoying a fairly well-paying job for a migrant, landscaping in Beverly Hills. But when Maria died and he had to get a second job at a restaurant, he sent Dad away to his brother in Bakersfield, the eighteen-hour days sucking all the joy out of his once-beloved landscaping job.

And surely the fact that Miguel was unable to keep Dad because of those long hours drove him to a mysterious end, an end that I am all too familiar with at this point, an end that really isn't an end at all, an end that doesn't have a corpse to reassure the living that the loss is real, an end that only seems to prove that death is some sort of cruel, never-ending hoax perpetrated by a world conspiring to make life intolerable. Miguel's end is so common in the story of my family that an actual death—even if it were a drawn-out torture by some bandits down in Tijuana—would have been preferable. If he had been found chopped up in several different pieces, maybe he wouldn't have left a legacy of false endings. But as it was, Miguel simply disappeared into the Los Angeles night in August 1946, establishing—or carrying on—a tradition of obscure history and imperfect endings.

There had already been years of strife between the brothers. Juan, ten years older, was bitter that Miguel wouldn't stay near the remaining family, was even more bitter that his brother insisted on staying in Los Angeles when decent jobs on the oil derricks awaited in Bakersfield. The stories Juan told of Miguel spoke of an irresponsible man looking for pleasures and vices instead of taking care of his own boy. This was when Dad started to laugh at his uncle's absurdities. He laughed when his uncle wondered out loud how Miguel could abandon his own blood, his own child. Dad started laughing in his teachers' faces, finding absurdity in all they taught in history and literature, seeing it for what it was: an arm of the apparatus that kept people in line. At a young age, Dad left school.

He said goodbye to his aunt and went off on his own to laugh in the faces of business owners and bosses, disturbing shit as he made his way north, often on the lam. People always took his laughter as happiness. They didn't know any better and liked the sound of it during and after and at the beginning of their brutal toil in the fields and processing plants. And, to a fault, Dad did nothing but laugh until just before he had to quit each place, leaving little time to convince people that they didn't have to put up with the injustice. In each group he worked and lived with, he did nothing overt until the very end because he enjoyed the camaraderie, the family he had at these places. But when leaving each job, he tried to plant the seeds of realization in the minds of some of the brighter laborers. Then he got tired in Ralston-Modesto. And he wanted more than to just plant the seed; he wanted to see the results of his work and talk.

For the first years at Giordano Estates as the lead grounds superintendent, he got along well with the owner. Don Giordano seemed to admire Dad's laughter, for instilling happiness in both himself and among the workers he employed. But as Dad got to know the don better, he realized the same absurdities existed at Giordano Estates as on the other plantations and factories he had worked over the years. Dad understood the business model all too well. Though the don never seemed to notice the change, Dad's laughter became completely different, again reverting to laughter at the absurd: running a business that made money from the last pennies of the destitute under the guise of some sort of refuge—the label on the bottles even showed grapes in the shape of a cross.

Dad was astute—more astute than the don—and knew the difference between one kind of laughter and another. He knew the don's amiability was just a way to keep Dad—and therefore all the workers—in line. So over the course of a few months, Dad began preaching, helping the other workers realize that the exploitation going on up and down the state was also going on at the Estates. The don's henchmen started sniffing around, and Dad knew it was time to leave. He took Mom, pregnant with their boy, out of that community and into an uncertain future with a mixed-race kid. By doing so, he also saved what little reputation Grandpa had.

That's right. Their moving to San José had little to do with Dad's allergies.

After Dad told me his story in his own words, I was pulled into the ranks of the existent, the living. You're probably saying to yourself, *Poor thing needs to be recognized by a man to "exist"—poor thing still doesn't even have a birth story of her own and now we hear a second version of her father's.* Well, let's just leave you and Gloria's women's lib out of this. Let's move on by saying that I'm still not entirely sure why Dad told me his "real" story. I like to think that my story of scalping Marlene allowed him to see his former self in me. I began to realize, though not fully, the power of storytelling, how the omission or inclusion of one detail or character can change the story entirely. I mean, when Dad listened to my rendition of the Marlene incident, I felt that I'd finally been able to show who I was and, in doing so, had enhanced Dad's life, and Alma's.

During my suspension, Alma came home from school and told me and Dad that people were acknowledging her, and not just for the rumors that Marlene had been spreading. The attention Alma got for her drawing in the newspaper, with a few people telling her they liked it, was fleeting, but it somehow sustained her. Alma was much like me: in general she preferred people not notice her, but she had stirred a tiny revolution. People noticed her for something other than her destitute, loner-dyke reputation.

―――――――――――

In an unlikely turn, Dad began spending time after school with me and Alma when his work hours would allow. Over the next couple years, he added to our ritual by joining us outside with two cups of coffee. Alma sketched in her books, charcoal pencil under her nails. I would read aloud from the *Mercury News*, ink on my fingers. Before we went in for dinner, Dad would pour out the remaining cup on the sidewalk next to the steps, a sweet, sticky, earthy brown stain running down the sidewalk. But we never asked why.

At one point, our after-school ritual was interrupted, the *Mercury News* unable to keep up. We were inside Mr. Henry's furniture shop those days, in front of the television to watch the first hours of the Gulf War and the hours that followed. We sat on Mr. Henry's floor-model leather sofas and plush armchairs and watched grainy video and reports of a clean war, of the precision-guided bombs hitting only military targets. I remember thinking, as the Iraqi army was being destroyed in front of my eyes, that this was a good thing, technology. Technology from companies in the Silicon Valley had finally made it possible to avoid the huge cost of innocent human lives of past wars. I'd learned about those wars in history classes and from Grandpa. It seemed unfair that so many people who were just living their lives could be disintegrated, condemned by proximity and geography. During the Gulf War, I thought the bad people were getting what they deserved and babies and families wouldn't be wiped out.

But Oso seemed to realize something was missing from the narrative on TV. He was gone for two weeks at the end of January, up in San Francisco, marching and almost getting arrested, spinning away from a cop in riot gear and hitting him with his NO BLOOD FOR OIL sign before running and hiding in a dumpster. Eventually, he came home, the war ended, and we returned to the street corner to watch the homeless and their daily late-afternoon exodus.

During these afternoons, the city around me seemed to change yet again. For the most part, the comings and goings at the Mission and the rise and fall of traffic congestion had only colored my imagination. But now the sounds were live, had a source. It was like seeing a musician play rather than listening to the music on the record player. While preparing dinner, Oso added color and depth to the news stories I read to Dad and Alma. The cops' regular sweeps of Saint James Park was an effort to beautify the city and push the homeless to less visible areas. Ironically, Oso's homeless friends ended up going through the Naglee Park neighborhood and camping on the banks of Coyote Creek. They'd complain to Oso in varied tones, sometimes all at once:

Walter reported, "The last time we was pushed out of the park like this was when the Russkies was looking real scary and a few companies got big ol' gov'ment defense contracts and the pop'alation boomed and the cement spread 'cross the valley."

Norm railed, "After the Cold War, those moneyed people spent

their time figuring out how to use the internet—a military tool—on
the people in their own homes. Anytime now, they're going to pull the
trigger; they've figured how to manufacture necessity out of the internet."

And Winny screamed, "He's right! He's right! The internet's a fucking
Trojan horse!"

Walter said, "Nothin' we can do about the money floodin' in. And
this valley fertile! You seen them big ol' cranes sproutin' up all over."

Norm complained, "Nobody needs these buildings, but they'll grow
like weeds (pardon my cliché). I mean, a hockey arena? In this climate?
And the more new money moves in to grow more money and grow their
babies, they're going to keep lobbying the older money to do something
about us—the refuse of society—so their kids don't have to see us. But
we're not going to disappear just because of the internet."

Winny bellowed, "A Trojan horse with Pandora inside! Pandora and
her big fucking brother! And they're coming to put you in their box!"

Dad still went on his walks but didn't often stray off the most direct
route to the church. So I imagine hearing Oso talk about the characters
they both knew from their time wandering the streets together was like
gospel to Dad. Crawling King Snake, a man in his late forties who looked
like he was in his mid-sixties, would lie in the grass on his stomach,
kicking his army boots in the air, conversing with himself and puffing on
discarded half-smoked cigarettes. One time, his monomaniacal search for
nicotine was interrupted when his eyes fell on Oso.

"Hello, how's school going?" was all he said.

Oso was a well-known character among the Saint James Park cast,
and they all knew Oso was a month from graduating high school. But
Crawling King Snake had never talked to him before.

Oso said, "School is better than it's ever been. I got my first A on an
essay. It was only American government, but an A anyway."

The Snake got his answer and moved on.

"What about Raven Lady?" Dad asked. "The one who squawks into
her hand and sits across from city hall at the base of that stupid statue of
McKinley?"

"That damned statue," Oso pontificated. "Forever looking west with his cross, his torch, his cannon, his eagle, his food. His abundance couldn't save Raven Lady. Now her friend, the Thinker, sits alone, none of her squawking to keep him company."

"That's too bad. What about Walker?"

"He's still making his rounds, over and over again through the university, around the park, up First Street in front of the newest buildings, saying hello to the hordes of UPS and Federal Express drivers."

Oso graduated high school without much fanfare. He worked jobs delivering the *Mercury News* in predawn Naglee Park on a bike too small for him and making cappuccinos for the impossibly hip, grungy, flannel-wearing university students at Café Matisse, he and his shoulder-length curls and bushy beard fitting in well enough. Dad continued to work and sit with us on the sidewalk after we got home from school; he'd begun to look a bit older. Alma and I tried to forget about school, she with her drawing and I by reading the newspaper. I read out loud like a news anchor telling stories of near and far: IBM and Apple troubles. Sinéad O'Connor rips up the pope's picture. FDA approves AZT. The Ruby Ridge shootout. Clinton elected. The World Trade Center bombed. Waco burned.

By this time, Oso had become more focused on the homeless issue. He got his shifts covered at Café Matisse so he could join demonstrations at the university and in Saint James Park in support of his friends. He became so focused on this one cause—the well-being of his friends—that he hardly reacted when I told him that César Chávez had died. Just a couple days before, a close friend of his, Tammy Tourette, had spun away from university cops' attempt to arrest her; she was hit by a car and killed instantly. He said that she wouldn't have died if it weren't for the "intolerant" residents of Naglee Park, who had complained for months about the disorganized vagabond caravan using their quiet, tree-lined streets as its garbage dumps and their flower beds as its urinals. Kicked out of Saint James every evening, they tramped their way to William Street Park, trying to hide in their lean-tos, trying to rest, trying to stay clean on the banks of Coyote Creek.

Our street corner was frequented by the ousted tramps and vagabonds, all of whom stopped at least for a brief while to say hello and talk to Dad. I played a little game with Alma: we tried to guess the names of the various drifters as they floated by those afternoons, and Dad would verify our suppositions, complimenting us on our astute matching of details to the colorful names. One of my favorites—and a regular visitor to the stairs of our apartment—was a Vietnam veteran, Nolan, and his dogs, William and Wanda. Nolan would tell his stories about the park dwellers, and I was fascinated and confused by his different details about them all.

Sometimes while I was in the middle of reading an article to Dad, he would get off the sidewalk and look at Alma's drawings. When Dad brought chalk home one day, Alma's medium of choice changed, but her subject didn't; she would draw larger-than-life ears on the sidewalk of all different shapes—and now colors. Day after day, they would be scuffed up or washed away. Day after day, she'd do her work over again.

I might have been jealous of the occasional extra attention Dad gave Alma. You might say that's pitiful, seeking the attention of a man who had ignored me most of my life, not to mention had treated Mom like crap. To hell with him, right? But I don't know what to tell you: it was Dad—and Oso—who helped me through those days. I still found comfort when Oso played Grandpa's LPs every night, the classical and urban sounds twisting me off to sleep. And when Dad worked the first shift, I would wake to the sounds of him getting ready. Before leaving, he'd come to our room, the sickle of light from the bathroom hanging over his pompadour. I would give him a little wave. He would smile in the faint light, wave back with his four-fingered hand, and turn to go. I'd go back to sleep for a short time—the most restful and dreamless that I can remember. I never told Alma or Oso about my morning ritual with Dad.

The daily migration from Saint James Park to William Street Park seemed to be part of something Dad was once involved in, in one way or another, but he was passive. Since Mom's disappearance, his concern about his old friends from the streets had diminished into a muted sulkiness. Dad became relatively peaceful because of his genuine interest in each of his children. So I was baffled by his sudden violence.

When red-haired Nolan appeared across the street, he was always accompanied by his two playful, yapping dogs: William, a large black mutt with copper coloring under his chin, and Wanda, a medium-sized blond mutt. They were always off-leash but never far from Nolan, except when they saw me; the mass of Lab/Rottweiler/cocker spaniel fur bounded across the street to lick my face and get belly rubs.

Rearranging his blue flannel over his belly, brushing the lettering of his name on the breast of his worn green army jacket and pulling at its collar, he would say, "Howdy do, Joey. That coffee for me?"

Dad would fidget, check his hair with his hands, stay quiet.

Tugging on his long, reddish-orange-and-white beard, Nolan would say, "So is the plight at the cannery the same?"

"What's it matter to you, cabrón?"

"I ain't no billy goat." Nolan would chuckle, take off his beanie, and run his fingers through his hair three or four times.

Sometimes Nolan took a different approach, saying something like, "You never told me as much, but I can read it in that tight brown face; behind those smoldering black lenses, your eyes say, 'Things need changing down at the cannery.'"

"What are you, maricón? Do you want to kiss me? Reading my face. Looking at my eyes. Damn, maricón. You don't know nothin'. Nada."

Ignoring the comment, Nolan would say, "Your eyes are sayin', 'Those management bastards ain't got the faintest on how to do their jobs.'"

"They did something right. They fired you, after all."

During this kind of routine exchange, Alma and I would scratch behind the ears of the dogs. As Nolan paced a few steps left and a few steps right, telling his stories about the city-versus-park-dweller saga, I'd look at William's lazily blinking eyes. I liked him the best.

"Just look at those mutts. Happier than pigs in shit," Nolan would say at all the attention we gave them.

Nolan was a lot like Oso, but I got the sense that him passing the time telling anyone's stories to his fellow wanderers and veterans was a way to keep from talking about himself. Whatever the reason, I liked Nolan the most out of all the tramps who visited us. He never asked me about school, seeming to know how boring it was for me. He would indulge my retelling of *Mercury News* reportage and short stories in old issues of *Harper's Magazine* that Oso swiped from Café Matisse. The intense, genuine attention Nolan showed to my interests was a simple happiness after my anonymous days at school. Alma seemed to feel the same way, eagerly showing Nolan her drawings, looking for his approving smile. We both held on to what we could, never sure when Dad's interest in us would go away. Our precarious existences—always in danger of blending into the scuffed exterior wall of that old apartment building or soaking into the sidewalk.

One day, as Nolan told his stories, William began to hump Wanda. Out of nowhere, his thing, looking like a partly squeezed tube of pinkish-red paint, wanted in somewhere, anywhere. And almost as quickly, Nolan kicked William; the hollow sound of the boot against William's ribs made me shudder.

"Goddammit, William. You're such a motherfucker," he said, and laughed, looking over at Dad for some sort of reaction but getting none. William cowered near the wall, and his mother sat there panting, looking as if she were smiling. Nolan continued: "Damn, William. Scarfin' up that crap in the park. Ain't got no daddy. Lickin' yourself. And now this."

Dad just sat there, watching the traffic go by.

"You're nothin' but a shit-eatin' bastard son of a bitch, a dick-lickin' motherfucker."

Alma laughed uncontrollably for a minute or so. It seemed she'd lost her mind; since Mom's disappearance, she'd almost become mute. Dad frowned in Nolan's direction. The ferocity and suddenness of William's assault on his mother shocked me. But Nolan's assault on William was what stuck in my mind. Somehow, I felt sorry for him for being unable to control himself.

I reached for William, stroked his head once. Before I knew what was happening, Wanda had sunk her fangs into my arm. I still have white scars. See?

She took hold of my arm and wouldn't let go. She locked her rust-brown eyes on mine and snarled. And I just watched. You believe that? I didn't scream, I didn't cry, I didn't hit Wanda. I don't remember even feeling much pain. I just watched, as if it were happening to someone else.

"Get off! Get off, you crazy bitch, off!" Alma was pulling on Wanda's tail.

But Wanda held on, her teeth gripping tightly and giving way only as my skin and flesh were dragged away from the bone.

"Wanda! Stop! Let go!" Nolan yelled, trying to pry her jaws open. But Wanda held on and stared straight at me, bearing her teeth down.

Then Dad's big, rough, brown four-fingered fist came down on the back of Wanda's head. She released my arm and slumped to the ground.

Dad spat curses in Spanish. Nolan moaned, incessantly ran his fingers through his hair as he sat on the sidewalk, probably having been shoved by Dad. The blood poured out of my arm onto Dad's calloused hands as he and Alma helped me up and started guiding me toward the stairs. Finally, the pain and the fear set in and I began to cry.

A deep sound came from inside Dad and he whirled away. Dad kicked Wanda square in her ribs. Again, that sickening hollow sound accompanied by a yelp. Wanda went cringing down the sidewalk, ears back and glancing behind her. Dad was in pursuit for a few steps, his hair now disheveled. William barked a couple times. Dad stopped and took a few steps toward William, who in turn crouched along the wall as he, too, slipped away, looking over his shoulder.

The dogs out of reach, Dad ran toward Nolan, who was now standing. Nolan turned away to absorb the kicks and punches; he stumbled, fell to his knees, and tried to get up. But a left fist hurtled Nolan onto the cement, his head snapping back and hitting the sidewalk with a dull thud. You ever seen that? Someone whack their head on cement? Dammit. Now I won't be able to stop seeing it in my head.

Anyhow, Nolan looked up at Dad, eyes unfocused, lip fat, hair fiery wild, the NOLAN on the breast of his jacket bloodied. Dad kicked him once more in the ribs before coming to help me.

We came back down a little later to go to the hospital, my arm wrapped in a towel. I half expected the police to be there, or an ambulance. At the very least, I expected Nolan to still be lying there, his dogs waiting for him to wake up. But they were gone.

Despite all of this violence and drama, I began to miss the visits from the man and his dogs after a couple weeks. I wondered where they were; I wondered what Alma would say if I told her that I wanted to go to Saint James and William Street Parks to look for him. My mind put them in all sorts of scenarios: Nolan dying from a concussion on the banks of Coyote Creek, the dogs starving. Or creek bandits beating Nolan, stabbing him, taking anything worth stealing. I imagined Wanda barking her fool head off until she, too, was knifed and left for dead.

I tried to laugh about the whole situation, saying to myself, *If only William weren't such a motherfucker, none of this would have happened.* But I didn't go out looking for the missing three. Too afraid to do anything, too afraid to find out something I didn't want to know.

Besides, I was pretty sure Alma wouldn't go for it, and I needed her support. Of course, Oso wanted to hurt Nolan, but he adhered to the park dwellers' code. And in those days, part of their code was to attract as little attention as possible. Being at obvious and increasing odds with the law, it was important that they didn't argue as loudly or have too many fistfights to settle disputes.

The result was, as Oso told us, that Saint James Park was a little more peaceful in the mornings and afternoons. The young, newly moneyed parents came more frequently with their kids. To show they weren't animals, the park dwellers would either leave or go take shelter in the neglected RFK monument or the edges of the park, letting the home dwellers have access to the open spaces of grass and the fountain that was sometimes used as a bathtub in the evenings by the likes of Walker and Crawling King Snake. But, as Oso told us, Nolan would violate the unspoken agreement by talking with young mothers and fathers and befriending children. (It's not what you might think; their parents were always close by, smiling, watchful, silent.)

According to Oso, Nolan once befriended the towheaded son of a fidgety young man. As the boy scratched Wanda's belly, he giggled at William's warm licks. Nearby, Nolan watched as the dogs and the boy wrestled for a while in the grass. The boy trotted off to find a stick, and Nolan stayed near the boy, assuring the father with a silent gesture to stay seated. The boy investigated tiny bugs in dog crap, discovered the smell of dog crap, and quickly lost interest; he found some tiny daisies in the grass, smelled them, put a few in his thick hair, and ate the rest. Seeming to like the taste, he brought a bunch for Nolan to try. Nolan laughed until his sides hurt. At Nolan's direction, the boy took the flowers to the fretful father. Still laughing, Nolan waved to the boy and his father and walked away, Wanda and William trotting closely behind.

It was this kind of anecdote that seemed to sum up Nolan. So we were all sad when Oso told us that Wanda had died a couple days after the incident with Dad. Then a few days later, William was hit by a light-rail train as it left the stop at Saint James Park. And Nolan left town on a bus—maybe headed to his parents' home in Southern California.

Over dinner one night, Oso spoke of Nolan as if he were giving a eulogy. "Despite his annoying nature and telling stories that people'd heard a hundred times or that they'd read in the headlines, Nolan was an important part of our park community." Oso held up his hand when Dad began to protest. "As lonely as we could find ourselves," Oso continued, channeling Grandpa's florid way of speaking, "Nolan always showed interest in individual problems or pursuits. To the forced solitude of homelessness, he brought to people a sense of living, a sense of being that not many others could bring. That and a warm lick from a friendly dog."

Dad's lip quivered as he scratched his stubbly chin.

A couple days later, Dad didn't return home until after dinner. As Oso was getting ready to go out looking for him, Dad stumbled in the door, covered in mud and cuts and bruises, his face contorted with an unspoken, unnamable pain. Alma's fierce obligation resurfaced, and she cleaned Dad up, helped put him to bed. And in the coming weeks, she looked after Dad. I couldn't help but think of how she had cared for Mom after Grandpa died. Where she found the energy to deal with another shattered parent, I'll never know. But she knew what I knew: that Dad's state left us on the edge of homelessness or another foster home.

As urgent as that was, my imagination paralyzed me. After Mom disappeared, I was able to fight through the dreadful visions of her unknowable demise. But the likes of brazen Holst on the record player would nightly click and drop after the ending of something like eerie Shostakovich passages, concocting new images to tangle with the ancient ones. The fray in my mind now included the dogs being kicked, Nolan's head bouncing off the pavement, the deaths of William and Wanda. Nolan's sadness. Nolan's departure. Falling asleep, I worried about what happens to dead dogs. Sleeping, I had nightmares about what happens to people at the other end of a long bus trip. I was crippled, my mind filling in the spaces where there were no answers.

Dad stopped coming by the bedroom to share a wave with me in the mornings. He and I didn't even share stories anymore out on the sidewalk; I read the *Mercury* to myself. And I actually missed him, this man who had for much of my life made me invisible with his indifference. Just out of earshot, I would occasionally glance at yellow-haired Alma seated next to graying Dad and try to figure out their odd companionship: this girl who, with a middle school history textbook, had brought down this man who, with indifference and violence, had terrorized us for most of our lives for getting in the way of what he felt he was owed. Whatever it was they were discussing—culpability, a confession, a treaty—I convinced myself my involvement would make things worse. I never asked Alma what she and Dad talked about. I had the overwhelming feeling that the more I moved, the more I talked, the more I tried to change things, the greater the chance something else would disappear.

So I read the newspaper. The United States bombed Iraq again. Lorena Bobbitt. Somalia. Don't ask, don't tell. NAFTA. Shannon Faulkner. Bosnia. No matter how still I stayed, the world continued.

And the people in that world continued laboring in it and talking about changing it. And they were changing it.

═══════════════

Oso continued to involve himself in small protests—and some larger ones—against the local government and its treatment of the homeless. By winter, Oso had been jailed four times, yet quickly released each time with no charges. To this day, I don't know how he escaped ever having to appear in court. He had buddies who were arrested once or twice and ended up in court, paying fines; one of them ended up doing a little time for punching a police horse. Oso even laughed about that one: "Floyd never was a bright fella."

Alma and I started our sophomore year as Hoover High School Hawks, but we could have been Hoover Hyenas for all we cared. And hundreds of new faces didn't seem to make a difference in our experience of school, either. Quite honestly, had it not been for Oso's reputation, I don't think the school experience would have changed at all. When he was there, Oso was well known among the teachers and the younger students. He always argued with his teachers—mostly his history teacher, Mr. Beck—about how homelessness was a problem of the entire community. While Mr. Beck agreed it was a problem, he disagreed with the way Oso wanted to make change. Oso had been reading Marx and Guevara—as any young revolutionary does, I guess—and this fueled his founding of his own country.

Yes, a country.

When we were his students, Mr. Beck told us of Oso's failed country, a story Oso never told us. He'd taken a thick red piece of Alma's chalk to school and drawn a border in the same corner of the quad every day at lunch. He welcomed anyone who wanted to discuss how to solve the problem of homelessness and listen to him talk about how the cranes and the new buildings and all the businesses were making homelessness a worse problem. The selfishness and thoughtlessness of the newly wealthy were everyone's problem.

"He was a little misguided," Mr. Beck told me and Alma. "But he had more passion than I'd ever seen in a student. I really hope he can find some direction, a way to make real change. I just hope he can do it without an armed uprising."

And it almost came to that.

In his final year, Oso decided to expand. Every day for a month at lunch, he found the previous outline and redrew the border, gradually taking over a larger and larger portion of the quad, not permitting anyone wearing corporate logos to pass through his country. At one point, Oso had more than a few followers; people saw them as a gang. On a number of occasions, they almost brawled with various Adidas-wearing students for infringing on the borders. Finally, the principal, Mr. Hanson, forced Oso back to his original borders. From his corner, Oso continued to hold court with a dwindling number of students until only four remained. He lashed out, calling his former followers sellouts, threatening them.

Again, Mr. Hanson had to step in, this time with the help of Mr. Beck. Together, they convinced Oso of other ways to persuade people to see things his way: they gave him a black Bic pen and a notebook.

"Your brother was so angry," Mr. Beck told me. "He graduated before I got to see if the writing developed. One of the biggest regrets I have as a teacher is not getting through to him sooner. How's he doing?"

I'd never seen Oso with the pen and notebook and never asked him if he had trashed it. Now I wonder if he hid it, afraid I would edit the contents of his notebook with the same red pen as I did his school papers. In any case, the Oso I knew at that time had become a sort of family man, trying any way he could think of to keep the family together. He contributed to the household routine, when there was one: the nightly feasts he prepared out of nothing; the DJ-ing he did in the evenings with Grandpa's LPs. What my brother had been involved in could never have been called activism, I don't think. The evidence—occasional cuts and bruises and popular protests and the stories that he told of his days in Saint James Park—seemed like something else completely. But I started to suspect, after I heard the history of his failed country, that Oso chose his stories carefully, selecting ones where he could mold or select the details. He did this not for the reasons that Dad told his story, to make himself into a hero. No, I think he was a little more like Grandpa, trying to teach with carefully chosen details.

Mr. Beck took some interest in me, visiting me and Alma in the same corner of the quad that Oso had set up as his country years before. And I liked him. He didn't try to get me to celebrate Cinco de Mayo, Lunar New Year, Chicano Heritage Day, or any of that. He did persuade me to go to some club meetings, though. None of these clubs were openly hostile, but none were particularly welcoming. When I showed up to the Latino Student Association meeting one day, people tittered: it seemed the middle school rumors that Alma and I were romantic had preceded me. I might as well have tried to join the Associated Korean American Student Body, but they would have stolen looks at me and whispered because I certainly wouldn't have been Korean enough. I would have done just as well to try to join the Vietnamese Honors Society, but I would have been met with the same mistrust, only this time, among other things, it would have been that my parents weren't refugees.

If a group for people like me had existed—people who had no parents, or had different-colored parents, or who liked boys and girls—maybe I could have been comfortable. Then again, maybe I needed a group that had *all* these characteristics. In that unlikely event, then what? Would we gather to celebrate that we found each other, that we had each other, that we had a voice in student council? Would that have been enough? Probably not. I'm not sure much really changes when you find a group to insulate yourself with.

Mr. Beck tried to convince me that chess club or AV club might be more suitable. But I had made up my mind. I returned to Alma's side. And Alma was busy expanding her focus: charcoal and chalk her medium, profiles of people her subject. The students. The students with a backdrop of brown lockers mounted on the gray moon-rock-textured walls of the school. Then, in the middle of our junior year, all that stopped. We met Loskie. But I'll get to that in a bit.

Though Oso was delivering newspapers in the early morning and slinging coffee during the day, he'd still wander before coming home to cook us dinner. So Alma, Dad, and I kept our ritual on the sidewalk in the afternoons. I read the news, as usual. And I would occasionally try—and fail—to draw full profiles of Alma and Dad. I was so frustrated, wanting to draw what I had never seen before: Alma in midsentence while Dad listened. My drawings sucked, and I was unable to capture the sadness, maybe resentment, in Dad's eyes; he scanned the traffic of park dwellers on their daily resettlement, now keeping to the other side of the street, scared of or pissed at Dad for what he had done to Nolan.

One day, as they were talking, both Dad and Alma looked as if they wanted to say something and to listen at the same time. Then Dad's face contorted. A tear streaked down his cheek from behind his dark glasses. His lips quivered. The face of speechless disappointment still haunts me, like so many other images.

Dad got up and walked against the light. A car swerved around him and jumped the curb. The driver, a fat man with a huge deep voice, yelled at him.

"Wait!" Alma shouted after Dad. "Dad! Wait!"

"Yeah, wait," the fat man said. "Look at my wheel. It's whacked. Is that wetback your old man? Go get him. He can't just—"

"Shut the fuck up," Alma growled as she looked to cross the street.

"What happened?" I asked.

"Nothing," Alma said. "Go upstairs."

"B-but . . ." I stammered. You believe that? I stammered, and something was wrong with Dad, the man I was only just getting to know.

"He can't just do anything he wants!" the fat man yelled.

"Shut up or I'll rip your throat out." Alma stared at him for a moment more and then ran across the street.

"I shoulda hit him!" the fat man yelled after her. "I'll be back with the cops!" He mumbled to himself and looked at me. I looked away, and he got into his car and drove off. He never came back. Neither did Dad.

When Oso came home that evening with the groceries, I told him what had happened.

"Well, let's go look for him, goddammit." He was right to be pissed. I'd done nothing, and I feel terrible about that to this very day. Maybe if I had, things would have turned out differently.

Sorry. Give me a sec. I'll be right back.

═══════════════

Okay. I'm fine. But I'll give you the short version of what happened. Granted, this was a pretty big event in my life. And it brings up a lot of baggage. Like how I've always done or not done what I thought was right. In not doing something, you still do something, it seems to me. I mean, look at the mess my family became. They're all phantoms. And my action—or inaction, as the case may be—has always seemed to negatively affect outcomes.

Okay, for example, I never told Mom how I was almost ready to go in the water with her, go into the surf and beyond the waves with her and Alma. Before I could, Mom was gone. And to this day, I still wish I'd told her; maybe she wouldn't have disappeared. But my anger at her for disappearing has not allowed me to forgive her. Stupid, I know, not forgiving a dead or disappeared person.

Sure, maybe I can come to peace with it someday, but it's just one albatross of many. When I finally get the nerve to see Oso, I have to let him know that I should have done more to keep him around, that it matters to me that he took off. I wonder if he has given up on me at this point. What's it been? Nine months since he flew me out here? Anyway, maybe if I can tell him what he means to me, I can cut that big old dead bird loose from around my neck. Then I'll have to move on to the next one.

I mean, from early on I knew that bastard Loskie was wrong for Alma. After a whole lot of shit, she had to break from him all by herself. But before I get to that, let me tell you what happened with Dad.

Oso and I went to the church first, talked to Father Khoi and a couple people who said they saw Dad kneeling—knuckles buried in his eyes—in his customary spot in the back during the readings, Gospel, and homily. But then, as usual, he was gone. We searched the other normal spots—Saint James Park, William Street Park—but no one had seen Dad.

I got tired after a few hours and went home, leaving Oso to wander the streets. I fell asleep on the couch in the empty apartment, the sounds of the bar and the jukebox and the late-night traffic allowing fitful sleep at best. Somehow Oso slipped inside the door and quickly fell asleep on the floor next to the couch. He was muddy and scratched up. I wanted to ask if there was any news, but I just took off his boots, covered him up, and let him sleep.

For hours, I lay there on the couch, trying to find inspiration in the wet-wool-and-mud fumes that wafted from Oso's sleeping body. I tried to convince myself to go back out. Look for Dad. Find Alma. Help her. Or bring her home and feed her, get her to rest. Then Alma came wearily through the door.

"Any news?" I said.

"He's fine. I found him at the church and we talked for a while. Now he's talking to Father Khoi. He misunderstood something I said."

"Really? Okay."

"No," Oso said, seeming to fill the room as he rose from the floor. "It is not okay. What the hell did you say to him? And he should be here. You should have brought him home."

He looked down at her, pulling his hair out of his eyes.

"Oso, he's fine," she said, and took a step back. "It's best for us if he has some time to talk with Father."

"So, you know what's best for us? I'm going down there to get him."

"No, Oso. Please don't. I really upset him. For hours he's been thinking that I said I helped Mom escape." Alma was on the verge of tears, pulling hard on her ear.

"What? Why would he think that? Why would something like that even come up? Why would she have wanted to leave anyway? Wait. Did you actually help her?" He turned to me. "And you. You were there."

I froze.

"Keep her out of it. Mom's gone and there's nothing we can do about that. Maybe she left on her own, maybe she jumped off the bridge, maybe she died. We'll never know. What I asked him was if he thought her disappearance was a good thing, in a way. I meant good between him and me."

"Why the hell would that matter? You're not even his kid."

Alma winced. So did I.

Oso continued: "And how'd he think that you helped her get away?"

"I don't know. But I screwed up bad. Real bad." She swallowed hard. Alma shrank away a little when Oso came even closer. But he simply wrapped his massive arms around her. Alma continued: "Do you guys want to go with me to get him tomorrow? He told me he wants to spend the night there. Father Khoi's got a spot for him."

Oso chuckled. "Sure. I know that spot well. Okay, we'll do that."

Just as normal as all that. The formerly vagrant father was allowed by his children a night away from home. They permitted their father a night of comfort in his old ways. And they became orphans because of it.

The next morning, we found him on the front steps of the church, curled up in nothing more than his usual jeans and flannel button-up. His glasses rested on his forehead, his body was still warm. With blank brown eyes, he stared into a streak of rising sun reflecting off a new tower.

Oso looked as if he wanted to hit Alma; but he stormed up to the church. Alma crumpled to the steps below my dead father and drove her fists into the cement until they bled. I knelt beside her and pulled her hands to my stomach, dabbing her knuckles with my sweater. In that instant, it was clear that the roles in my ever-shrinking family had changed. Yet again. Dad's blank, sunlit stare penetrated me, touching the same spot that had urged me to action after Mom disappeared. Dad's lifeless eyes communicated a simple message: *Don't leave Alma or Oso alone for long; people do stupid things when they think they're alone in the world.*

And keeping the three of us together while keeping the two of them apart was no easy task. But this was the imperative I was faced with at the age of sixteen. When a frazzled, pale social worker came by the apartment, Oso and I convinced him that it was best to keep the family together even though Oso was only twenty-one years old, that Alma was there as a friend of mine to comfort me in my time of despair. I even cried, throwing myself into Alma's arms, to make it more convincing.

Yes, it was that easy.

I kept Oso away from Alma by convincing him to wander, to blow off the steam of anger and mistrust by talking and walking with his friends at the park. And I tried my best to get Alma to draw something, anything, to keep her from dying of guilt. I considered rousing her with some of Grandpa's LPs but decided against it, wanting to see what happened if we experienced this ordeal in silence. In this muted urgency, I ushered the three of us into a new life. At least for a brief time. On top of all that, I had to make arrangements to put Dad in the ground.

Luckily for me, Father Khoi lived up to his reputation. A diminutive Vietnamese man with clipped English and mysterious white scars reaching from beneath his black hair and halfway down his forehead and temples, he showed such patience, love, and guidance. For a man who knew me only through what Oso had told him, Father Khoi seemed driven to help me in particular, having identified something in me. He must have seen me as some sort of refugee, a refugee like he once was except that he left home on a boat with his whole family and arrived here with only his brother and mother. I loved Father Khoi as much as you can love a person you don't really know. And the comfort he provided during those heady days had me thinking about becoming a practicing Catholic. But I figured that if Father Khoi couldn't provide answers that Dad needed, there was no way he could help me.

There's not much I can or want to say about the funeral itself except that it was simple: killing Wanda had cast Dad out of the outcasts, so no waywards showed up. Other than Mr. Henry in a black suit and tie, only the three of us kids were there. None of us wore anything but our usual flannel and denim. None of us talked. None of us cried. Father Khoi read something. I can't remember what it was. He and Mr. Henry left us graveside. Oso turned to go.

"Don't go," I said.

"Why not? I've got other people. You two seem to do fine by yourselves."

"Oso, I don't know what you think happened, but you're wrong."

"Then why'd he kill himself?"

"Do you mean by looking at the sun to make his heart explode?"

"What else could it have been?"

"Someone could have come by and lifted those glasses. You know, to wake him up or something."

"Or something. Or something. Everything's always open to convenient interpretation."

"Oso, goddammit. Why would we want Mom to go away? Why would she leave us? She loved us. You may not believe it, but she loved you, too. She kept you from hurting yourself all those nights you sleepwalked. To this day, you still don't believe us. But Alma and I were there when you'd turn on those lights, talk to us about nonsense, and try to get out of the house. But Mom had a way with you. And Dad, too. Then she just disappeared. That's it. Interpret it any way you want, that she left because of Dad, that she abandoned us, you. But the fact is she's not here. Neither is Dad. It's just us. We have to make that work somehow."

That night, after Alma fell asleep, Oso and I sat in the dining room, the light coming from three candles stuck in the necks of empty green wine bottles that'd somehow survived since Grandpa lived with us. We watched the traffic on the intersection below and poked the red wax, the red wax that dripped down the black-and-white bottle labels, the bottle labels with sketches of vineyards, vineyards that looked as if they were pooling blood or wine on the table. The flames cast weak shadows and flickered when Oso teased them with his thick, calloused fingers. Oso wanted to play some Bach, but I asked him not to. The sounds of the city washed over us for a long moment.

"Where would we be if Mom and Dad didn't do what they could for us?" I asked. "I mean, they did what they thought was right. But I wonder what things would be like if Dad had been home more. Or if Mom had said more. Or if Grandpa had not died when he did. Or what my life would have been like if . . ."

I swallowed hard. I wasn't sure if Oso was looking at me; the faint light now threw deep shadows through Oso's twisted, wet-looking bangs.

"It's weird to talk so much about Mom on the day of Dad's funeral," he said, "but it's like we laid her to rest, too."

We sat with that idea for a minute or two.

"What would life have been like if I'd gone with you to Santa Cruz?" He snuffed out the candles with thumb and forefinger.

"What?"

"You thought I didn't know?" his silhouette responded. "Well, Mom always let me know, in her quiet way, that I could come along if I wanted. But I . . . I . . ."

The silence and darkness in the room harmonized with grating gears and a muffled jukebox.

Wanting to give Oso an out, I said, "I wonder if getting Alma to the beach would help her a bit."

Alma said nothing on the bus over to Santa Cruz; at our beach, she sat in the sand, wrapped up, only her head visible, hair whipping above our old thick beach blanket. She just stared at the water, choppy on that windy day. Oso and I walked along the water's edge, me telling him about Mom and me and Alma there at the beach over the years. When we came back, Alma was still sitting there, staring at the waves as they grew, yawned, and expired on the shore. Her silence was contagious as we watched the sun go down. A couple days later, Oso and I agreed that the little trip to the ocean had washed us clean of something. But the ocean and the air didn't have the same effect on Alma, her vapidity increasing over the next year. Staring at walls, lolling in bed on school days until the last moment, doing nothing when Oso again started his nocturnal ramblings.

With the little money we had left from Dad's small life insurance payout, Oso came home with a beat-up green 1966 Pontiac Bonneville. "Now you can take her to the ocean whenever. Oh, and I'll need you to go to the grocery. I just need the car to deliver the papers; they just doubled my route."

Nothing helped Alma, who seemed to have assumed all the responsibility for both Mom's disappearance and Dad's death. New driver that I was, I braved Highway 17 and its hurtling, twisting madness over the hill to where my mom's pale apparition waited at the water's edge. Alma and I sat in silence on the beach for hours, and I wondered if Alma saw Mom, too. Maybe if she had, she would have entered the purifying waters. Maybe I should have walked to the water and waited for her to take my hand. But my mother floated alone beyond the breakers, unable to convince me to take that first step, with or without Alma.

Despite my seaside failure, it was our concern for Alma's well-being that kept Oso and I tight, unified in our desire to help her. Surrounded by Oso's classical music selections and smells from the kitchen, I read Alma's homework to her in hopes that something would sink in. And let me tell you, another person's depression is exhausting. By the time the day was over, I slept dreamlessly. But not before focusing on the woven sound of the city, the music, and Alma's sleep-breathing, as if that would help me figure out what to do next.

It wasn't long before Oso started sleepwalking again, and the dreams of severed fingers and bloody hands and gnarled vines twisted in and out of my shallow sleep. I took to the couch, trying to keep Oso safe from himself and the things he couldn't be held responsible for. But Oso would often get out, never forgetting his driver's license—my brother running and yelling in the January rain down Eighth Street, or pissing on a car on a particularly sweltering night, or talking to homeless men.

His sleepwalking even got him in jail a couple times, but no charges were ever filed. Oso was quite well known—even respected, I think—by the cops: in his waking hours in Saint James Park, Oso must have imposed some sort of order on the ranks of the homeless, making the cops' jobs easier. But the cops still tested him for drugs and booze; none ever turned up. Still, though, it amazes me—as it no doubt amazes you—that the law wasn't more involved.

When he got home, he and I would exchange the same kind of absurd banter he and Mom used to have, though I was not so playful.

"I am Oso with a side of greatness."

"What?"

"With a side of grapefruit."

"Turn off the light."

"Great loot. And I will not turn off the light. Zach said I could leave it on."

"Turn off the light, Oso."

"But Zach said I could turn it on. You want to ask him?"

"Turn off the light."

"Okay, but Zach said I could leave it on."

I had power over Oso in his dream state. And it was astounding to me.

She writes without stopping, filling in postcards. When she finishes one, it's like she's turning the page of a book.

Say: I don't think I could write postcards.

"Why not?" She looks up but doesn't stop writing.

Say: No one to send them to.

Staring, writing, she asks, "Why are you here?"

Tell her.

"I know her." She finally stops writing. "She says you grew up deprived of sleep, devoted to those stories."

Say: Headless chickens and fingerless hands, vines and a screaming child.

"She was devoted to you."

Say: Then why did she leave?

"Someone with a questionable past needs a new audience when there's no one left to hold her accountable."

Wait. Is that you, Alma?

She goes back to writing postcards.

8.

JULY 4, 1997. How will it be remembered? The day that Pathfinder and Sojourner landed on Mars? Or the day Kat Campos got locked up for intoxication? The real question is, will it be the first or the last time?

Yes, it does seem like I'm hearing voices, but I don't remember them. Something or someone is telling me to do these things, though.

Maybe it would be better if drugs or booze were found in my system. Then we could understand a little about why I screamed at some poor backpacker in front of the hostel on 103rd and Amsterdam, distraught enough to grab her by the shoulders. But, for all I remember of it, I might as well have been on Mars. One minute, I was walking from home to meet up with Oso in Washington Heights, and then I hear the Twenty-Fourth Precinct cell door clang shut. Up to that point, they tell me I was repeating, "Is that you, Alma? Alma, is that you? Alma? Alma! Talk to me!"

Hey, at least there's the bright side for you: if the backpacker decides to press charges, I may be forced to see a headshrinker.

You're telling me you've never heard voices? Nothing from your older sister, your twin brother, your dead parents? What about Gloria? She must haunt you. You were together for so long. She was your first love. And you two had made plans for the future. Then things fell apart.

She was leaving the next day to see untouched land before it was gone. Birds soaring, jetliners roaring. Jackhammers and spray-painters and traffic pounding, hissing, droning on the Henry Hudson Bridge. Fresh asphalt permeated your nostrils. You and Gloria walked in silence until pavement gave way to dirt paths. You meandered under the red-orange-yellow-purple-brown canopy of Inwood Hill and decided you would live together here in the city and have three kids; you even gave them names. Parents dead and siblings thousands of miles away, you would have no obligations to anyone but your own little family. After a few years, maybe you and Gloria and the kids would move to Europe. Both of you wanted to someday live among ancient, real culture. Paris, London, Venice. You two were so sure of the future that you felt each other, tasted each other, smelled each other, heard everything, saw each other among the gusty winds and the floating leaves. How do you not hear her voice? You were each other, after all: pressed into each other pressing into the trees and the soil, and twigs and pebbles and plants and mud were in your hair and on you. She must be whispering to you.

And then she traveled the world. Alone. You had to work. When Gloria returned, she said the Great Wall was only a testimony to the futility of self-preservation. Rome and the Colosseum were empty even of history, or the imagination thereof. The pyramids were not the greatest tributes to the dead; rather, they were monuments to slavery. And Gloria couldn't see raising kids in New York City anymore—or any city. While you saw exposure and immersion as ideals of cultural education, she saw them only as states of being for the homeless and the drowned. Besides, she had said, people get flattened in their cars on collapsed freeways, bodies plummet from burning buildings. All she could see in a New York City future was twisted, melting flesh entwined with rebar. All she could smell in the subway was rotting carcasses and poison. All she could distinguish and inhale on the streets was homeless folks' piss or dogs' shit or people's trash. To Gloria, if you tried to raise the kids here, they'd be paved over, buried in refuse. Gloria began disappearing for weeks at a time. So when not at the hospital, you began to console yourself by planning the neighborhood clinic.

It's only been five years since she left you, and you're telling me that you are not haunted by the voices of Gloria and the kids you never had together?

Well, the voices in my head, if you want to call them that, are urging me not to go see Oso yet. So I won't.

———————

Oso eventually left Café Matisse and the newspaper delivery job when he got work in construction; San José was continuing to grow, mostly upward and somehow still outward, big homes dotting and snaking up the foothills. On the weekends, the three of us would go on short walks together, smoking, Oso and I trading stories about work and school. Alma smoked her cigarettes down to the filter in near silence. A few times, I think I heard her mumble to herself. Oso and I became more worried about her, but we had no idea what to do; and if we told the social worker, we were afraid she'd be taken away from us. We continued to do what we'd always done, hoping that something would bring her back into the world of the living.

As usual, Oso played the LPs as we went to sleep. But his sleepwalking was getting more frequent. One night, I heard him talking. I got up from the couch, and as I approached the room, he mentioned the sweet melodies of Dad's laughter and the deep tones of Grandpa's voice. I saw his silhouette through the crack in the door, backlit by the yellow streetlamps outside. I pushed the door open, the night-light from the bathroom casting my faded shadow onto Alma's fully covered sleeping body. Oso was sitting next to her on the bed. I stopped at the door, wondering for a brief moment the same thing you're wondering. But I had faith it wasn't like that, that it never had been. I led him to bed, exchanging a few nonsensical wordplays. Just as my mom had always done.

I never told Oso or Alma. Or anyone. Until now.

We held together. For a while.

One spring night in my junior year, Oso was down at the Cav, having a beer with some guys from work. I'd overheard someone at school talking about a party in Santa Cruz near the university. I was so tired of Alma's mood that I decided we should go.

Yeah, a party. My thinking was that an out-of-the-ordinary social situation would, at the very least, throw her into some sort of revolt against me, raging against being in a room with so many people she didn't know and didn't want to know.

The party was a bunch of mellow beach-bum hippies—yeah, the stereotypical California people: a strange mix of high schoolers, university students, and a couple guys looking like professors. Not that it would have mattered, but I didn't see anyone from our school. So, as everyone got high and listened to unending Grateful Dead guitar solos, Alma and I blended into the wall. And after she came back from the bathroom— almost scowling, almost smiling—Alma started talking. It may have been the alcohol, and she didn't say much except thanks for taking her there. At any other time, I would have asked why she had such a look on her face. But I was just happy to hear her string sentences together. After several more drinks, Alma wanted to go for a swim before going home, saying the chill of the water would sober us up.

Swimming for sobriety. That was Alma's logic over the coming months, as if she'd been too long underwater without oxygen.

It wasn't our usual beach. We parked and left the headlights on to light our way to the water. As simple as that, Alma stripped off all her clothes and went in. I waded into the shallow surf, trying to keep an eye on her, the thought of losing yet another person drawing me into the cold, dark wet that had always terrified me.

I was as much at risk of drowning right there onshore as Alma was out there by herself. So I stripped naked. *She is out there by herself.* I waded in until the water was at my knees. *She has never been out there by herself.* The water swelled around me, sprayed me, rose above my hips. *I have to go out there.* Shivering, I was about to go beneath the next wave when out of that very same wave came Alma. She walked past me, glowing pale in the lights of the car. And I didn't say anything, stunned at what I was beginning to realize. Swimming beyond the breakers was some sort of baptism for the women in my life, a baptism in the tumultuous water that sustained life and took it away.

The waves surging, I stood astonished, staring at the black swells. Then I heard the engine start, so I ran to the car, pulling on random pieces of clothing. Possessed by some perversion of her former self, Alma drove, though she didn't have a license. I was still reeling. Again, I said nothing when I should have. We could have died, but my mind was back at the beach. Anything I could have said would have been swept out through the wide-open windows anyway.

Alma swerved and twisted us back home over Highway 17. When we stopped for cigarettes a couple blocks from home, Alma went in by herself, hair still damp and tangled with bits of seaweed; I was still half naked under a towel, trying to get the sand out of my crotch, a chill remaining in my bones. I wanted to ask Alma what it was like to go in the ocean and why she did it. But Alma came back to the car and told me about some guy she'd met at the party. She seemed quite taken with him. So I didn't say anything. I still wonder if, had I asked her about the ocean, got her to think about what it might mean to her, I may have saved her, myself, and even Oso from the coming events.

The next morning Oso found the car with one wheel up on the curb and facing the wrong direction on Third Street.

"It's obvious you were drinking," he roared, looking at Alma, looming over her. "What were you thinking?"

"It was me. I was driving," I said. I was a little surprised at myself.

"Why would you do that?" he bellowed, his hair falling in his face. "It's shit like this that could get me in a lot of trouble. And it could take you two away from each other."

It's clear to me now that Oso recognized how rare it was to have a person by your side through your entire life. Not as a spirit. Not as a memory. Not as a myth. There, in actuality, slogging through all the din with you. He may have felt that Alma and I somehow were the core that would help him through his own din.

You're right. I also thought it was his friends in the park who had given him that stability. But the park friends were always dying, getting thrown in jail, or moving on to the next possible warm bed. Alma and I were supposed to be there for him. Even if Alma was somewhere distant in her mind, at least Oso and I could focus on our shared goal of getting her to the other side of whatever she was going through. But I failed him. So now I have to see him—soon—to find out if this woman, Camille, is able—or willing—to deal with his restiveness, to be his core.

For another year and a half, Oso was on edge. And rightfully so. He would never admit it, but he was likely just as scared as I was, knowing we were one stupid mistake away from some dumpy foster home. When Oso was around, he was silent—as was the record player. The hulking absence of his voice and the classical music made the apartment seem smaller. It was unbearable, and the pull of social forces was too much to resist. Well, it was really only one social force.

———

Loskie was a massive ship churning through a small, shallow harbor: eyes were drawn to him as his wake tossed smaller vessels. The waves on the surface distracted from submerged things he stirred up and carried behind him.

The disappointment at not being accepted to the Naval Academy five years earlier had led Loskie into the restaurant business, having been exposed in his earlier life to the bakery owned by his father, a politician in a Southern California town. Loskie had big ideas about being owner, chef, and bartender of his own restaurant, making money off the tech fat cats in and around San José. When we met him, he had a job as a prep cook and was awaiting acceptance to a culinary school up in San Francisco.

And Loskie's stories of his dead mother and father were both peculiar and familiar. Because of his parents' saintliness, Loskie saw himself as a descendant of "inevitable success" as a restaurateur; his plan to fly fighter planes—or play pro ball or be a philosopher or hike the entire Pacific Crest Trail or scale the face of El Capitan—was an unfortunate diversion from the true calling instilled in him by his father during those long early-morning hours at the bakery. Loskie's predestination seemed all the more real with his numerous stories of sweet-talking his way out of DUI busts and ditching cops when smoking dope in public.

I first saw him at another party not far from our apartment. Alma came back from the bathroom and sat next to me, our backs against a wall. She was scowl-smiling again.

"What's that look all about?" I asked.

"I just had sex." Alma was smiling more than scowling now.

My guts clenched. "Really? Who with?"

"That guy over there." She motioned toward a tall man across the room in a red Hawaiian shirt. He was gyrating his hips, moving to a meandering guitar solo. "Name's Loskie."

"You just met him?" I stared at the side of Alma's face as she studied Loskie.

"At that party last week," she said, not looking at me. "He smiled at me as I was walking by; I smiled back. He was singing and dancing to hippie music. He followed me to the bathroom and closed the door. I watched him in the mirror as he bit my ear and my neck a little, his hands everywhere. I was scared, but I liked it. Next thing I knew, my elbows were on the counter and my pants around my knees. When he put it in, it really hurt and I was about to tell him to stop. But then it was over. It was pretty much the same thing tonight."

"That doesn't sound so great" was all I could manage to say.

"Yeah. I'm trying to figure out what the big deal is. Maybe it'll get better."

"You're going to do it again?"

"Sure, why not?" She turned to me. "Besides, he's got a free spirit. When have I—when have we—ever been around someone like that?"

Over the next few weeks, as I tried to figure out what this new person meant to the world I knew, I went mute. And when Alma didn't ask me why, I went deeper into silence, a silence accompanied by rage, a seething rage, trying to understand life without Alma watching me with those dark eyes, those dark eyes on me and that arm across me in the mornings, in the mornings, evenings, nights, guiding and comforting me through all my hesitations and uncertainties. The only people who knew or cared about my existence always died or went away. So, if Alma was consumed by Loskie, I was convinced my disappearance was inevitable, that I would vanish from my own life because I soon wouldn't live in the minds of others.

Maybe it was out of necessity—a sense of survival—that I managed my fear and anger so I could stay as close as I could to Alma. Or maybe it was Loskie himself. You'll think this is a bit depraved, but I soon found familiarity in his idea of himself; attraction to his sturdy frame, blue eyes, and unending supply of second chances; intimidation in his swagger. I couldn't deny that I wanted to know more about Loskie, figure out what this attraction was all about. I had been attracted to boys at school, watched them from a distance. But I found myself pulled along, unmoored by the same force that had somehow tugged Alma out of the mire she'd been in since Dad died.

Over the next year or so, we would meet Loskie in the afternoons between his shifts. In Plaza de César Chávez, the Fairmont Hotel looming across the street, we sat smoking and watching business types avoid proximity to the eternal park dwellers. Loskie told us his stories of carousing the night before, of drama at the seafood restaurant where he worked, of his virtuous parents. And we told him short versions of our stories, though Loskie would inevitably compare and contrast whatever barbarism or tragedy we were talking about with an episode in his own life. Before Loskie went back to work, we'd take short walks, dodging convention-goers, skirting the men and machinery at work building the tech museum and the Adobe tower, expecting to see Oso at the 303 Almaden Boulevard construction site where he was working at the time.

We never saw Oso, but he may have seen us: Alma holding Loskie's hand, me arm in arm with Alma, Loskie kissing Alma before going back to work, me turning and taking a few steps away.

If Oso ever saw us with this strange man, he never said a word about it: he would come home dead tired, eat a little, and go to his room—Mom and Dad's old room. Alma often quietly left around eleven and came back around two. I wanted to go with her, but I stayed in bed, thinking about what they were doing, what it would be like to be with him. But it didn't make me feel like you have shown me, like you have shown me how to feel even if you're not here, not here to touch me. Thinking about Loskie and Alma made me freeze, plagued by a shallow dream. But instead of the usual bloody hands and chicken heads, I saw my parents, my parents and their loneliness in each other's presence, their sadness, their violence, their doing what they did to each other in service to an unknown ideal, an unrealized happiness. But I still hung around, wanting to protect Alma while at the same time trying to come to terms with my attraction to Loskie. And I certainly couldn't risk losing Alma altogether by talking to her about how I was feeling about Loskie. We had liked the same boys at school, but the physical part of the relationship changes things.

Sometimes Loskie wouldn't show up to the plaza in the afternoons. And, as if in tribute to comforting old rituals, we would take in the city scene, Alma sketching in silence and listening to me read from the *Mercury*. Cobain dies. Nixon dies. Mandela elected. The Rwandan genocide. Woodstock '94. The MS *Estonia* sinks. Aristide installed. The Great Hanshin earthquake. The Oklahoma City bombing. And at weekend parties before Loskie arrived, we would sometimes have a few quiet drinks; retreating to a new but familiar corner, we were unapproached and unapproachable, content just to be next to each other. Then Loskie would show up, strung out after a dinner shift and maybe a bump or two of coke. He would make a pass at the two of us. But before I could fight my way through the possibility of loneliness, sadness, or violence in a room with them, Loskie and Alma would vanish for an hour or so. And I'd be left to wonder if this solitude was worse than if Alma were to disappear completely.

One time in a customary corner, Alma and I sat in the afterglow of our high school graduation, not really caring that we had done it but happy that we were done with it. Now we would really figure things out, and we would figure them out together. And the booze got the best of us. And we cried. And we hugged. And when Loskie found us like this, he took it the wrong way. And he was furious, at first.

Then Alma said, "Oh, it doesn't mean anything. Don't worry about it."

Those words almost made me evaporate. So in a drunken haze I found myself in some room, making out with Loskie while Alma gave him a blow job. When he was done, he grunted at me, "We gotta do that again."

Suddenly repulsed by the heat from his tangy whiskey-cigarette breath, I turned to look for Alma, but she'd already gone to wash out her mouth or have a smoke. I walked home without another word. When I got to the apartment, I found Oso in the back of a squad car. I thanked the officer and led Oso inside. By the time we got into the apartment, he was fully awake. And tears welled in his eyes. He told me he had gotten a job at a motel in Yosemite. He was leaving the next day.

Confronted with the departure of yet another person, I said nothing.

Nothing.

Goddammit.

And like so many times before, I turned away at the sight of something I didn't understand or didn't deserve.

I don't know what it means.

I don't know why.

No, I won't blame it on the booze.

Then Oso was gone.

I told myself I would visit him in the mountains. But it never happened.

It doesn't matter now! He left! That's all I can tell you!

I can't tell you why I didn't try to keep Oso from leaving. A lot was at stake, and he just up and left before either Alma or I could find jobs or a place to live. Oso may have been pissed at us for how we acted during our senior year. Why wouldn't Oso have anything but mistrust of me? Why would he open his new life here in New York to me? How do I know that he even gave me a second thought after he left a year and a half ago?

You're right. I don't know. I must have faith. In the days after Dad died, Father Khoi said that faith is meant to be questioned; the act of questioning strengthens faith. I thought this was a strange thing for a priest to say. I didn't—still don't—understand it. I mean, if you question faith too much, you put that faith in danger, right?

Even if you agree with Father Khoi—even if it was in fact a verifiable truth—there's still a huge risk of being hurt by the very things and people we have faith in. It's a wonder there's any faith at all in this world.

Look, I'm sorry I yelled. Telling all this has raised more questions about my place in this story than it has answered. But I don't want you to be sorry. It's just that . . . I never expected this. Never expected to have to answer to anyone. Never expected you.

———————

Mr. Henry helped me get a job answering phones at his lawyer friend's downtown office, but Alma and I couldn't cover the rent that summer. Alma, who had gotten a hostess job through one of Loskie's friends at the Tied House Cafe and Brewery at San Pedro Square, moved in with Loskie and his roommates not far outside downtown. Luckily for me, Mr. Henry put up some of the deposit for a furnished bedroom in a small white house on Twelfth Street, just inside the Naglee Park neighborhood. At first, oddly enough, I didn't really miss Alma. And when she and Loskie didn't show up after promising to help me clear out the old apartment, I wasn't surprised or even that annoyed; we had been drifting apart for months. Mr. Henry, bless his good Catholic soul, had his deliverymen help me take everything—all the furniture he had given us over the years, clothing, dishware, cookware, even Grandpa's LPs and record player—to the pawnshops in Relics.

I gave the movers a few bucks before they left; the clerk counted out the cash for my stuff. I did the math and realized I would have enough money to cover the rest of the security deposit. In fact, I had a bit of a surplus, so I poked around the store.

"What's this band?" I asked the clerk, and held up a battered Discman with a faded sticker of a black cross circled and slashed by red.

"Bad Religion," the short, dark-skinned man said. "You know them?"

"I've mostly only listened to the classical records I just sold you. Well, that and a beat-up Nirvana tape."

"Can you believe it's been over a year since Kurt died?" He took off his fedora, revealing a pompadour.

"I barely remember him dying. Too much other stuff going on."

"Well, I can understand that."

"No, you probably can't," I said, putting the Discman down and walking toward the door.

"Wait. Don't you need a CD player now?"

"I guess."

"All right. How 'bout some music?"

"I figure I'd go to the library."

"I doubt the library has a very big punk rock selection." He rummaged in a bin full of wigs and handed me my first CD: *Suffer*.

"That one's on the house," he said. "Chicks aren't usually into Bad Religion. But what the hell, right? I can find some good women artists for you, too. I also work at Streetlight Records. You should come by sometime. Ask for me. Name's Hector."

"You hitting on me?" I asked.

"Nope. Tammy's my girl." He pointed at the tattoo on his forearm. "I just like helping people discover new things."

I sat outside, smoked, and listened to the whole CD, staring at the album artwork. I studied the lyrics and tried to make sense of the image blazing through the hazy scratched and cracked jewel case: an immolating blond boy standing defiantly on some American suburban sidewalk. And I was hooked. You probably wonder how I could become addicted to music by men. But their rage and dissatisfaction helps give me some idea of where the discontent of men comes from.

The world began to look different over those several months. I settled into a routine with my new roommate, Lisa, a short, rotund university librarian. Every night, she brought home stacks of books on California history; she sat, read, and wrote notes under two chemist lamps as sandalwood incense laced through the shafts of light, the shuffling of paper the only sound. Sometimes I stopped and looked through her open door, wondering what she would do with all that knowledge. But I never asked her. Instead, I'd go to my room, soak in the silence, and read a *Harper's Magazine* or *Mercury News* I'd swiped off the tables at Café Matisse on my way to work earlier in the day. But on Saturday nights, after long walks to Streetlight Records to trade in the music I didn't like, I'd sit in my room with my earphones on and listen to the latest used CDs that Hector had steered me toward. If lyrics were printed in the liner notes, I'd ponder those; otherwise, I'd puzzle over the album covers, judging whether the artwork fit the music.

With the exception of classical music, I sampled everything. Jazz in all its forms. Blues. Classic rock. Rap. Hip-hop. Pop. Punk. New age. Techno in all its genres. I then listened to everything alternative/modern from Seattle to New York and beyond: Alanis Morissette and Ani DiFranco to Tool; L7 and the Cranberries to Nine Inch Nails; Tori Amos and Fiona Apple to Moby; Hole and Björk to Dr. Dre. I ended up obsessed with Hector's favorite hard bop jazz artists and grunge bands. Yeah, yeah. I know you'll have trouble squaring that with what you think you know about me. And you're probably thinking I'm far too open to suggestion from the men in my life.

Don't get me wrong: I still listen to women artists. Hector taught me to be curious about what all artists were doing with their music. But there is stratification in John Coltrane, Ornette Coleman, Thelonious Monk, and the men from Seattle; in the dark narratives, distinct off-key notes, and distortions I can hear them wrestle with something they have in common: the drive to get at their angst and to solve it. Or at least explain it. I don't need my own take on things muddying the waters. I mean, why stop with my own limited perspective? Why start with it, for that matter? Besides, how could I understand men unless I tried to see the world through their eyes? So I started imagining what Oso or Dad or even Grandpa might think of Chris Cornell's lyrics or Alice in Chains' gloom or Charlie Mingus's arrangements. Like I said before, I don't think the music by these men means anything to me directly—how could it? But at least their music seems more relevant than classical music.

I felt as little sentiment about the classical music of my youth as I did about the old apartment. This may seem strange to you, but the music and the apartment both were reminders of the unsolved lives—yes, unsolved lives—deaths, and disappearances in my family. Everything about my new room—its eight-foot ceiling, desert-sand-beige walls, carpeted floor, small windows, and relative quiet—was such a stark contrast to the old apartment, the apartment where the random paint-roller strokes were tallied, tallied and suspended on the high ceiling's crown molding, crown molding where the stray ghosts of stories and empty wine bottles would float, float after coming at will through the panoramic windows to mingle-mix-weave with the sound, the sound of revelry-cars-buses-trucks-city-orchestra, and the smell, the ancient phantom smell of sweat-iron-flowers-fruit-vegetable-horseshit-dirt-dried-lead-paint-diesel-fumes.

I had moved only a mile from Third and Santa Clara, and I was protected from all of it. But as it turned out, the loss of Alma was not as easy to get over. But she was happy for the first time in a long while. When I did see Alma and Loskie, I still forgave his whiskey absurdity; as pitiful as you may think that is, somehow it was still charming. Then they were gone, moved to an apartment in Santa Cruz so Alma could do some sort of work-study for a couple years at the junior college before transferring to UCSC.

For months, I fended off a growing urge to change my hair, buzzing it like Sinéad O'Connor but keeping my long bangs. I took a class at the university paid for by my boss. Working, reading, listening to music, drinking the occasional twelve-pack of cheap beer, I tried to keep busy. Then late one evening, Alma hopped on a bus over the hill with a backpack and a fifth of Popov. There on the porch, pinching her forearms, she wept.

"He said he didn't want me to come see you . . . I left him . . . He told me to get out . . . I told him to go to hell . . ."

That night Alma curled her warm, drunken body next to me. Breathing beside me. I heard sirens in the distance as I lay awake in the dark. Not even considering my roommate Lisa, I wondered if Alma would live with me. Sorrow so often struck Alma over the next month or so that she'd curl up next to me and cry herself to sleep, mumbling, "All that devotion," and "Now this." These repeated words seemed to spook Lisa; she started coming home, closing the door to her room, and not coming out. Then with no warning, she cleared out all her stuff on New Year's Eve and was gone. I can't blame her.

Worrying about making rent and Alma's withered state, I didn't sleep well for weeks. I helped Alma get a job at Café Matisse, quietly managed my own responsibilities and Alma's anguish, all in a vain attempt to exhaust myself to oblivious sleep. For so much of my life, I'd found it pacifying to sleep near Alma, her breathing a part of a symphony, a sonata, a concerto. But now my questions and speculations were specters swirling in the darkness without a sickle of light, swirling in oppressive silence. Loskie could find a way to recapture Alma. Alma could once again become immersed in the man who had raised his fist at her the night she got on the bus to see me. I stayed awake and quiet and saw myself as vigilant and self-sacrificing. But I sacrificed the freedom that truth brings. Even with Alma sleeping next to me, I was alone in my nightly willful self-deception in which Alma and I knew what all the struggle meant, that we were finally defined so clearly that we could explain it in a way that other people would understand.

One night in early February '96, Alma went to the supermarket. In an old issue of *Harper's*, I read a thoroughly confounding short story called "Ad Infinitum"; then I fell asleep, thinking of a line toward the end of the story: "The story of our life is not our life; it is our story." I had a dream that I was standing with my back to a wall inside a small, perfectly square room. It was bright and without sound and entirely white. In the center was a wooden stool painted white. On the stool was a white vase with a single white daisy tilting to the right, unsettling all symmetry in the room. Then double doors opened on the wall opposite from where I stood. A silhouetted female figure beckoned me. I hesitated. When I woke, I was overwhelmed by the dream. Its beauty. Its obscurity. It was urgent that I tell Alma about it. But the house was still vacant. All except for the distant wailings of ambulances.

Later that night, the dream recurred. But in the middle of the dream, I was awakened by the sound of Alma's moaning. Then I heard a long stream of piss in the toilet. I went rigid. Loskie's voice permeated the walls. The door to the other room closed, but I still heard the muffled sound of him talking. Then I heard Alma laugh. For months, I had nursed Alma's broken heart. And now Loskie, the cause for Alma's despair, was the source of her joy. How could Alma let him back in?

All-encompassing hatred consumed me. I hated myself, having let myself believe Alma and I had found our definition. I hated Loskie for somehow maneuvering his way back into Alma's life. But I downright loathed Alma. Over the months before, Alma couldn't take care of herself, was barely able to breathe through the ceaseless crying, couldn't see herself living without Loskie. She was so far from where she had once been. As the laughter in the next room turned into droning snores, I fell into a deep sleep, again dreaming of the woman motioning me forward.

The next morning, I got up to go smoke outside. As I walked toward the front room, I heard the TV. And laughing. I stopped, uncertain which emotion would show itself when I saw the reunited couple, how I would react when I heard how the estranged lovers had gotten back together. I fiddled with my smokes as I shuffled in front of the TV. With an unlit cigarette in my mouth, I listened to the couple tell about their destined reconciliation. I knew it was a lie: Loskie had not just happened to hop a bus to San José, he had not just happened to see Alma in the Cav, he had not even had to convince her to forgive him. But that was how they told it. He had told Alma he was sorry, that he had screwed up. Alma laughed and twirled her hair, black eyes shining.

Damn right, she was pathetic.

I was relieved. At least a little. But not because I was glad that my friend was happy again. All those months of Alma's self-pity and incessant sobbing had made the house humid with melancholy. I never thought it could happen, but Loskie's arrival helped me breathe easier. I was able to forgive Loskie. And with all his generosity in the following weeks, my hatred for Alma subsided, too.

Unable to get his position back at the seafood restaurant, Loskie found a job as a short-order cook at a greasy spoon. For the next couple weeks, he cooked us food we had never imagined before, elaborate meals of roasted chicken, barbecued filet mignon, seared ahi tuna, Swedish meatballs, reductions, sauces, gravies, stews, gratins, salads, sautéed vegetables—all of this was preceded by expensive cheeses and fresh fruits and crackers and followed with twenty-year-old port. Loskie fiercely declined any sort of repayment. I have no idea how he could afford this, but I always suspected he sold drugs to townies and ex-cons down at the Cav. Anyway, he cooked the meals and cleaned up after himself. A reef of generosity sometimes emerged through the confusion and vapor of tormented alcoholic waters that relentlessly crashed upon him.

Alma continued to work at the café, and after a couple weeks of staying at the house, Loskie agreed to pay a portion of the rent. I tried to get back into a routine with work and my spring semester literature survey course at the university. But Alma and Loskie started fighting again. As I tried to read in my room, the sounds of bickering and yelling bounced off the walls. I could have told them to move out. And I could have found a student to fill the room. I could have had peace and quiet. But I was paying only a third of the rent. On my limited budget and with my CD-buying habit, this was a lot of money. Besides, I would have been lonely otherwise. So I found a way to get used to their fighting and screwing. It was just another set of sounds to live with. I'd done it all my life, so this wasn't that different. At least that's what I made myself believe.

The three of us started going out a few times a week. Loskie had joined a weekly billiards team at the Cav, and after our bellies were full on Loskie's rich cooking, Alma and I sat at the bar every Thursday night and pretended to care about his games. Mostly, we talked about our shared desire to travel and live completely alone. We could never agree on the best places to live. Alma hated cities and never understood why I wanted to live in one. Alma was a lot like Gloria, in that she wanted to live only in remote places. The Amazon, the Dingle Way in Ireland, the Sahara. But she couldn't figure how exactly to live self-reliantly in those places. She laughed, cursing the fact that there were no 7-Elevens in the middle of the desert.

It was over these long, vodka-soaked conversations that I came to a better understanding of Alma's weakness. I thought at the time that maybe some people simply need other people to make them feel complete. And then I heard Alma's hope for autonomy in her plans to see the remote places of the world. So for the time being, I allowed Alma her state of dependence. I even saw a connection between Alma's return to her normal self and Loskie. But I gave him far too much credit. I soon started to feel like I was under a camera lens. A fish-eye lens distorted with booze and envy. Whenever Alma and I were together, we were always in Loskie's line of sight. At the Cav and at parties, he kept his warped, furtive eye on us.

At a house party one night, Alma and I sat with tonic and a small bottle of Gilbey's at our feet. Arm in arm, we talked about what else might be outside our small world. When Loskie arrived, having stopped at the Cav for a few drinks after work, he wandered through the crowd of people, looking for us. When he saw Alma and me tucked in the backyard, he said we were trying to hide from him. Then he had a drunken idea: another opportunity to try to screw us both. Loskie and Alma fought. I walked home alone.

They made up and left the party together. And Alma drove Loskie's little Geo Metro into a telephone pole going thirty-five. The car was nearly split in two; the cops said there were no tire skids. Both of them were in the hospital for a week, barely conscious. Loskie developed slowness in his speech and Alma sustained a bit of a limp.

After they got out of the hospital, Loskie made jokes about how Alma had almost killed him. I wished she had, realizing right then that

Loskie always believed it was someone else's fault. His inability to get a decent kitchen job, his repeated failures to move out of an area that he always bitched about—it was even someone else's fault that he wasn't smart enough. So I was certain he hadn't put up much of a fight when Alma drove on the night of the accident. Clearly, he was to blame for almost killing Alma.

I didn't sleep at all while Alma was in the hospital. Ever since that night, I've worried about Alma like never before. I wanted Alma to know that Loskie was incapable of maintaining a selfless thought. I had also occasionally seen flashes of something else that Alma was still blind to: the angry, distorted lens with which he watched us. But I never said anything. I was afraid that she would misunderstand my honesty, that I would force her into a choice between me and Loskie, the choice between lifelong friendship and grotesque love. If I moved out, I might be able to keep Alma in my life. But leaving—and leaving her alone with that bastard—seemed stupider than staying.

Then in early April, Loskie threw a party at our house. It was like all the others: his friends hanging about the yard like a bunch of convicts in a prison yard. In the middle of the party, Alma went to her room to change her shirt. Alma called me into her room and closed the door as she tried to find a shirt that looked good with her jeans. Loskie came in as Alma was changing her bra. He turned red when he saw me in the room.

"If this door is gonna be closed and two chicks are getting naked, I should be there, too. It's my house, after all."

I wanted to say, *Your house?* Now, after almost a year with you and Gloria's legacy, I might scream, *You colonized this fucking house!*

But I said nothing.

Instead, Alma simpered. "I got beer on my shirt, honey."

"Sure, sure. Hey, wait." He paused and leered at me. "Let's finish what we started that one time." He stepped closer to me. "I know you want us both."

He dropped his pants, grabbed his dick, and waved it in my face. He laughed. And Alma just stood there, shoving her nails into her palm.

A week later, I moved into a tiny room on the other side of campus. I saw Alma one last time at the end of that summer, at the party Loskie threw for her when she got out of jail for her second DUI.

The day after I moved out, I went to an old barbershop full of old men. From the moment I walked in with my straight black hair down my back, the men stared. I almost turned to go. But I waited and read an article in the *Mercury* about Israel's Operation Grapes of Wrath. I felt their eyes on me. When it was my turn, the barber—burly, with a gray flattop and an anchor-eagle-globe of faded green tattooed on his forearm—didn't hesitate to set in with the clippers. Within five minutes, I was walking toward the door, brushing tiny bits of hair off my newly shorn scalp and pushing my bangs out of my eyes. I smiled in the mirror and the men still gawked. Realizing I was late for my poetry writing class, I rushed out the door. Twenty minutes later, I was following Thalia to her shop.

The spring sun warmed my scalp in a way I had never felt before. And I saw Thalia, her twisted, sun-kissed brown hair and rich olive skin drawing me along behind her. Her long legs glided under a paisley skirt, sandaled feet carrying her through the crowd. Thalia's ears sparkled, loaded down with studs and hoops. I suppose I wanted to draw them. But my drawings were just as bad as my wilty poetry verse. So, without a plan, I was urged past my classroom by the sweet sun-heated blooms of spring.

Over the previous year, I had been walling myself in—music on my Discman or magazines and newspapers in my face; I guess I'd walled myself in for most of my life. Only Miss Femi, all the way back in middle school, had an effect similar to Thalia's. But Thalia's allure was much stronger. I followed Thalia as if pushed up San Carlos Street by the warm breeze, across the light-rail tracks, past Plaza de César Chávez. The new business towers, the new and old hotels, and the almost-finished tech museum stood and watched me. In a cloud of diesel fumes and blossom aromas, I followed Thalia into Relics. She went into the shop called Don't Look. I hesitated but entered.

Bent filling in a ledger behind the old cash register, she didn't notice me. My hands were shaking as I examined the surrealist paintings from the university's art students and tried on a tan suede jacket that smelled of mothballs and tar. It looked good on me, but I put it back. I eased into a polished black leather antique chaise and took a breath.

"This is a great shop," my voice squeaked. "It's not like the others."

"Well," Thalia said, releasing her twisted pile of hair. Her earrings jangled. "I can't figure how those other guys stay in business selling useless crap. So I try to appeal to those who have a little more taste."

"I think you have a good idea here," I said, still squeaking, intimidated by her apparent age and obvious beauty. "It just amazes me that Relics hasn't been torn down to make room for condos."

Thalia gathered the long curls into a ponytail. "People will always have a fetish for crap they can't or won't use. People like clutter. And they'll always appreciate a break from the madness of Valley Fair Mall crowds. There's something special about haggling with shopkeepers. The tech revolution is a coup that will fail."

I stared at her, puzzled.

She continued: "Consumers like to experience something before they buy it. Who would buy a pinot noir online rather than taking a day trip up to Napa or Sonoma for an actual tasting? I mean, if you're making a salad, do you really want other people choosing your lettuce for you? Do you want someone else to determine what constitutes a good tomato?"

I stifled a giggle. "Well, I guess you've got it all figured."

She blushed and tugged at a small hoop earring. "Sorry 'bout that. I spent a lot of time thinking about these things before opening this place. Is there something I can help you with?"

As if possessed, I said, "Would you model for a sketch I'm working on?"

She pulled again at the hoop in her ear. "Me? What's so art-worthy about me?"

That night, we met at the Cav. It just so happened that one of Hector's favorite local bands, the Odd Numbers, was playing that night. In that tiny bar, the band was deafening. Thalia and I sat side by side in a corner so we could hear each other. Our arms touched, the neon from the beer signs distorting our skin, turning hers darker and mine paler. I downed the vodka cranberries Thalia bought for me. I talked a little about my classes at SJSU and even less about growing up downtown.

She stirred melting ice cubes in her gin and tonic and leaned in, breath on my ear, to tell me about crazy customers at her shop and the vacations she'd taken for thirty years to her parents' summer home on an island in the Aegean Sea. Every time she made a storytelling hand gesture, I thought I smelled lavender, but I don't think it was her; it was hard to tell through the cigarette smoke. At her place a few hours later, she knelt in front of me, taking off my pants. I was shivering, and I smelled a hint of Tiger Balm. With my bare backside against the cool wall, my kneecaps shook. Soon, I was grasping the nearby closet doorknob for balance, green clouds undulating on the backs of my eyelids. I experienced a certain relief for the first time in my life. This happened three more times, and I wanted to do something for Thalia. But I had to confess that I didn't know what to do. She smiled, laid me down beside her, and told me to kiss her ear and neck. Shortly, she inhaled, held it, and slowly blew out a giggle, all this almost without sound. I fell asleep amazed that she had done that for herself. I'm still amazed.

The next morning, we drove up the coast to a parade in San Francisco's Castro District.

Yes, one of those kinds of parades.

All summer, we drove on scenic Highway 1 to San Francisco in my beat-up green '66 Pontiac Bonneville with the ripped ragtop down. Along the way, we would stop so Thalia could go for a swim at Pescadero State Beach or so we could get naked in the back seat at the Año Nuevo parking lot. Thalia paid for most of our adventures. But when we broke up after a few months, I realized how much I actually spent shopping in Santa Cruz, having coffee in Davenport, filling the old '66 with extra gas, driving to Duarte's Tavern so Thalia could warm up with artichoke soup after her swims, buying books at City Lights, eating and drinking in the Castro. I could have done without it all, but I should have kept the car.

As some sort of self-torture, I slept in the back seat of the Pontiac for a while after we stopped seeing each other. But the haunting smell of leather, gasoline, and sex was too much. So I sold the car.

I don't think I loved Thalia, but I missed the way she could make me feel, rubbing my stubbly scalp as I drove or lying across the bench seat, gazing up at me while I tried to focus on the road ahead.

*I*t's dark outside.
  A woman slips out the door.
  First, feel wounds.
  A motel room.
  Alone.
  In the glow of the streetlamp, a razor blade.
  Next, make fresh wounds. Put head back and close eyes.
  The blood drips.
  Now, look down at nothing. Finger the large wound.
  Sigh. Again and again.
  Then walk in a forest.
  Noise.
  Finally, emerge from the woods and touch scars. And then touch nothing.
Gaze across the river. Hear only the birds.
  A disembodied voice.
  "Katherine?"

9.

I'M EXHAUSTED, NOT CRAZY. I did just wander Manhattan for three days, remember?

But no matter how much I wander, I can't seem to sleep. But I feel better than I can ever remember.

The cuts? It's a simple explanation. Self-punishment. Self-pleasure. Like the cigarette burn on my back. What do you think it means?

Well, I realized a few days ago that it had been exactly a year since I saw Alma. It all of a sudden felt urgent to see Oso. So I left a message on his machine and started walking to Washington Heights.

———————

Louder Than Love repeating on my Discman, I walked well past Oso and Camille's apartment on 163rd, trying to ignore all the people glancing at me like I had flaming Martian eyes and burning Martian hair. Even here in New York, the pallid tinge to my yellowish-brown skin seemed to glow fiercely. Or maybe my music was too loud and too wrong, everyone on Broadway deciding that a woman like me shouldn't be listening to Soundgarden. I was all the way to 110th Street before the judging eyes pushed me underground.

As the subway lurched north toward 163rd, I shivered from the air conditioning and anticipation. In the nearly empty subway car, an old man stared out the window into the darkness, a young guy read a big hardbound novel, a young woman in a miniskirt rubbed bruised thighs, an old woman inspected her passport. I rubbed my hands together, and the old woman peered at me, pulling her luggage closer. Covering my head with my hood, I folded my arms and leaned back to listen to "No Wrong No Right" for the fifth or sixth time.

When I got off the train, the smell of dried piss and piss-made mud greeted me. The yellow wall tiles that formed the station street number were fading, the formerly white tiles darkening with layers of dirt. I treaded up the stairs on a bed of black dried gum and took off my earphones. Lincoln town cars honked at possible fares, buses hissed their air brakes, trucks downshifted their gears. And music I'd never heard before—strong, sexual beats—came from a shop just up the block, the security guard doing double duty as a hawker: "Buy this. Buy that. Hey, kid, get away from that; you break it, you buy it," alternating between Spanish and English.

I blended into the music, the shops, the noises, more than I ever expected to. No one stared at me. But I didn't feel invisible, either.

A man yelled, "Five-oh, yo! Two-five-two!" I don't know what "two-five-two" is, but I'm sure "five-oh" means cops. Undercover cops? But all I saw was some tall bald guy with a blond goatee walking on the other side of the street. Hiding in plain sight, I guess. Whatever the case, he was more out of place, more noticeable, than I would ever be in that neighborhood. Before the fuss over the goateed guy settled down, a couple boys no older than sixteen said something to me in Spanish. I didn't quite catch it but heard a word or two that I knew referred to my ass.

I spun around. "What did you say?" I locked eyes with one of the boys.

He said something laced in bravado. Palms up, I shook my head, looking for an answer.

"Bringing inglés up in here."

Then I got the gist of what he meant, and turned to leave. What could I say? No hablo español. Lot of good that would have done me.

The years of grime left the bricks of the five-story walk-up apartment building a deep rust tone. The gates off to either side of the main stairway led to two basement-level apartments, the barred windows eye level with the gum-blackened sidewalk and obscured by garbage cans. Living in those dungeons would screw up your perspective on things, so I was relieved Oso and Camille weren't living down there.

I snuck through the security door and climbed shiny green stairs through muted light and the odor of fresh paint. The smell got stronger as I approached 5C. I knocked.

"Yeah?" a woman said from inside.

"I'm looking for Oso," I said, out of breath. I pushed the hood off my head.

"Katherine?"

The door opened. Paint fumes and a bright light rushed over me; all I saw at first was an outline of a figure slightly taller than me. A dark woman with a small pointed nose stepped out of the silhouette. Camille hugged me like she knew me, like I was her sister. Her cheek against mine, I inhaled a mix of faint body odor, patchouli, and paint fumes; for a moment, my mind slipped off to Alma and Mom. Camille's long paisley skirt and black tank top fit her snugly. I could still feel the cool of Camille's cheek on my face as she led me into the small studio apartment.

"Your hands are wet." She stood in front of me, clasping my hands, gazing at me with amber eyes.

"Little nervous." I looked away. Everything was covered in plastic. From somewhere in the room, a sonata played quietly.

"You've nothing to worry about, sweetie."

"Where's Oso?"

"Come sit. Sorry about the plastic. I finally had to paint this place. Lazy landlord. All dirty white walls, even some faint, dirty handprints when we moved in."

"The colors are warm." I sat in the office chair, plastic rustling under me. I dug my Discman out of my pocket and put it on the desk, Bad Religion's logo glaring.

"Amazing what a little 'desert sand' can do to the walls. And I just finished the first coat of crimson on the ceiling. But my neck is killing me. I can't stand the thought of doing another coat."

"Why not just leave it?"

"Well, for one thing, it looks like a three-year-old's finger painting."

"I can see forms in the roller strokes."

"Really? Like what?" She flopped herself on the bed, the plastic crinkling as she settled onto her back.

"In the middle. There's a side view of a naked man holding a torch."

"Where? Oh, I see it. Uh-oh. He looks a little excited."

"Yeah, I didn't want to mention that. And right above me, a one-winged butterfly next to an old man's scrunched face."

"Good Christ. You're right."

That was all she said for a while. And I was calm. Camille had let me into her home without ever having known me. She introduced me to a small part of her world and listened to my interpretations of her ceiling— all of this after being with my brother for about a year. Considering the hospitality she was showing, it was uncertain how Oso had rendered me. As she lay there on the bed, she traced in the air, outlining possible figures and shapes she saw in the bloodred roller strokes. I noticed her slightly swollen belly.

"Why are you here?" she asked.

"Your letter. The plane ticket. You and Oso wanted me to come."

"I wanted you to come. There's a reason for that."

"You're pregnant."

"I invited you over a year ago, Kat."

"I've been working through some stuff." I paused. "Where is he?"

"LES, Lower East Side. His squat family needed some help installing a staircase in an abandoned building that they took over. He actually wanted to bring you along, but there's a rumor of a police raid tonight. So he thought it was best you stay away for now. He'll be here tomorrow if things are calm enough down there."

She went on to tell me that after he left San José, he got on a bus to Yosemite. When he got off the bus for a transfer, he instead purchased a ticket and began a seventy-seven-hour bus trip across the country.

"What changed his mind between San José and Modesto?" I asked.

"He said his mom's and dad's ghosts sat next to him on the bus and rehashed old stories."

"What kind of stories?"

"The ones about lives half lived, where José stayed just long enough in jobs to cause problems, where Clara never left the vineyard until she was pregnant and responsible for another mouth to feed. When José and Clara met and fell in love, they never imagined they would fight about their entirely different ideas of family and parenting. Oso said Clara finally left because she was tired of fighting."

I stiffened. "She disappeared."

"That's not how Oso tells it."

"He's wrong."

"Those years must have been tough for you. As a kid, you believed anything your Mom wanted you to. Your love made it easier for her to manipulate you."

Bristling, I said, "Manipulate?"

"Well, it's true. She was selfish."

"I don't think so. Oso didn't know her like I did." My head was spinning. I was shocked by the familiar way Camille talked to me about these things.

"It's me who thinks she was selfish. I mean, look at what she did."

"She just disappeared."

"Really? Why do you defend her?"

"I ask myself that question every day. Look, I don't know what Oso told you. What I do know—what I believe—is that my mother sacrificed for me, for everyone."

Raising an eyebrow, Camille said, "We are still talking about Clara, right?"

"I was led to certain other conclusions about her life."

"How?"

"I'm not going to say."

"Why not?"

"What's the point? I've come to terms with the fact that there's no absolute truth in history, only curated perspective. She died. Her death was accidental. She disappeared."

"Well, Oso doesn't see it that way."

"He didn't know my mother."

Again, she asked, "Wait, are we talking about Clara?"

I was terribly uncomfortable, but I couldn't move. "How'd you and Oso meet?" was all I could manage.

Graciously, Camille let her line of questioning go. "We met at a protest against the city for brutally cracking down on the squatters who had been living in a row of three abandoned buildings in LES. In fact, Oso was one of the squatters. When he got here, Oso had no plan. But he didn't really expect it to be so difficult to find a place to live or to find a place to stay that first night. He ended up in LES and slept in Tompkins Square Park.

"A few months later, the city started a new push to clean up and even demolish the abandoned buildings. After a friend of Oso's was beaten and jailed in another squat a few blocks away from his, people started protesting and writing letters in the *Times*. Oso was out every day in Tompkins Square Park and in the neighborhood, forming alliances with LES renters and owners. He wanted me to support the cause, but I told him I was observing the park's inhabitants for a paper I was writing for my last sociology class at Columbia; I was graduating the next month. But he convinced me to take a stack of pamphlets back to campus. He said thanks as he suddenly ran off, having seen a couple cops approaching.

"A few days later, I spotted him at the rally. His eyes glowed as he told me about the positive response the squatters were getting from other residents in LES.

"'It's tough,' he said. 'But it's not that tough.'

"'How so?'

"'I promise them neighborly cooperation, and they're much more willing to open their mind to the idea that everyone deserves shelter and a chance to foster creativity—a life, a work of art, a business idea.'

"'Do they buy that bullshit liberal idealism?'

"'If they don't, I get more practical. I ask them if they would rather have junkies and drug dealers in these empty buildings than us.'

"He spoke to me like I was one of his squat family. But when I told him I grew up in St. Charles, Illinois—a nice western suburb of Chicago—his demeanor changed. He was still polite. But he was blunt.

"'Have you ever considered how many ideas go unnoticed because they die quite literally out in the cold with the person who originated the idea?'

"'Not exactly,' I replied. 'But my parents worked their asses off— twice as hard as white folks—and earned their home and the way of life they wanted to give me. They weren't given anything.'

"'None of my squat family were, either. Some of them are squatters because they have no choice. Others are here because of ideological reasons—you know, to hell with corporate America and all that. But every squatter will tell you that shelter is a basic human right no matter what you want out of life.'

"He paused and then asked what I was going to do after graduation.

"'I want to study the effects on society as the gap between rich and poor expands and retracts over time.'

"'Could you do that important work without the very basic need of shelter? Winters are not easy as a squatter, but people still huddle under their blankets and study and write. They couldn't do that very well living out on the street. All problems stem from the lack of affordable housing. If we don't have money, we can't eat, we can't sleep, we can't go see the doctor. And why? Why? Because all our money's gone to pay for the basic human need of shelter. Why should one need be met and so many others go unattended?'

"I had never considered things this way," Camille told me. "But think of it. The progress of humanity—not technology, that's not what I'm saying—but humanity has slowed because there is so little shelter for people and their ideas to better their own lives and the lives of others. You're probably thinking that I have too much of an agenda for a social scientist. But what was I supposed to do? Just observe and report to the city council? What good would that do?

"And that's the thing about Oso: he can compel you to imagine. But he's no salesman, he's no missionary. He believes everyone could be as passionate as he is about this if only they weren't so afraid of losing the inessentials, not to mention the essentials. And that could change the world."

You're right, Lilly. I *am* always asking what the point is; I've been asking long before I met you. But if things change no matter what, why not try to influence the change? If someone hadn't sacrificed a couple generations ago, people like Oso—and you said this yourself—people like Oso would be thrown in jail by the likes of Joe McCarthy. So maybe Oso and the squat families can change the world for the better. And look at what you're doing here in Marble Hill and Inwood. You give people a chance to do something meaningful by helping them stay healthy.

Don't you understand that what Oso sees as possible changes everything for me? There might actually be a point to all the striving people do. Maybe I can help Oso and the movement.

You're right. I do sound like an idealist.

I don't know why you're reacting this way. I mean, it doesn't surprise me that you say men have an outsized influence on me—you've said it many times before. For you to say it at this point, though, tells me that you think my ideas are completely unoriginal, that I have no clue what I'm talking about. Why is that? Is it because I haven't seen what you've seen, read what you've read, done what you've done?

Sure, go ahead and tell yourself that. Whatever makes you feel better. It doesn't change the fact that, after hearing about my interest in what Oso's up to, you said the only change that's possible happens, at most, in your own little neighborhood. I thought you would be more supportive of my emerging ideas—my ideals. And they are just that: ideas. But for the first time in my life I find myself thinking there might be something worth standing up for other than myself—something that's bigger than my immediate surroundings—and then I hear you say that I'm being unrealistic. It's so out of character that it makes me think you're just trying to keep me from leaving. Or is it that you don't want me going off to work on someone else's agenda?

With what I know about you, I still don't understand how you got so cynical as to think unseen forces—forces stronger than any of us—tell us what to think. But maybe you're right. Maybe "the imperatives of the unseen hand are so strong" that realizing a dream outside our home or neighborhood is impossible.

Anyway, I was getting a little light-headed from the paint fumes in Camille's apartment. I opened the windows wider and let in Washington Heights' traffic sounds and merengue beats. Camille, still on her back, looking for figures in the red paint, continued.

"The building Oso stayed in, Umbrella House, was a fairly well-established squat with young families and single squatters, all living fairly clean lifestyles—drugs were prohibited in the squats and a sort of vigilante justice kept the drug dealers at bay. All the squatters had regular part-time and full-time jobs in addition to being activists and vigilantes and novice pipe fitters, amateur bricklayers, and inexperienced carpenters for the improvement of the squats.

"And in his own room, Oso had just put a new coat of paint and was growing basil, cilantro, and parsley on the fire escape outside. It wasn't much more than that for him and his roommate. Two twin beds, an old lamp on a night table between them. This simplicity of life based in 'laws of common sense' that rejected popular ideas of happiness appealed to me at first. We spent the night together, just talking. And after that, we were inseparable, splitting time between my dorm room, his little squat, and the long subway rides in between.

"When I finished school, I got a job doing research with one of my professors. It didn't pay much, but I was able to move into this apartment. We had a fight about that.

"Oso said, 'You're defeating the very purpose of what I stand for.'

"'It's just not sensible. We need more stability if we want to have kids.'

"'Don't you remember what I told you? It's actually part of the city ordinance: if the building is made better on a regular basis, then, after ten years, squatters could legally own the spot. So our concerns will be gradually met.'

"'Ten years? And when was the last time the city obeyed its own ordinances? Or court rulings? I don't know that there will ever be any kind of certainty in squatting. I mean, I don't want to risk actually being homeless. And if we had kids, the city could take them away.'

"'I'll never let that happen.'

"'Why don't you just move in with me and still remain active in the movement?'

"'If I don't live the life I am fighting for, people will see me as an imposter. Worse yet, I would see myself as an imposter.'

"So Oso's ideals and my dreams led to our breakup. But a few weeks later, he showed up here, distraught. He had a friend, an old Vietnam vet from California, uh, Nolan?"

I was floored. "You're kidding. They just met up here randomly?"

Camille responded, "He only told me that he was from San José."

"I had no idea they had stayed in touch."

"You knew him?" she asked.

"Long story."

"Anyway, Nolan froze to death in Tompkins Square Park.

"'Such a senseless death,' Oso said. 'Those goddamned cops kicked him out into the cold. He didn't have anything like this squatters' movement in San José or San Francisco. That's why he came here in the first place, to see what could be done. He had some great ideas for the squats.'

"Oso had a look in his eye that said he was going to run off, to disappear again only to reappear banged and bruised. He had come to me a few times before with his mysterious wounds, and I'd taken care of him—even if he couldn't tell me how he got hurt—and I wasn't about to turn him away just because he had different ideals. I was—I am—in love with him, his mind, his resolve. Even if I didn't yet fully understand his ideals or agree with the way he wanted to pursue them, I knew he needed me.

"I let Oso in that night, and we talked until dawn about the things he'd seen on the streets and in the parks in his youth, about all that he tried to do for friends like Nolan, the friends who fought him and fought each other and fought the cops. Sure, some were there in the park because they were addicts; but he learned that their addictions were usually symptomatic of dreams never realized or a government abandoning its veterans. Oso talked at length about being exposed to these people early in life, and he told me about his dad befriending the people in the park and preaching about how the Church was the only place where social change could happen. But it was Nolan who told Oso of the squatters' movement in New York."

Why am I telling you all this? What I'm saying is I am oblivious-dead. I've been sleepwalking all these years, trampling through, past, and around idealism. I prevented injury when I should have caused it. I caused injury when I should have done more to prevent it. I don't know how to change that pattern. I'm petrified with the idea that I'll continue to destroy, that everything I try to make better will just continue to dissolve. The only difference now is that I'm at peace with the cycle of creation, abandonment, and destruction.

When I left Camille a couple nights ago, I was in a daze. I walked through the grind of gears and engines, of merengue music and people, wondering if I would recognize Oso when I saw him the next day.

And I did what I normally do. I trudged all over this crazy island

and rode the subways. Then I went to see Oso. Now I'm so exhausted—physically, mentally, emotionally. Don't be surprised if I fall asleep before I finish telling you what happened.

Camille was asleep upstairs, so Oso met me outside. He gave me a big hug and kissed me on top of my head. I stayed in his massive wet-wool-scented embrace for some long moments.

We didn't talk for a while. We walked through a strange park in Washington Heights. Highbridge Park. We went up and down some neglected and crumbling stairs, under a group of bridges and roads. All these paths were new to me; not for Oso. We crossed Washington Heights Bridge and looked into the Bronx and at Yankee Stadium and, farther south, to hazy buildings in Midtown. Next thing I knew, we were heading north on University Avenue. And I felt more at ease than I expected to.

Finally, I said, "I missed you. How did you end up here in New York?"

Oso undid his frayed ponytail and scratched his head. "On the bus out of San José—what, over two years ago now?—I thought of killed idealisms. And when I got to that town of Modesto, the center of what Dad liked to call the Garden of the Sun, I thought of the decisions I'd made and how I'd never really seen anything through."

"But you helped your friends from Saint James Park."

"A lot of good that did." He pulled his black curls into a tight ponytail.

"And after a certain point, you practically raised me and Alma."

"But I left. I left because I was frustrated with my life. And I didn't realize how stupid I'd been until I made it halfway to Yosemite. What the hell was I going to do there, anyway? So I came out here to New York to find Nolan, to try sticking to something, to try influencing the direction of others' lives.

"When I got here, I found Nolan, we got involved in this squatters' movement, I met Camille, Nolan died the way that he did, and I started to question, again, my own resolve to really make anything happen in the relatively small world that is Manhattan, much less my home state, the country, the world. Then Camille told me that she was pregnant, and I had hope again, stirred by the thought of changing the world by raising my daughter the right way. I don't have much at all in the way of money. What I have are my ideals. And I need to be around if I want to teach my kid that dialogue with one's self is the most important, that what happens to her is not completely beyond her control, that faith in herself lies within herself—unlike what the Church would have us believe."

"Do you think guilt is the only reason people do what they do to—or for—other people?"

"I don't think so, Kat. But I guess I never thought about it that way."

"I've been struggling to figure out what to do to make things right in the world."

"And then you have to struggle even more when you start to think of the perceptions of others. Do they think you were wrong? Do they think you were right? Well, Camille and our baby have helped me come to peace with all that. And that's why I'm trying to see good things through. That's why we bought you the ticket out here. And I want you to know how sorry I am for abandoning you and Alma."

"You have nothing to be sorry for. I think it was us—or just me—who abandoned you."

"How could you think that?"

"Once Loskie came around, we—"

"Oh, really? C'mon, Kat. He may not have been the best person in the world, but you and Alma really never had any friends. And in the end, you finally got away from him. Right? Please tell me Alma left him, too."

"I hope so. I think she left San José a week before I did."

"Why didn't you go with her?"

"Long story short, she asked for my help in leaving Loskie, asked me to come with her. I think she was questioning some things about herself."

"That doesn't answer my question."

"I don't know. I guess I thought it was best for her to figure things out on her own."

"Was it that easy for you?"

"In a way, yes. It was easier since people usually ignored me."

"There's no way that could have been easy, though. Why didn't you ever tell me? Did you ever tell Mom?"

"Everyone was too wrapped up in their own worlds. Me being bisexual didn't seem that important. And everyone was unpredictable; I was afraid of being ignored even more than I already was. And I was terrified of being put out on the streets, of going crazy like so many of your friends had."

"The ones who were a little off were usually that way before they became homeless."

"Well, I had Alma to lean on, even if our closeness was the reason people at school speculated about me in the first place. Anyway, you shouldn't feel bad about leaving."

"But you two were so young still."

"We weren't the only ones."

"Yeah, I know. But let's face it. I had been out on my own much longer than you two had. Dad and I never really hung out after I turned twelve or so, when it occurred to me that the canneries weren't open year-round. So I followed Dad to the church one day, where he sat for eight hours. When I confronted him, he confessed that he got unemployment checks for five months of the year. You can imagine how shattered I was to find out that my heroic, self-reliant father no longer resembled anything like the man of dissent I had grown up idolizing."

"What a phony, prideful man he was," I said. "Why didn't you tell us?"

"I guess because the fiction was easier to maintain by that time. Anyway, I should have been around more, especially when you were growing up. I mean really. The adults did a number on us. All we are left with now is trying to figure out how they became how they were so we won't become like them. And how are we supposed to do that? You sure as hell couldn't trust those stories that Dad told. Embellished hero. All I could do with Dad's stories was try to make them meaningful."

I blurted out, "Why don't I have a birth story?"

Oso stopped walking. Across the street were Bronx Community

College and a public library, so people were all around us. Oso put his hands on my shoulders. Pale splotches emerged on his dark skin.

He said, "I can't believe I never told you. Dammit. I'm so sorry. It must have gotten crowded out over all those years of Dad's stories, my stories."

Suddenly, I was weeping. Oso guided me to a cement slab under some trees. And he said, "I was out walking the streets and came around a corner to see the whole thing."

"You remember at four years old? And you were wandering the streets at that age?"

"It doesn't matter. Do you want to hear this or not?"

"Yeah." I laughed and sobbed at the same time.

"All right, then. Hush." We sat side by side and watched the traffic and people flow by. After a few minutes, Oso continued. "Throughout the entire pregnancy, you didn't move in your mother's belly. Even though they'd had another kid before you, I guess idiosyncrasies can make each pregnancy feel like it's the first time. She and your father became terribly worried even though you were growing in there. One afternoon, three weeks into the tenth month of the pregnancy, your father thought it would be a good idea to go on a walk with your mother. Your dad kept saying, 'Oh my God, get out of there, baby. You'll kill your mother.' He repeated this like a mantra. Then you were born before the ambulance got there, right there, with your mother propped up on that brick wall of the Mission. Your father was pale. No noise came from you. Not a laugh, not a normal cry, not a bearlike roar. But you—your eyes were open, looking around with concern.

"Your father bent close to you. Your breathing was deep. But he was scared as he wrapped you in his flannel and handed you to your mother. The sirens wailed and the people gathered and the blood seeped out from underneath her, but your mother just sat calmly, sobbing quietly through a smile as she gazed at you. You and your concerned face. But your father backed up in fear. He saw the world in terms of black and white. He believed that a person is a product of their environment, but what really defined a person was the way they reacted to their environment, suggested, of course, by the noise they made when they were born. So when he saw you come into this world on that sidewalk next to the bar with nothing but a calm, worried look on your face, your father was terrified. It was the circumstance—not you—that he was unprepared for. He had seen dozens of births over the years, but the way you came out was so unexpected that it shocked him into a silence, a silence that left him unable to tell you his story—or your story."

Yes, it was curious that he said "your mother" and "your father." I do know that none of the birth story could be true. But it was somehow satisfying. And I know you'll be distressed to hear this, troubled that it was a man who made my life . . . my story complete. But think about it. Aren't you distressing, troubling in your own way? Pitying me for not feeling differently about a man's influence on my life. Or being upset that I don't tell my story differently. Why bother at all if you've already made up your mind about me?

I know you didn't say any of this. But we've been together long enough. I know you're thinking it.

Anyway, Oso and I stood and continued our trek up University.

"Then why didn't Mom tell me my story?" I asked.

"She was quiet for her own reasons."

"Which were . . . ?"

"I don't know," he said.

"I think something happened to her in San Francisco when she ran away at fourteen."

"What? Grandpa told me she never left the vineyard until—"

"Oh, good ol' Grandpa," I said, savoring that I knew a piece of history that Oso did not. "He was a convincing storyteller. But he subtracted. He added. He multiplied. Details for didactics is how I've come to look at it. But so what? What does this have to do with Mom?"

"I don't have an answer for you."

Oso and I continued silently north for an hour. We crossed over Fordham Road toward Kingsbridge Road. Along University, buildings were six or seven stories tall, slightly varying in the drab color of their bricks, bodegas every block. Nothing out of the ordinary. But I could tell that Oso was looking for empty buildings, searching for potential squats.

Then he asked, "Why don't you come help out down in LES? I could help you find the right squat family."

"It's not really my scene."

"What is your scene, Kat?"

"That's what I'm trying to figure out. And I don't think I'll be able to figure it out if I get wrapped up in your scene."

"That's the thing. It's definitely not my scene, either. It's everybody's scene. It's for everyone who has ever been isolated for being different. Take the kids, for example. It seems like every third teen in LES is there because their family kicked them out for being gay."

"There's more to me than being bisexual, Oso."

"You're right. I'm sorry."

"Even if I did get involved with those kids, I wouldn't know the first thing about helping them."

"Well, let's get you back in school. Camille could help with that."

"Oso, you can relax. I don't need to be saved."

And that was about it. At Kingsbridge and University, Oso's pager buzzed. He called Camille from a pay phone. He told me everything was okay but he had to go do some things for her. Another long embrace and he was gone on a subway. I know it's sort of anticlimactic, but our story is not finished. Not even nearly finished.

I knew you would be skeptical, Lilly. But this is the way it happened. And it got me thinking as I walked all over town last night and today. Maybe the way we tell stories is wrong, wrong because they have endings. Stories—real stories—never really end. People are born, people live, and people die, and life continues to go on in a series of letdowns, excitements, joys. I'm starting to look at life more as a tidal cycle; the brevity of the good and the intensity of the terrible things are becoming easier to accept. The problem arises for me when—regardless of the tide—I'm waiting at the water's edge for my family to come ashore. But they stay out there for longer and longer periods, becoming so accustomed to the cold and the danger that they could grow gills and fins to coexist with all the unknown creatures, finding contentment in uncertainty.

Something is happening, but I don't know what it is. I need to sleep, but I want to know. I'm not making any sense. No. No, I am making sense.

You love me for what I've told, seeing the emergence of some butterfly—your cliché, not mine. But I've been trying to spin away from you without tearing those clichéd wings, those clichéd, undeserved wings. You have said, after all, that my story sounds stolen in some parts. Or made up. Or whitewashed.

Yet you still want me to make a life with you. And we always argue about what life might look like. You want to adopt. But your need to be a savior contradicts your own philosophy when you say you can "redirect kids' predestiny by taking them in." You can't save them because you could never understand them. You could never understand what it's like to have your first memories be of your own screaming, waking every morning to a terrifying boy jumping up and down on your bed. You could never understand how Alma lying there next to me, gazing with her lifeless yet comforting black eyes, ushered me through the horror of those mornings with that little demon Ricky, another foster kid like Alma. A foster kid like me.

That's right. I was a foster kid. You thought you had me summed up nice and neat on a little placard next to my likeness in the American Museum of Natural History, that you had—as Berlin would have said— accurately interpreted me from curated contexts. And by the way you're looking at me now, I can interpret a hell of a lot about how you have interpreted me. I can only imagine how you've retold my stories, if only to yourself. I can tell you that the *where* I am from is real. And *most* of the people I've told you about are real; the legends, myths, and cautionary tales really are *what* they told me. It's the *who* I am from that must be messing with your head—just imagine how it messes with *my* head; I mean, it's to the point that I sometimes wonder if I would really feel any less messed up if I actually knew who my parents were. Good people? Bad people? Ashamed people? Unfit people? Dead people? Career people? Poor people? And where were they from? China and Korea? Spain and the Philippines? France and Vietnam? Japan and Korea? Japan and China? Japan and Vietnam? Vietnam and Cambodia? America and the First Nation? America and Honduras? America and Mexico? America and the Philippines? America and Japan? America and Korea? America and Vietnam? Maybe none of these.

Yes. Maybe all of these. You would love that, wouldn't you? The melting pot fantasy. Love conquers all.

Yeah, yeah. I know. But look, I didn't tell you I was a foster kid because I didn't want to be a charity case, a tragic homeless woman you—and everyone else—can't help but stare at while trying not to get caught looking. It's bad enough that you look at me with pity for all my wanderings, a refugee from my own mind.

Besides that, you wouldn't know the first thing about raising a kid who's had ghosts and monsters for foster parents. My last set was quite a duo. Cheri was a woman who did the bare minimum in her daily hungover gasoline-and-dirt haze, but put a ton of effort into keeping up the illusion, the most important thing for a foster parent who has ulterior motives. And through a fault of the system and overwork of its agents, most of the social workers I met were like blindered saviors at best. Blindered: reacting to only the most obvious signs of abuse. Saviors: providing a mistreated child a moment of relief from abuse and neglect, the foster parents' preparation for the social worker's visit offering a glimpse of how well they should be treated. Our social workers simply had no time to inquire past obvious signs of a cover-up. If misfit and poorly mended clothes were called "play clothes," that's what they were. Maybe this is the way it is with everything: if things appear okay, that's the way they are.

How would you even deal with a kid who had a foster mom like Cheri, much less a foster dad like Skip? Cheri would head off to the bar after Skip came home smelling of grease and sweat from work. While we ate our bland dinners, he leered at Alma from behind his darkened glasses. How would you know what to do with a kid who is so messed up that she more than once hoped she would be the one absconded with in the middle of the night? Add that to the overwhelming feeling that she was rejected by her parents, and you get someone lying awake at night, saying, *What is so wrong with me that even a monster wouldn't want to touch me?*

I don't know if Alma even woke when Skip came to take her away at night, her breathing unchanging. I hope she did sleep through it all. If she found a way to remember, I wonder if she blames me for not doing something. If she does blame me, I hope she has forgiven me. I will probably never know.

The point, Lilly, is that you think José and Clara—the only halfway decent guardians I ever had—are beyond forgiveness. But just like I don't want your charity, I also don't want your judgment. Or your guidance. All I want—all I need—is a chance, the space, the time to figure things out on my own, to succeed or fail without being dependent on you, without trying to live up to your standards of success or failure. Now, I have to move on . . . I mean, I have to sleep . . . but first you should know that it was your story—and everyone else's throughout my life—that I was thinking about when I found myself, as I have so many times over the last year, committing to a long walk. After Oso left on the subway in the Bronx, I walked down University Avenue, lost, trying not to look lost, searching for the 4 train. I wasn't ready to come home yet even though a headache persisted and I hadn't slept for days. Or was it that I knew that more questions had yet to be answered? Was I hungry? I'm so hungry. I know we need to talk more. But I'm so tired. I don't want to argue, but I need sleep . . . going to sleep now . . . but I can't. I can't stop wondering if I'll ever see a good thing through. These questions swirl like debris in my head when I wander the streets, when I sleep, when I wake . . . Mix in some ideas that float . . . I see no other way forward but to leave, travel back to California with my savings. Now I've got to see the places in between, to stop just talking . . .

The torture of the headache is an experiment. I want to know the cause of it. I get some aspirin from a bodega but decide not to take it. I walk through the Bronx and past a few neglected and abandoned buildings shrouded in greenery and finally find the 4 train and find myself in the Upper West Side, and I only have enough for a cup of coffee. I write a letter to myself. Yes, a letter to myself, writing "you" instead of "I," as if some other person in this world knew me as well as I know myself. I wrote that way because when I address myself and then read it to myself, there are no excuses for all that is wrong in my life.

After I write the letter, I leave the café and get on the 1 train, this time intending to go home. Instead, I get out at 157th Street and walk to the Hudson River, Riverside Park. I sit on the shore and think of whether I have ever seen a good thing through, and I swim through a vague idea of who I am amid this massive city, wondering at the high-rises that sprout up from the New Jersey foliage on the opposite bank. I see a massive barge moving slowly upriver. I sit there until the barge is parallel to me, and then I walk beside it, but it soon outruns me, and I kick a dirty old tennis ball. Somehow I get off the asphalt path and find myself walking nearer to the banks, and I see fishing rods propped up, lines in the water, a tarp, and a cleaning station for fishermen. A home? Two figures loiter near the makeshift tents. I don't know if they're homeless, but I can't approach complete strangers and ask for some food. Damn, I'm hungry.

I find myself on the asphalt again, the George Washington Bridge looming large above me. I am growing tired, so I find my way through a few small tunnels and up innumerable steps and again under the spans of the West Side Highway, under the off-ramps and on-ramps, under the sounds, and under the thoughts that follow me everywhere. I find another café, sit with my Discman, and listen to Bad Religion's *Recipe for Hate*, just to escape the irregular noise of kids and people talking and that annoying, loud pop music. And I manage to escape it, for a moment, that is. But as the guitars shred, the drums drive, and the bass rumbles in my ears, I feel trapped between my music—is it my music?—and the noise of the café, and I wish I were back at the river's edge or that I'd taken the

LIRR out to Jones Beach where the only noise is the regular crashing and receding waves washing over my ears, the sound of my soul breathing. My soul? What the hell is that? I'm used to the sounds of traffic, but they are never to be loved: the pounding of trucks, the hissing of air brakes, the squealing of metal on metal, seems to chase me out of town, chase me out of my mind, chase me out of range, makes me want to scream for help because I'm soaked, steeped, immersed, marinated in the drone of these sounds . . .

. . . Have I been talking? Have I been sleeping? Who will tell me?

Then it's dark outside.

A woman takes money from the side table and slips out the door.

I stand facing the wall and twist my arm behind me and finger the fresh cigarette wound on my backbone. I grin.

A motel room.

Alone.

In the glow of the streetlamp, I find a razor blade and look closely at the sealed scars on top of my forearm.

Next, I make them fresh wounds. Then I put my head back and close my eyes. The blood drips down my arms.

Now, I look down at nothing. With one hand, I finger a large wound, exposed nerve endings. With my other hand I scratch my forehead with the back of the razor blade.

Then I sigh. Again and again.

Then I walk in a forest.

The noise of jackhammers and spray-painters and cars and jetliners is intolerable.

Finally, I emerge from the woods. And I touch my scars. And then I touch nothing. Midspan on the bridge, I gaze across the river into New Jersey. Giant monoliths stare back with thousands of eyes. Heavy with electricity, they blink slowly and then close. The pounding and the hissing and the droning stop. I hear only the birds roaring in the distance.

A disembodied voice seeps from the gloomy stillness of a moonless night.

"Katherine."

9/5/1997

Dear Kat,

It has been easy for you to play a cameo role in the lives of people. You'll continue to do it until your money runs out as you go from city to city, spending fragments of time with travelers in the hostels. Boston. Portland, Maine. Montreal. Chicago. Vancouver, BC. Seattle. Portland, Oregon. Ashland, Oregon. You'll go to all those places as a fragment, maybe even a figment. But you are no stranger to this.

In the not-so-distant future, you'll be on the shore where you once stood and watched a woman and a girl, nude, enter the surf, bending, ducking, swallowed by white foam, taken by the terrible crash of water upon itself, folding endlessly. A brief moment as a child alone, an orphan of all life on Earth. A cameo. A fragment of time as the infinite roiling sea flattened around your feet and you sank to feel each granule of sand embed itself in your knees. This happened once, this happened incessantly. This incessant fragment that is played in your head more than any other, more than any other fragment from other people's lives, the lives that you witnessed or heard about and had as much control over as you had over the tides.

In the not-so-distant future, you'll be on that shore not forty miles from home, the only home you knew, the only one you ever loved; all you will have to do is go over that mountain pass that is shrouded in the green-canopy wilderness of trees, through and by the lives of mountain lions and deer, constrained by the twisted ribbon road that leads back to the scene of many scenes, scenes that unfolded in those staccato fragments of a life that you've had, the life that led you to do injustice or <u>perceived</u> injustice. It is that ribbon of constricting road that straightens out in that valley, the valley of small pieces that add up to one colossal jigsaw of your life, life that you told of, you distorted, you denied yourself, you denied others, you refused to live, you refused to stand up for; a life you've lived vicariously.

The ceaseless varying vicarious story you have told, on more than one occasion with countless mistakes and inconsistencies, has been dangerous. Berlin, Lilly, both wondering if you could be taken seriously, if you really were who you said you were. If you were. What has led you to tell all the stories is as much a mystery as who your "real" parents were, why they gave you up, why you had to fabricate your bloodline to explain why you were the way you were, are the way you are. Why you look the way you do, defined by others only by traits that are not even your own. Or are they?

You'll go from one side of the country to the other, careful of what you say, listening to stories of other travelers, hopping from city to city, in and out of the lives of countless short-term companions. And you will end up back at the water's edge in your native state. Naked. California. Naked California. It is there you will try to get back to the true, native You. You will track your journey and put your life down into your private words. Your words will be prophetic. But only to you.

Will it be enough simply to have made it back alive to your native state, to stand on that longed-for shore alone to see hundreds of familiar people, silenced, limping, walking, floating, fleeing parallel to and just beyond the breakers, alongside millions of less familiar people? Will it be enough to know that you have toiled all your life through the sounds of others—and yourself—to reach that shore alone?

Yours,
Kat

AUTHOR'S NOTE

IN WRITING THIS BOOK, it has never been my intent to be the voice for any one group or any specific set of intersectionalities. How could I presume to be? I am, after all, a white heterosexual male from a suburban middle-class nuclear family. What started nearly two decades ago as a method of exploration beyond my level of experience grew to something much more than that, mostly because the world has changed in such dramatic ways in that time. So have I. And I will continue to do so. To that end, I am willing to discuss my shortcomings in writing this novel, this experiment. If I have helped guide a few conversations into uncomfortable places, I will consider the experiment a success.

REFERENCES AND SOURCE MATERIAL

WHEN I FINISHED the first draft, it contained little more than scant information from the Foundation for Advancement of Illegal Knowledge's *Cracking the Movement: Squatting Beyond the Media* (1994), and a modicum of material based on an anonymous pamphlet entitled "Squat the World!" (1995) found in the online journal *Not Bored*.

The final version of the book has been enhanced by exact words from two articles in *Social Justice* newspaper (1934, p. 84); Oso's quote (p. 119), lifted from a monument to a 1968 speech given in San José's Saint James Park by Bobby Kennedy, which Kennedy himself borrowed from George Bernard Shaw's *Back to Methuselah*; background from Vincent Harding's "Interview with Dolores Hureta: Early Family Influences" (n.d.); inspiration from Tool's "Forty Six & 2" (1996, p. 124); quote from

John Barth's short story "Ad Infinitum" in *Harper's Magazine* (January 1994, p. 196); and background from Ash Thayer's *Kill City* (2015) and Alexander Vasudevan's *The Autonomous City: A History of Urban Squatting* (2017).

ACKNOWLEDGMENTS

THIS BOOK WOULD NOT EXIST without my wife, Nicole. En route to her PhD and career, she somehow summoned patience and insight during my countless rewrites. Her faith in my vision sustained me through several fits and epochs of doubt. For this and so much more, my love for her is boundless.

I owe a debt of gratitude to Dr. Susan Shillinglaw at San José State University, who gave me so much in my formative years as a reader and writer. I'd also like to thank Prof. Salar Abdoh at the City College of New York for his sage observation about the constipated nature of the first 100-page draft (AKA my thesis). The feedback I received on the first (bloated) version of the manuscript from Cara Cassidy, Jaclyn Neal, and Jennifer Holmberg was indispensable in the eventual culling of tens of thousands of words. And great thanks to editors along the way, Heather Jacquemin, Nancy Tan, and Hannah Woodlan.

The immense generosity and belief in this project shown by Aaron

Amaro and Kyoko Nakamaru, Jeanne Anderson, Alex D'Anna and Peri Kabbani, and "Mama" Sarah Johnson reaffirmed my efforts.

For their crowdfunding generosity and for engaging book club discussions to come, thanks to Jan Campion, Kimberly Halsey, Jennifer and Lyal R. Holmberg, Linda and Lyal Holmberg, Pam and Lars Holmberg, Josephine De Guzman Kingsbury and Sean Kingsbury, Coral and Rob Kline, Dr. Kyle Murdock, Mia and Andrew Murphy, Jaclyn and Erik Neal, Julie Ann O'Connell, Andrea and Kyle Rosenthal, Susan Shirley, Christine Wehrli, and Dr. Heather Winnan.

I also want to recognize the crowdfunding support of Jan and Rick Allan, Dr. Melissa Bailar, Yuhao Chen, Nada Cusin, Dr. Micah Ioffe, Dr. Mark Matuszewski (RIP), Dawn and Stan Miller, Dr. Lynsey Miron and Dan Knewitz, Beth Peters, Rachel Schmit, Kelly Siefering, Amber and Dr. Andrew Sims, Drs. Erin Stevens and Joe Bardeen, and Jonathan Yap.

Additional recognition must be given to Ahmed Al Hamad, Juan Alvarado, Marybeth Anderson, Neil Buettner, John Campos (shared excellent '89 quake details), Amanda Champany, Mata Dreliozis and Konstantinos Kreonopoulos, Susanne Dryer, Judy "Mama Fish" and Tim Fisher, Amanda Fitzpatrick, Emily and Dr. Andrew Flannery, Vicki Gall, Janelle Gray, Hailee Hake, Christine Holloway, Jon Holmberg, Brita Holmberg, Shirley and Joe Holmberg, Marta Holmberg and Scott Brewer, Meg and Adam Hoog, Byeongyeob Lee, Katie Jensen, Dayle and Ken Johnson, Anne Kemp, Dr. Lindsey Knott and Rory Crossin, Jaebue Daniel Lee, Jack Lelko, Maria Martinez, Hae Hun "누나" Matos, Dr. Kathleen McCraw, Nancy and Peter Monday, Diane and Victor Monday, Patty and Tom Monday, Marissa Moser, Sharon Nagy and Sal Lee, Dr. Elisabeth Narkin, Christine Northup, Dr. Jesse Passler, Erin Pitman, Christine and ChristopherRamirez, Gail and Eduardo Ramirez, Michelle Rausch-Neary, Kristen "T" and Jason (RIP) Redding, Brendan Rosenberg, Michael Santistevan, AJ Sellarole (shared excellent '89 quake details), Tara Serrato, Erin and Dr. Andrew Sherrill, Shelley Shirkey, Janine Stanlick, Dr. Melissa and Andrew Terry, Rose and Ed Wehrli, and Matt Williams.

And for additional support, thanks to Janelle Adelman, Shannon Ahrndt, Osama Alharthi, Nancy Barrock, Dr. Deba Mitra Barua, Geoff Bourassa, Joyce and Larry "Mike" Bradshaw, Cara and Diron Cassidy, Linda Dano, Tim Donlon, Tim Gerstmar, Dr. Edward Hansen, Dr. Jacob Holzman, David Kelly and Terri McMahon, Barb Kissinger, Lynn Kissinger, Eunjoo Lee, Dr. Melissa London, Naga Madhavapeddi and Bharath Krishnaswamy, Eucario Matos, Heidy Matute, Jami Messinger, Elena Niola, Donny Olewinski, Dr. Emily and Greg Padgett, Daniel Piper, Jason Ramirez, Dr. Laura Richardson, Alexandre Selhorst, Tamara Wade and Hector Marin, Julie Waechter, and Torrie Zambon.

Finally, I have deep appreciation for my parents, Kathy and Charles Holmberg, who indulged my undergraduate degree in English and therefore fostered my dream of writing stories.

CPSIA information can be obtained
at www.ICGtesting.com
Printed in the USA
BVHW080213070322
630719BV00002B/12

9 781646 636198